THE CRYSTAL RUN

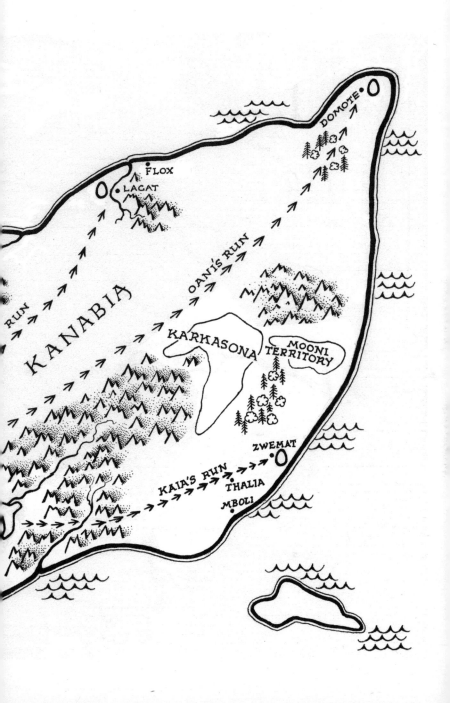

The idea for *The Crystal Run* had been rattling around in my head for a few years before I decided to write it. It's a very different type of book to the ones I've already written because it's an adventure story set on another world, and the two main characters are teenagers. I didn't set out to write a book for younger readers; all I wanted to do was tell the story, but the more I thought about it, the more I realised that the book would be stronger and more interesting if Joe and Kaia were in their teens.

One of the things I like writing about most is how people react when they find themselves in unexpected situations. Nothing could be more unexpected than the situation Joe finds himself in and it was great fun taking him, and Kaia, on their journey.

Books were a huge part of my life when I was younger, and I loved to spend time meeting new characters who later became familiar friends to me. I want anyone who picks up *The Crystal Run*, no matter what their age, to get the same sense of adventure and excitement I do whenever I open a book. I hope you enjoy Joe and Kaia's story and that they become as real to you as they are to me.

THE CRYSTAL RUN

Sheila O'Flanagan

Hodder
Children's
Books

HODDER CHILDREN'S BOOKS

First published in Great Britain in 2016 by Hodder and Stoughton
This paperback edition published in 2017

1 3 5 7 9 10 8 6 4 2

Text copyright © Sheila O'Flanagan, 2016
Map copyright © Geoff Taylor, 2016

A CIP catalogue record for this book is available from the British Library.

ISBN 978 1 444 92708 5

Typeset in Goudy by Avon DataSet Ltd, Bidford on Avon, Warwickshire

Printed and bound in Great Britain by Clays Ltd, St Ives plc

The paper and board used in this book are made from wood from responsible sources.

MIX
Paper from
responsible sources
FSC
www.fsc.org   FSC® C104740

Hodder Children's Books
An imprint of Hachette Children's Group
Part of Hodder and Stoughton
Carmelite House,
50 Victoria Embankment,
London, EC4Y 0DZ

An Hachette UK Company
www.hachette.co.uk

www.hachettechildrens.co.uk

With much love to David, James, Hugh and Oisin.

This one is for you!

PART ONE

SANCTUARY

1

The two boys were at the corner of the street. They were standing close to each other, not talking, just watching. They were both dressed the same, in grey trousers and blue hoodies. The grey trousers were part of the school uniform but the blue hoodies were their own. The boys were tall and broad and muscular. They looked like they played sports, or worked out. They looked older than the boys in Year 9.

Joe Hunter didn't look older than anyone else in his school year, and he didn't look like he worked out. He knew that even if he spent hours in the gym he never would. He was lean and gangly, all arms and legs. He wasn't good at sports. He was also slightly hard of hearing. Which meant that guys like Greg Nolte and Niall Keller saw him as a bit of a target.

Joe didn't want to be a target. He liked to steer clear of trouble. So when he saw Niall and Greg ahead of him, he crossed the road. He felt a bit of a wimp doing it. But it was the best option.

He readjusted his headphones as he passed them on the

opposite side of the street. Joe didn't wear earbuds because of his hearing problems. The trouble was that he struggled with softly spoken words or hearing people who were more than a couple of metres away. He needed sounds to be close and clear. Usually he got on all right but occasionally it was a bit of a struggle. He wore invisible hearing aids to make things easier.

He was closer to Greg and Niall now. They'd stepped out from the wall and were looking at him speculatively. Joe glanced around. The road was a quiet one, a short cut home from the school which circled some waste land and disused buildings. There was nobody else on the street. He gritted his teeth and kept walking.

'Hunter!' Greg called to him. 'Nice headphones, man.'

Joe slid the headphones from his ears so that they were around his neck.

'I said nice headphones, Hunter,' repeated Greg as he and Niall crossed the road. 'Jeez, what's the point in you having good cans if you can't hear anything?'

'I can hear,' said Joe.

'So why didn't you say something?'

Joe shrugged.

'Hand them over,' said Niall.

'What?' Joe looked at him warily.

'You mean pardon.' Niall laughed and so did Greg. The two of them slapped each other on the back as though they were each the funniest people they'd ever met.

'Hand them over,' said Greg.

'Why?'

'I want to try them.' Greg took his iPod out of his pocket.

Joe weighed up his options. There was no way Greg would give them back. But there was no chance they were going to let him walk by either. Joe looked around again. The road was still deserted.

'C'mon,' said Greg. 'Hand them over.'

'No,' said Joe.

'I'm warning you, Hunter.'

Joe didn't know what to do. It wasn't worth getting into a fight over the headphones. But his dad would be furious if he found out that they'd been taken from him. They were expensive.

'Give me a break,' he said. 'They were a present from my dad.'

'Where'd he get them?' asked Greg. 'I thought your dad was out of work.'

'Part time,' said Joe. Maybe if they thought he had no money, that the family were down on their luck, they'd back off. 'Everyone's on shorter hours. Money's a bit tight.'

'Yet he wasted it on buying you these.' Greg shook his head. 'And it's a waste cos everyone knows that if you can hear at all, you listen to crap.'

'Give them over,' said Niall.

'No,' said Joe again.

As he spoke, Niall lunged towards him but Joe, without even thinking about it, twisted away from him and began to run.

'Hey!' yelled Greg. 'Get back here, you moron!'

Joe ran faster. He wasn't a speedy runner but he had longer legs than either Greg or Niall. The thing would be to try to make up a bit of distance in front of them. But he wasn't sure he could do it. He ran down the road and then turned sharply left, hoping to shake them off even though he knew it was impossible. Worse than impossible, he realised with some horror, because he'd chosen Taylor's Lane to run through and it seemed to be blocked at one end. It shouldn't be. He knew that it joined the road he'd just left with another one which snaked around the disused buildings. He'd been down this lane hundreds of times before and it had never been blocked. He wasn't entirely sure what was at the end of it. It seemed like a wall of shimmering metal right across the gap where the road should be.

Was it a solid object? If it was, perhaps he could climb it. If it wasn't, then there was no question that Niall and Greg would catch up with him and beat him up. If it really was solid metal it would be shiny and slippery and difficult to climb. But it was the only means of getting away. He could hear them shouting behind him. They hadn't missed him turning into the laneway. They were catching up.

He ran faster, putting on a spurt so that he would have some energy behind him when he launched himself at the shining wall. He kept his eyes firmly on it as he got closer and closer and then he leaped as high and as hard as he could, his fingers totally extended as he reached for the top.

A jolt of electricity surged through him and he was dazzled by a brilliant white light. He felt his body slam into the wall. And then, almost in slow motion, he began to fall.

2

His head ached. That was the first thing. So did his back. His arms too. Joe couldn't remember anything after hitting the wall. He didn't know if Greg and Niall had caught up with him. If they'd taken his headphones. If they'd given him a beating at the same time.

He tried to open his eyes but, right now, they were gummed shut, as though he'd been asleep for a long time. Maybe he had. Maybe he'd been beaten up so badly that he'd been knocked unconscious. Or maybe he'd been momentarily stunned by slamming up against the wall, and even now Greg and Niall were standing over him and about to begin the going over that he was sure they wanted to give him. He swallowed hard. He rubbed his eyes and they flickered open. He was afraid that he'd see them looking down at him, ready to stamp on him or kick him. But they weren't there. Not yet anyway.

He took a deep breath. No point lying here like a fool waiting for them. Better to do something. And if he wasn't flat out in the laneway, better to know if he was in hospital and how hurt he might be.

The light was very bright. So bright that initially Joe thought that he was actually on an operating table. That he was being put back together after whatever had happened and that he'd woken up in the middle of it. Which, he thought, was going to be very painful. But there were no voices and he couldn't make out any people around him. Plus, he realised, he wasn't on any kind of table or bed or chair. He was lying on the ground. Yet it wasn't the muddy ground of the laneway. It was a smooth, tiled surface, slightly warm to the touch.

Joe blinked a few times and then pulled himself into a seated position. He was sitting on the floor of a long covered passageway. The tiles were mosaic in vivid shades of green and white. The walls were covered in the same mosaics, but these were multicoloured and formed a variety of patterns which Joe eventually realised were depictions of bizarre animals along with unrecognisable symbols. There were tigers with wings, birds with huge, serrated beaks and creatures he couldn't even begin to identify. As he studied them the animals seemed to shimmer and move, and the symbols pulsate. He rubbed the back of his neck, squeezed his eyes closed, then opened them again. He looked along the passageway which led from a closed arched door at one end to an open space at the other. He wasn't sure what was outside – from where he sat it seemed to be a type of courtyard. There were more doors off the passageway, and large urns filled with enormous multicoloured flowers either side of them.

Where the hell am I? wondered Joe. And how did I get here?

He moved his head cautiously from side to side. The ache was beginning to disappear as was his slightly blurry vision. He stretched out his arms and legs, then got to his feet cautiously. Despite his aching body he seemed to be in one piece. He picked up his headphones which had somehow slipped from his neck and ended up a little further along the passageway. He felt in the pocket of his trousers for his smartphone and took it out. He looked at the screen. He'd charged it before leaving the house that morning so it still had an almost full battery. What it didn't have, though, was a signal. Not even a faint one.

Joe began to walk slowly along the passageway. His steps seemed bouncier than usual, as though his body somehow weighed less. It was a strange sensation. He looked around him, half expecting Greg and Niall to appear and demand his headphones again, but he was completely alone. It was a relief to have escaped them, he admitted to himself, but where exactly had he escaped to? He examined the intricate designs on the walls but they gave him no clues.

He was still confused and disoriented when he reached the courtyard. It was about half the size of a football pitch, partially covered by a tiled roof which was supported by slender pillars. Like the walls and the passageway floor, they were covered in mosaic tiles. This time, they were shimmering white. A rectangular pond, with clear water, ran almost the length of the courtyard. There was a fountain at each end of the pond, although neither of them was working, so the water in the pond was perfectly calm, without a single ripple. In the centre was a flat, round stone with a hole in the centre. It was supported out of the water by sculptures of the winged tigers he'd seen in the mosaic tiles. These were undoubtedly some kind of mythical creatures from a story he couldn't properly remember. The ground around the fountains and the pond was filled with small, coloured pebbles which glistened and sparkled beneath the warm sun. And that, Joe realised, as he looked upwards was another thing. The sun was shining brightly but there was also something else in the sky – a wide ribbon of light that arched across it. Joe had never seen anything like it before. It was like a pure white rainbow.

It was so hot that he didn't need his maroon jumper. He took it off and at the same time undid the top button of his white school shirt. He left the jumper draped over the side of one of the urns of flowers that surrounded the courtyard. There was a strong scent from the flowers, somewhere between sweet and citrus. It was a pleasant smell, although Joe didn't recognise it.

He walked slowly around the courtyard, in the shade of the tiled roof. He could see that there were doors leading into the building that surrounded it, but all of them were closed. He tried to open them one by one, but they were all locked too. The windows were shuttered, which made him think the building was deserted. He sat down on a stone seat and rubbed the back of his head. He still had no idea where he was. Or how he was going to get home.

3

When the noise came, it frightened him so much that he leapt up from the stone seat. It was the sound of a bell. Not a tinkling, cheery bell, but a loud, thunderous tolling bell. It rang three times and then stopped. Out of the corner of his eye Joe saw one of the doors at the end of the courtyard begin to open slowly. He ducked down behind one of the huge tubs of flowers.

A tall woman (taller and thinner than any woman he'd ever seen before) walked out of the door. Her hair was blue-grey and pulled high on to her head. Her face was long and narrow and her eyes were a piercing blue. She wore a full-length silver dress which caught the light of the sun. She was followed by a boy and a girl, both of whom seemed to be about the same age as Joe. They were dressed identically, in shimmering green tunics over cropped green trousers and flat black trainers. The boy's dark hair reached his shoulders and was pulled back into a narrow plait, held in place by a green ribbon. The girl's hair was much longer, blond, and also held back with a green ribbon, although in her case her plait was a far more complicated style. The woman stood at one end of the rectangular pond, the boy and girl either side of her, their palms pressed together as though they were about to say a prayer. Then the bell tolled again and a group of four boys and four girls, all of a similar age, walked through the door and lined up on the opposite side of the pond to Joe. He crouched down even lower behind the ceramic pot as he looked at them. They wore the same tunics, ribbons and trainers, only in white.

The tall woman raised her arms above her head and began to chant in a language Joe didn't understand.

The group of eight knelt by the water. They bowed their heads towards it. Then seven of them stood up and turned around so that they were facing away from the pond.

The woman stopped chanting and clapped her hands.

Another door opened and four men walked out. They were dressed entirely in black and carried short black canes in their hands. They stood beside the fountains in pairs. Then they pressed on the engraving on each fountain. There was a whooshing sound and an arc of water spurted from each one. Only it wasn't water, Joe realised. It seemed to be a translucent wave of energy, because bright lines of blue and green flickered up and down its length like a force field. The men pressed another engraving on each fountain. The wave flattened out, so that it was like a sheet over the pond, stretching further so that it also covered most of the courtyard. Then a final press of the engraving and objects appeared on top of the force field itself. At first they were transparent but after a few minutes they seemed to solidify. A beam. A wall. A climbing net. Shining silver balls and then more beams, this time spinning. Joe realised that it was an obstacle course.

A final object appeared at the end of the pond. It was a huge square with large blue dots making a circular pattern in the middle of it like a clock face.

The girl who had remained kneeling now stood up and walked to the opposite end of the pond. She removed her white tunic and trousers and placed them neatly on the ground. Underneath, she was wearing a white one-piece suit. The bell rang again, once. The girl ran towards the first object in the obstacle course, which was the beam. As she began to cross it, Joe saw that the dots were turning red. He guessed she was being timed.

The girl was quick. She hardly touched the surface of the beam as she ran across it. Then she climbed the net with ease. She skimmed the silver balls, scrambled beneath more netting, ran across the spinning beams and then threw herself at the wall. But even though she was tall she couldn't reach the top. And she couldn't find anything to grasp to pull herself higher. She tried jumping, but she couldn't get enough height in the jump. She pressed her hands to the wall, pushing it as though she was trying to find a hidden hand hold. But it was too smooth.

More and more dots on the square were turning red as she tried and tried to climb the wall. Eventually they were all red and the assault course suddenly disappeared, leaving her standing on the force field. She stayed there for a moment, a beaten expression on her face.

'*Doza*,' said the tall, thin woman.

13

The girl took a deep breath, then bowed slowly and walked to the woman. She stood in front of her. The woman removed the white ribbon from her hair and handed her a black one which the girl used to tie back her hair again. She bowed once more and rejoined the group, standing at the end of the line and looking in the same direction as them, away from the obstacle course.

The next person in the row stepped forward. A boy this time. His hair was short but he wore his white ribbon around his forehead. It made him look tougher, harder. His bow to the tall, thin woman was short and quick. Then the men in the black tunics pressed the buttons on the fountains and the obstacle course appeared again. The dots on the timer were reset and the boy took a deep breath before beginning the course. But as he ran across the beam he lost his balance. He wobbled for a moment, trying to regain it, before he fell. A siren sounded, the obstacle course faded, and he stood up, a grim expression on his face. The tall, thin woman waited until he approached her, then exchanged his white ribbon for a black one, just as she'd done with the girl.

Each person in the line tried to complete the obstacle course. One by one they failed, had their white ribbons exchanged for black ones and rejoined the line, their backs to the course.

The final attempt was made by the smallest of them, a girl, and Joe didn't rate her chances very highly. No matter how good she might be over the beams and the netting, she'd never conquer the wall. He watched as she bowed to the thin woman and then started her run at the obstacle course. She was quicker than the others and lighter on her feet. She barely touched the obstacles as she crossed them. Then, as she approached the beams, she slowed down. Her hands went to her hair and she undid the white ribbon, twisting it around her wrist as her unbound hair cascaded down her back in dark waves. She hesitated for a moment then ran at the beams. But instead of sprinting across them as the others had done, she cartwheeled over them. As she reached the last spinning beam, she used its own motion to throw herself at the wall. At the same time she threw the ribbon, which caught the tiny spikes at the top of it. She used the ribbon as a rope to pull herself to the top where she stood precariously, gripping it with her toes.

There were still twelve blue dots on the square when she jumped from the wall and landed on a small circle. She pushed the button on a pole beside the circle and the obstacle course disappeared.

The bell rang. The seven others turned around. The tall, thin woman waited until the girl had walked back to her then placed her hands on her head.

'*Yisha*,' she said, then stepped back.

The boy and the girl in green stood in front of her and lightly touched their foreheads against hers. They stood to one side while the men in black surrounded the others and marched them back inside the building. A few moments later they returned.

The boy and the girl bowed to them and walked to the far end of the courtyard where they opened a door and went inside.

The girl knelt down again, her head almost touching the ground while the men pressed the engravings on the fountains again. The force field vanished. Then, out of the slab in the centre of the pond, rose a long, gleaming pole. It was like a thin spire shining in the sunlight. It reached about the height of a three-storey building. As Joe watched, spikes emerged about a quarter of the way up the pole, leading to a small platform near the top.

The four men stood beside it. The girl walked to them. Then one man made a cradle with his hands which she used to step on to his shoulders. She could just about reach the bottom spikes. As she took hold of them the man pushed her higher so that she was able to pull herself upwards. Joe watched anxiously as she managed to get a firm hold of the higher spikes and then curl her body so that her feet rested on the lower ones. She started to climb the pole.

When she got to the platform she stepped on to it. Then the men raised the black canes and cracked them like whips. As they cracked for the third time, black ribbons streamed upwards and wrapped themselves around the girl, pinning her tightly to the shining spire. The bell rang again. More spikes began to appear on the spire. These were longer and thinner and seemed to pass right through it. Joe realised, with a mounting sense of horror, that when they reached the girl they would impale her.

The blue dots on the square began to turn red. There were a lot more dots this time, so she clearly had more time to free herself before she was killed by one of the spikes. But it wasn't going to be easy. She was already straining against the ribbons with little effect, although her expression was calm and determined.

The men pressed a final engraving on the fountain opposite.

Jets of water shot towards the girl. She twisted and turned to avoid them, as they, in turn, changed speed and direction. Hard as it would have been to free herself before, it was twice as difficult now.

The men and the tall woman all bowed towards her. Then they filed out of the courtyard leaving her alone.

Except for Joe.

4

Was it a punishment of some sort? wondered Joe. But if it was, it was horrific. He had to do something to help her.

The spikes continued to come out of the spire like deadly needles, sharp and unforgiving.

Joe looked around. The courtyard was very definitely empty except for the two of them. But there was nothing lying around that could help him to help her. He stepped out from behind the big tub of flowers and walked towards the pond. His steps still felt springy and light.

The girl didn't see him. She was too busy avoiding the water jets and trying to free her arms from the ribbons. Joe could hear her groaning with the exertion. He went to the fountain and pressed the engravings as the men had done earlier, but the water continued to flow. And the blue dots continued to turn red on the large square.

Joe splashed his way through the pond to the base of the spire. The girl was now looking at him with a startled expression. Her writhing beneath the ribbons became even more frenzied.

'It's OK,' called Joe. 'Don't worry. I can help you.'

Although he still wasn't sure how. He looked at the tapering pole. The lowest spikes were at least two metres high, which was out of his reach. Even if he wasn't standing in water and could jump, he didn't think he could reach them. But he had to try anyway. He took a deep breath. He bent his knees and concentrated as hard as he could. Then he leapt out of the water, his hands above his head.

He didn't know how he managed it. He'd never jumped as high before in his life. Somehow his body seemed to be both lighter and stronger as he grasped the spikes and then, with his right hand, reached for the higher set. They were smooth and the same width all round, making it easier than he expected to pull himself up. Then he jerked back and nearly fell again as one of the sharper, pointed spikes suddenly shot through the spire and missed him by centimetres.

Carefully, but as quickly as he could, he climbed towards the platform.

'It's OK,' he called again as she worked frantically at the ribbons. 'I can help.'

She stared at him from big blue eyes. Her hair was wet from the spray of the water, and damp strands were stuck to her face. But the white one-piece appeared to still be dry. Droplets of water rolled off it and on to the pole.

'I can do it.' Joe tried to sound confident as he pulled at the ribbons which tied her. The girl looked at him in horror as the needle spikes came closer. Then the ribbons slid through Joe's hands, greasy and slippery like long strips of seaweed.

'*De uko bea?*' the girl gasped. '*De uko bea?*'

'I don't understand you,' said Joe. As he spoke, the last of the ribbons came loose. He felt himself slip and he reached out to grasp one of the spikes. The needle caught his palm, tearing at the skin as he missed it and fell towards the pond. But he didn't fall as hard and as fast as he expected. Instead, his fall was slow, giving him time to turn in the air so that he landed on his feet in the water. He wasn't hurt at all, although the cut across the palm of his hand was stinging.

A moment later the girl was beside him. She stumbled slightly and he put out a hand to steady her. She twisted away from him and then jumped out of the water and launched at him with a type of Martial arts kick. Joe was so surprised he didn't get out of the way quickly enough and ended up on his back in the pond. The girl stood over him, her fists clenched.

'What the hell did you do that for?' gasped Joe.

'*Voh am,*' she said. '*Voh am, Haaken Gizi.*'

'Stop!' Joe twisted out of her way as she aimed another kick at him. 'Are you crazy? I'm trying to help you!'

'*Haaken Gizi!*' she cried and leaped at him again.

Joe jumped away from her, out of the water. He surprised himself again with how high he jumped.

'I want to help you,' Joe told her. 'Look, let's be friends, huh?' He held out his hand. She continued to stare at him. And then she took his hand in hers. For a moment he thought she was going to squeeze it and he gasped in anticipation, because it was the hand he'd hurt as he'd slid from the pole, but instead she looked at the cut on his palm in puzzlement.

'*De uko bea?*' she asked.

'I'm sorry,' said Joe. 'I don't know what you're saying.'

'*De uko bea? Haaken?*'

'I don't know who Haaken is,' said Joe. 'I'm Joe. Joe.' He pointed at his chest and repeated his name. Then he looked at the big square in the corner of the courtyard. Fewer than half of the blue dots had turned red. Which he hoped was a good sign.

'*No uko bea Haaken?*'

'I'm sorry,' said Joe again. 'Look, I don't want to seem rude or anything but shouldn't you get the hell out of here before they return? Before those dots turn red? Because I'm sure those guys will be back then. Expecting to take your body down from that pole.' He wondered why he was bothering to say anything at all. He didn't understand her and she didn't understand him.

He could see uncertainty in her eyes. Then she put her hand into a hidden pocket in the white one-piece and took out an object that seemed like a tiny shell. She handed it to him. He looked at it and shrugged.

'*Joq.*' She pointed at her ear and then his. '*Mag ig Joq.*'

He shook his head. 'No. I can't.'

'*Joq.*' She caught his wrist again and lifted it to his ear.

'I have trouble hearing,' he said. 'I have hearing aids. I can't put this in my ear.'

He turned his head to show her. She touched both his ears and the aids fell out. Then she placed the shell inside instead. He scrabbled in the water for his aids but they were submerged in water. He began to panic.

She spoke again. '*Jour.*'

He could hear perfectly. Better than ever. He touched his ear. He knew the shell was in it but he couldn't feel it.

'*Jour.*' She indicated her mouth, opening and closing it as though she was speaking.

'You want me to talk?' Joe asked. 'You want me to speak to you?'

She nodded. '*Jour. Jour.*'

'What do you want me to say?' He glanced at the square at the end of the pool. It was almost completely red. And the spikes were nearly at the top of the pole. He was pretty sure that the men would return soon and he was equally sure he didn't want to be around when they did. So he started talking rapidly. 'My name is Joe Hunter. I live with my mum and dad. I have a younger sister. Her name is Susan—'

'*Jour. Jour,*' she said again.

'Who are you? Where am I?'

'Joe,' she said slowly, although she pronounced it 'Sho'. 'You are Sho. You are a Hunter.' She looked at him warily. 'The Haaken are hunting now? Hunting Carcassians?'

He looked at her in astonishment. 'How on earth did you do that? Can you speak English?'

'The Joq,' she said, indicating his ear. 'The Joq makes you understand.'

'It's like a translator,' said Joe. 'Wow. That's amazing. Who makes it? Apple? Google? Is this a secret testing facility? Am I in Silicon Valley?'

She looked puzzled. 'I do not know this apple or google,' she said. 'I do not know this Silicon Valley. I do not know you.'

22

'I don't know you either,' said Joe. 'Who are you? Where are you from?'

'If you are here you must know,' she replied. 'And if you are not Haaken . . . is this part of the test?' She shook her head. 'You *are* Haaken. You are a terrorist descendant of the Kanabians caught behind the Shield when it was erected. You must be. You are here to betray me.'

'I've no idea what you're talking about,' said Joe. 'I'm from England.'

'Eng-land? Is this a Haaken stronghold? We have not been told of it.'

'I wouldn't exactly call it a stronghold,' said Joe. 'The thing is . . . I don't know how far away England is. I don't know where I am. Or how I got here.'

'If you are not Haaken.' Her face darkened and her body stiffened. 'You are Kanabi.' She suddenly sounded horrified. 'A Kanabi spy. In Sanctuary.'

'I'm not a spy!' cried Joe. 'How can I be a spy? I'm still at school.'

'School?' She looked at him disdainfully. 'Do you think I am an ignorant child that you would say such a thing to me? You are too old for school.'

'Maybe here, wherever we are, you leave school sooner. But I'm at Oakview Secondary,' he said. 'Look.' He retrieved his jumper and showed her the school's crest. A large oak tree with the motto 'Together We Are Stronger' underneath.

She looked closely at it. 'What is this? This is not Haaken. Or Kanabi.'

'I told you,' he said. 'English. I'm from England.'

23

'Where is this Eng-land?' she demanded. 'Why are you here? How did you breach the Shield?' Her voice was hard but he thought she also sounded scared.

The Shield must have been the shimmering wall at the end of the lane. Somehow he'd passed through it, leaving Greg and Niall behind. But where had he ended up?

'I have wasted time talking to you,' she said not wanting for him to answer. 'This is part of the test. I must prove my worth to the Leaders of Carcassia by killing you.'

Joe stared at her. Being beaten up by the school bullies suddenly seemed a much better option. He stepped backwards but she grabbed his arm and held it tightly.

'I will kill you if necessary,' she said. 'But I will not do it unseen. That is not my way.'

'For God's sake, give me a break!' cried Joe. 'I thought I was helping you but all I want is to go home. That's it. Honestly.'

He meant it. Right now he wanted to be in his house on the Summerhill Estate, playing *Call of Duty* on his Xbox and eating the tea and toast his mum always gave him when he got home from school.

'You are lying,' she said. 'You are a Haaken Gizi and you have been sent to test me. The final round of the Gimalle is the hardest. Everyone says so. And now I know why. It is your life for mine.'

'If that was the case I would have let you be killed on that damned pole!' cried Joe. 'I wouldn't have rescued you.'

'You did not rescue me.' Her voice was full of scorn. 'I would have released myself and completed Gimalle.'

'I thought you were being punished for something,' said Joe.

'I thought you were in trouble. And stop calling me a Gizi. I'm not a terrorist.'

'Perhaps it is a coward I should be calling you,' she said. 'It is easy for you to scoff at our ways but you would be dead already if it was not for people like me.'

'People like you?' asked Joe.

'Do not pretend.'

'I'm not pretending,' pleaded Joe. '*Who* are you? *What* are you?'

'I am Kaia Kukura,' she said. 'I am a Carcassian Runner.'

5

'You're an athlete?' said Joe. 'And this is how they train you here? What distance do you run?'

She looked at him, puzzlement in her eyes. 'I am training for the Kerala,' she said. 'For the Crystal Run. You know this already, Haaken Gizi.'

Joe had no idea what she was talking about. He was totally confused and he reckoned that his arm would be black and blue from where she was gripping it. And his stomach, where she'd kicked it, was aching.

'I realise you'll be tired of hearing this,' he said. 'But I don't know what the Kerala is. And I don't know what a Haaken is. And I'm not a Gizi, I'm not a terrorist.'

'What else can you be?' she asked. 'You will not succeed in your mission. I will keep you here for them.'

'Them?'

'The Yeppuno,' she said.

'The men who were here earlier?'

'They protect the Runners,' said Kaia. 'To the death,' she added.

Joe didn't like the sound of that.

'This has nothing to do with me,' he said. 'All I know is that I was being chased, I got an electric shock, and when I woke up I was here.'

Kaia ignored him and glanced at the square. The last blue light turned red. The bell tolled again.

'They will be here soon,' she said. 'They will be surprised. They will be expecting to see my body as the time has run out.'

'What about me?' asked Joe.

'I do not know if they will be expecting to see you,' said Kaia. 'But if it is a case of you or me, I am alive and you are my prisoner.'

Joe didn't want to be a prisoner. Those guys in black, the Yeppuno, had taken this girl, tied her to a pole and shot water jets at her while deadly spikes nearly impaled her. And this was apparently some kind of training. If this was how they treated their own people, how would they deal with a stranger? Especially one they might think was a terrorist?

'They will question you,' she said. 'You will answer them as you have not answered me.'

'Kaia . . .' He looked anxiously at her and then the door at the end of the courtyard opened. The tall, thin woman walked in, followed by the Yeppuno.

All of them stopped when they saw Kaia holding Joe by the arm. The woman's expression was shocked.

'*Akka*,' she said.

The shell in Joe's ear didn't translate it. But he didn't need a translation to know that she was ordering the Yeppuno to arrest him.

They marched over to him and two of them grasped his shoulders. He squirmed and a third man cracked his cane. Black ribbons flew from it and wrapped themselves around his wrists and his ankles. Joe felt himself topple over but he was caught by one of the Yeppuno who held him upright.

The woman turned to Kaia, who bowed deeply to her.

'What have you done?' the woman asked in horror. 'You have not defeated the course. You have brought someone to Sanctuary to assist you. This is forbidden, Kaia Kukura. You have shamed yourself and all who run.'

Kaia shook her head. 'I did not bring him here. I did not ask for his assistance,' she said. 'I do not know him. I was taking the challenge when I saw him. I thought he was Haaken, sent to kill me. Or that he was a test.'

'Haaken.' The woman stared at Joe. 'He does not appear Haaken.'

'He claims not to be,' said Kaia. 'Perhaps he is a Kanabian spy.'

'That cannot be,' the woman said firmly. 'We are protected by the Shield. No Kanabian can pass through it.'

'He says he is from a place called Eng-land.'

The woman looked at him in astonishment. She turned to Kaia and began to speak rapidly. The shell was having trouble keeping up. But Joe caught some of it.

'I'm not a traitor or a terrorist,' he said, when he heard the word Gizi again. 'I told Kaia already. I'm not from here.'

There was more rapid conversation between Kaia and the tall woman. Then she turned to Joe.

'How did you reach Sanctuary?'

'This place? I don't know,' he said. 'I was coming home from school. I was being chased. There was a wall . . . where there hadn't been before. I tried to climb it and then suddenly I was here.'

'You climbed a Duqq to get into Sanctuary? That is not possible. You will be kept here,' she said. She nodded at the four guards. '*Akka.*'

They grabbed Joe by the arms and began to drag him from the courtyard.

'Kaia!' he cried. 'Where are they taking me? What are they going to do with me?'

But she turned away and didn't answer.

They brought him to one of the rooms which opened from the passageway he'd first found himself in. They unlocked the wooden door with a huge old-fashioned key. The room was dim and cool with a very high ceiling. The walls were whitewashed stone. The only light came from a window close to the roof. There were other windows in the room but big shutters had been closed over them. There was a long wooden table in the centre with wooden chairs around it. Otherwise it was empty.

Joe leaned against the table while the men checked that the shutters on the windows were locked.

'*Kash,*' said one of them, and then they left.

Joe heard the key being turned in the lock behind them.

He eased himself on to one of the wooden chairs. His hands and ankles were still bound by the black ribbons. The good thing was that they hadn't tied his arms behind his back and so he began to pull against the ribbon. It stretched slightly and a tiny tear appeared. He raised his wrists to his mouth and began to worry at the tear with his teeth. The ribbons had a slightly salty taste. When he'd freed Kaia, they'd been wet and slippery, but now they were dry and seemed to stick together. It took him ages of pulling and teasing, but eventually he managed to free his hands. Then he got to work on his ankles. He had no idea how long it took to undo them, but when he did he sighed with relief.

But he was still in a locked room on what appeared to be another world. And he couldn't see any way out. The only door was the one he'd come in through, the one that the Yeppuno (which the Joq had actually translated as 'protectors') had locked. The shutters on the windows were locked too. He rattled them just to make certain but they didn't budge. He was trapped. Unless he could somehow climb up to the window near the ceiling. But that was at least four metres high and, even standing on the table, he wouldn't be able to reach it.

Nevertheless, he had to find a way home. It wasn't that he wouldn't have liked the opportunity to find out more about where he was, but he didn't want to hang around for the whole 'being questioned' thing. Especially as they kept on mentioning the words 'terrorist' and 'traitor'. Terrorists and traitors always ended up in big trouble. And the way Joe looked at it, he'd had his quota of trouble for the day.

So. Jump to the window, climb out, find a way back home.

Easy.

Not.

He stood on the table. The window, which was close to the

roof and had a small ledge beneath it, was still way out of his reach. He lifted one of the wooden chairs. It wasn't as heavy as he expected and he was able to put it on to the table. Even standing on the chair, though, he was well short of reaching the window. He wondered if he could jump high enough to catch hold of the ledge. His first thought was probably not, but then he remembered how high he'd jumped to free Kaia from the pole. Higher than he'd ever jumped before. And it had been easy. Maybe he could jump higher here, in Carcassia.

He took a deep breath. He bent his knees.

Then he propelled himself forward, his arms stretched out above him.

6

It was as though he were moving in slow motion towards the window ledge. He had time to stretch his arms even further in front of him. It had been an unbelievable jump. He was going to make it.

His fingers touched the ledge and he held on as tightly as he could. Then he began to pull himself upwards. It wasn't as difficult as he expected. As before, he felt lighter than he normally did. Less weighed down by his own body. It was a strange sensation.

He continued to pull himself upwards until finally he was sitting on the ledge. He had to scrunch himself up to fit on it, but at least he was at the window. There was a round hook at the top of it and he pulled it. The window tilted and opened horizontally. Joe grimaced. If it had opened outwards, like his bedroom window at home, it would have been much easier to escape through. But this window swung on a hinge and so the gap was only half as big as it could have been. He was going to have to squirm out of it. And when he did, he would have to be really careful because beneath him was the sloping tiled roof that ran around the courtyard.

Joe couldn't see if the courtyard was deserted or not. But it was very quiet. He would have to be equally quiet if he was to escape unseen. Obviously there had to be a way out of this place and there had to be a way back home. He just hoped he could find it before the Yeppuno found him.

He took a deep breath and pushed himself through the window opening. It wasn't easy and his shirt kept getting caught on the hook. But eventually he was more out than in.

Joe held tightly to the edges of the red tiles and tried to manoeuvre his body into a safer, more comfortable position. But the tiles were smooth and it was hard to keep a grip on them, so he found himself slipping towards the edge. The squeak of his trainers on the shiny surfaces seemed to echo and he was expecting the Yeppuno to arrive at any minute and envelop him in their black ribbons again, but the courtyard remained silent. And even though he wasn't able to stop himself from tumbling off the edge of the roof and on to the stones below, nobody came.

He lay there for a moment, winded but not hurt. The fall hadn't been as fast or as painful as he'd expected. He hadn't quite floated to the ground but he hadn't crashed into it either. There was definitely something about this place that was working in his favour. As he got to his feet and dusted himself down, he knew that walking was easier. Maybe running would be too. But he hoped he wouldn't have to find out.

He made his way cautiously towards the passageway he'd

landed in when he'd first arrived. He walked slowly, stopping to examine the patterns in the tiles, looking carefully at the closed wooden doors, and keeping an eye out for anything that looked like . . . well, an escape route to another world. An escape route to home.

He didn't see anything. The passageway was just walls and doors. He'd have to try one of them sooner or later even though his heart beat faster at the thought. What if they all contained prisoners, like him? He wondered how long it would be before they found out that he'd escaped.

There were four doors in the passageway and each of them had a circular, wrought iron handle set into it. Taking a deep breath, Joe pushed gently against the first door but it didn't open, so he twisted the handle as softly as he could. He was afraid that it would squeak loudly and give him away, but all that happened was that he felt resistance against it and the door stayed firmly shut. Clearly, it was locked.

He tried the next door. It was locked too. So was the one after that.

He tried the fourth door. This time he felt the handle turn. He heard a click and he pushed the door open carefully.

This room was different to the one in which he'd been held captive. There was the same big wooden table and wooden chairs, but the shutters weren't on the windows and light streamed inside, making it much brighter and warmer. There were long drapes of white muslin dividing the room into different areas, as well as pictures on the walls and large urns filled with scented flowers.

It didn't seem like a way out. It seemed like a place where

someone lived.

'What are you doing here?'

The words were icy.

Joe looked around. He didn't see anyone.

Then she stepped out from behind one of the muslin curtains. She was wearing a red dress which reached the floor. Her hair was long and loose and flowed down her back. She was very angry.

'Kaia,' he said.

'How dare you come here?' she demanded. 'What is this magic you have that moves you from place to place?'

'No magic,' he said. 'I got out of the room I was in and I'm trying to find a way home.'

'You will not escape with whatever information you have come to collect,' she said. 'Nobody leaves Sanctuary. Except the Leaders. And the Runners.'

'You said *you* were a Runner. You get to leave?'

'I will not discuss this with you,' she said. 'The Haaken believe that the Carcassian way of life is wrong. But you still live within the protection of the Shield.'

'I'm not Haaken. I tried to help you.'

'You tried to sabotage me.' Her eyes showed her fury. 'You are still trying to sabotage me. And if Haaken have reached Sanctuary or the Kanabians have learned to breach the Shield . . . we are lost.' Suddenly she wasn't angry any more. She was frightened.

'I'm not trying to sabotage you, I promise,' said Joe. 'I haven't breached your Shield.'

'But you have,' she said. 'You are here. You are the first.

That is why you must be questioned. So that we discover your secret. So nobody else can follow you. You will be questioned and locked up for ever.'

'You didn't do a good job of that.' Joe was feeling more confident now. 'I climbed out of a window to get here.'

'There are bars on the windows.' She waved her hands at the windows and he could see through the open shutters that there were grilles on the outside. 'You cannot have passed through metal.'

'I didn't.' He explained about getting out of the window near the ceiling and she looked upwards and then at him again. Her eyes widened in amazement.

'That is impossible.'

'I thought so too, at first,' he said. 'Managed it though. Fell off the roof afterwards, but I got up again and now I'm here.'

'Nobody has ever got out of a locked room before.'

Joe thought there was a hint of respect in Kaia's tone.

'There's always a first time,' he said.

She walked over to the wall. 'And a last,' she told him. 'You should never have got out of that room and you should never have come to this one. I am calling the Yeppuno.'

'Why weren't they outside if they're supposed to protect you?' asked Joe.

Her jaw clenched. 'They are with the Sanctuary Leaders. Discussing you.'

'They should have been protecting you,' said Joe. 'OK, so I'm not a terrorist but someone else could be.'

'My protection is halted until they decide if I can make the Run or not. Thanks to you.'

'That's a bit harsh.'

'But I can call the Yeppuno now and they will come.'

'Don't,' said Joe. 'I'm not your enemy, Kaia. Really I'm not.'

'Of course you are,' she said. 'You have prevented me from Gimalle. From achieving the status of a Runner.'

'If I did, it wasn't deliberate. Let me explain what happened.'

She looked at him disdainfully. 'You can explain to the Yeppuno.'

'I want to explain to you.'

She hesitated for a moment then nodded. 'Talk.'

'OK.' He coughed a couple of times. 'Sorry,' he said. 'Dry throat. Comes from eating the ribbons.'

She looked shocked. 'You *ate* the Flagali?'

'Well, sort of.'

She stood up and went to a small table in an alcove. There was a jug on the table and a tumbler. She filled the tumbler from the jug and handed it to him.

Joe looked at the pale blue liquid suspiciously. In the action movies he liked to watch, spies were often offered spiked drinks by their captors.

'What's this?' he asked.

'It is the juice of the Umqo,' she said.

'Is it safe?'

'It is safe for me.' She took a mouthful and put the tumbler back on the table.

'Oh well.' Joe was thirsty but he sipped it cautiously. It had a sharp, citrus taste. 'So far so good.' He sipped some more. He hoped that he wouldn't pass out. If that happened, he knew that he'd never trust anyone in Carcassia again.

7

Kaia listened without speaking as he told her about running from Greg and Niall, but at the end she laughed.

'It seems that the Haaken traitors are making up ever more unbelievable tales.'

'It's true,' said Joe.

'If it were true, then why did you need to flee these boys?' she asked. 'You are fast and strong. You jumped to me from the fountain and you reached the high window of your room. I have never seen anyone who can do what you can.'

'I might seem fast and strong here,' said Joe. 'But back home, I'm not. Back home I'm ordinary and those guys would have caught me and beat me to a pulp.'

'Everyone is as strong as you in this Eng-land?'

'In England, I'm not strong at all. Lots of people are way stronger.'

She looked worried. 'If you are telling the truth then Carcassia is in more trouble than we have ever believed.'

'I think it was a fluke,' said Joe. 'A portal that opened up from my world to yours. I don't think anyone else is coming through.'

'The Haaken . . .'

'Tell me about them,' he said.

'You do not need to know.'

'According to you I'm going to be locked up here for ever. So it would be good to know why.'

She sat up straight in the chair. Her long hair fell around her face and she pushed it back. She paused for a moment and then began to speak.

'If you are Haaken you know already. If you are Kanabian you know already. If you are neither, your future is still in doubt. I will tell you. It cannot harm us.' She cleared her throat and continued. 'This homeworld is Charra. There are two main tribes. The Carcassians and the Kanabians. A long time ago they lived peacefully together; the Carcassians to the south and the Kanabians to the north. The Carcassians liked to develop and grow, to help each other attain knowledge. The Kanabians also liked to develop and grow but they preferred to steal knowledge and steal other people's work. More and more, the Kanabians came to Carcassia and tried to take things that did not belong to them. Especially the Kerala. The Kerala in the north is different to the Kerala in the south. Its power is weak. So the Kanabians wanted to take our Kerala for themselves.'

Joe adjusted the shell in his ear. Although he understood most of what Kaia was saying, it didn't translate every word.

'What exactly is the Kerala?' he asked. 'The Joq is translating it as crystal but crystals are just stones, aren't they?'

'Kerala makes things work,' she said simply.

'How?'

'It is from the ground.' She looked frustrated. 'With it, everything works. Our light. Our transport. Our . . . everything.'

'Electricity!' exclaimed Joe. 'But why couldn't the Kanabians make electricity themselves. With coal or water?'

She shook her head. 'This electricity . . . it is not made. It is from the Kerala-ka plant. It grows.'

'Wow!' Joe looked at her in astonishment. 'You mean it literally grows?'

'Yes,' she said. 'The fruit of the plant is called Kerala. Once the Kerala hardens it generates power. And we have learned to cultivate it to increase the power.'

'That's pretty cool,' said Joe. 'We'd like that where I come from.'

She looked warily at him.

'I don't mean I'd take it!' he cried. 'I told you, I'm not from Kanabia. It's just . . . well, we have energy issues at home and . . . look, sorry, it doesn't matter. Keep going.'

She took a deep breath before continuing. 'As I said, the Kerala-ka plant in Carcassia is much stronger and more plentiful than the Kerala-ka in Kanabia, and its Kerala more powerful. At first we shared our Kerala with the Kanabians but they wanted more and more and they tried to take them from us. And so there was a war.' Her face darkened. 'Many people were killed. The Kanabians are fierce fighters. They took people from their homes and killed them in the street.'

'Didn't you have better weapons?' he asked. 'If you had this power weren't you able to make guns or rockets or whatever?'

'The Carcassians do not make weapons. We have never

40

made weapons. We do not fight.'

'I thought you said it was a war?'

'We did not expect to fight,' she amended. 'When the Kanabians came we had no choice. But we were losing the war because we had no experience. We did not know what to do. The Kanabians were beating us into the ground. They had arrows. And they showered big stones down on our cities. Look.'

She got up from the table and went to a large cupboard in the wall. From it she took a huge book which she opened. Joe didn't recognise the writing inside but the drawings were familiar. They were like the drawings in his history books where mediaeval battles took place. There were pictures of men with bows and arrows, with swords and with giant wooden machines which Joe suddenly remembered were called trebuchets. They were like enormous catapults and they fired boulders over great distances.

'We were losing the war,' said Kaia. 'There was enormous suffering. So our leaders decided to erect the Shield.'

'This . . . this force field surrounds the city?'

'Carcassia is more than one city,' said Kaia. 'It is a country. My country.'

'Right,' said Joe. He frowned. 'This Shield must be big. It must use a lot of power. A lot of Kerala.'

'Yes,' she said. 'But keeping the Shield in place is the difficulty.'

'Why?'

'To power the Shield the Kerala is placed in a special device called a Loran. But Kerala must also be placed in other Loran in Kanabia for the Shield to be effective.'

'And the Kanabians are OK with this?'

'The Kanabians want nothing more than that our Shield fails so that they can make war on Carcassia again and steal everything we have,' she told him. 'And that is why the Loran are hidden from them. The Runners must find the Kanabian Loran and place the Kerala in them. Every cycle, three Runners pass through the Shield on this mission. I have trained hard to be a chosen Runner.' She turned the pages of the book and stopped towards the end. 'This is the Kerala we bring with us when we leave.'

The picture she pointed to was of an oval object, set on to an ornate stand. It looked like a highly polished egg.

'But there are three of you,' said Joe. 'So do you each place three crystals?'

'There are three Loran in Kanabian territory where the Kerala can be placed,' explained Kaia. 'And three Kerala are placed in each Loran. But only one is necessary for the Shield to work. The others add power and are backup if another fails.'

'So having three of them in one location makes the Shield stronger and last longer,' said Joe.

'The more Kerala, the more power,' Kaia agreed. 'But each Kerala has its own lifespan and we cannot say exactly what that is.'

Joe nodded. 'So you have to put these things in enemy territory. That's scary.'

'It is an honour to be a Runner and place Kerala,' Kaia told him.

'How long have you had the Shield in place?' asked Joe.

'Many generations,' Kaia replied.

'And in all that time you've never tried to negotiate a peace treaty?'

'The Kanabians do not negotiate,' said Kaia. 'They kill. Besides, we cannot communicate with them through the Shield.'

'When the Runners come back, do they say that the Kanabians are still intent on war?'

'Come back?'

'Return,' he said. 'When you've placed the Kerala and you come back to Carcassia, what happens then?'

'A Runner does not return,' she said.

'Why?'

'It is not possible.'

He stared at her. 'So what do you do? Live in Kanabia? How does that work if you might still be fighting them?'

'A Runner does not live in Kanabia.'

'Where do you go then?' he asked. 'Is there somewhere else?'

'No.'

'So what do you do?'

'We take the Muqi,' she answered.

'And what does that do?' he asked.

'It sends us to sleep.'

Joe was getting a bad feeling about this.

'And then?'

'And then we die,' said Kaia.

Joe was horrified. She was talking about dying as easily as talking about walking down the street.

'Why?' he asked.

She looked at him as though he was stupid. 'What else is

there?' she asked. 'I would be in Kanabia. Outside Carcassia. I cannot come home. So I will die.'

He couldn't believe what she was saying. 'Why isn't it possible for you to come home?'

'Because of the Shield. Nobody can come through the Shield.' She spoke slowly, as though to a child. 'You have not been listening to me. The Shield protects Carcassia. Without it the Kanabians would be here. Nobody can get through.'

'Not even people from Carcassia?'

'No. Once you leave it is for ever. But the Haaken believe we should be able to move freely through the Shield. They are continually trying to find a way to breach it.'

'Moving freely doesn't sound like a bad idea,' said Joe. 'And if the Haaken are the descendants of Kanabians like you told me before, why not let them go?'

'They would betray information about Carcassia to the Kanabians,' said Kaia. 'It is better that no one leaves and returns than allow the murdering Kanabian Chan the opportunity to invade our country again.'

'Perhaps they've changed,' said Joe.

She stood up. 'You had me convinced,' she said. 'While I spoke these things seemed new to you. But you are like the Haaken. You want the Kanabians to overrun Carcassia.'

'I don't!' cried Joe. 'I don't belong here and I don't understand enough about the situation. I just thought that it would be good to be able to pass through the Shield and come back. That would mean you didn't have to die.'

'I am proud to die for Carcassia,' said Kaia. 'All Runners have a special place in our world, in our history. I will be

44

honoured, too, if the Leaders agree I have achieved Gimalle and am the third Runner for this cycle.'

'That boy and girl in green,' remembered Joe. 'They're the others.'

'Yes. And I should be the third as I would have completed the test and achieved Gimalle.'

'But you could have been killed on that spire,' said Joe. 'What would have happened then?'

'The seven would have tried again until someone finished.'

'And if no one did?'

'There is always one from each troop who finishes. Always.'

'And the three who finish are supposed to place these Kerala and keep Carcassia safe?'

'Yes.'

'Maybe after such a long time the Kanabians really have changed,' said Joe. 'Maybe if you dropped the Shield you'd find that they were peaceful after all.'

'You do not understand!' She began to walk around the room. Her face was flushed and her eyes glittered with anger. 'They are animals, the Kanabians. They do not care about anything or anybody. All they want is our Kerala for themselves. So that they can enslave us. Then they will destroy all that is good and beautiful in Carcassia. And we will not allow this to happen. That is why our ancestors created the Shield and that is why it must be maintained.'

'OK. OK. But surely you can find a way of a Runner getting back to Carcassia. How can they just let you die like that? Wouldn't it be possible to . . . well to lower the Shield for a moment, just to let you back?'

Kaia shook her head. 'No.'

'So how do you leave? Surely you have to drop it to leave?'

'Anyone can go through the Shield from this side when the power has been decreased. But it is not possible to pass through from the opposite side. It must be dropped completely.'

'Oh.'

'And that is why you are a problem.' Her voice was worried again. 'You have come through the Shield, Sho Hun-ter, and we need to know how. Because there must be a weakness in it somewhere and if the Kanabians find it we are doomed.'

'I told you how.'

'But nobody believes you,' she said.

'I'm telling the truth.'

'How do we know that?'

'You have to trust me, I guess.' He shrugged. 'Look, it's obvious I know nothing about your lives and about anything that's gone on before. I understand why you have the Shield and why you do what you do . . . but I think it's wrong that they're sending you to your death. I don't want you to die, Kaia. I don't want to die either. All I want to do is go home.'

'So how are you going to do that?' she asked.

'I don't know!' His voice was despairing as he thought about it. 'I simply don't know but I have to find a way.'

8

They were sitting in silence when the door was flung open and two Yeppuno burst into the room. Immediately, one of them raised his arm and the black ribbons – the Flagali – flew through the air and wrapped themselves around Joe and the chair he was sitting on. Kaia stood up and looked at the guards.

'I thought you would be here long before now,' she said. 'This is a failure.'

'I apologise, Runner Kaia,' said the first Yeppuno. 'We spent some time with Instructor Vasila and the Leaders discussing the prisoner.'

'You would have been better served guarding him.' There was anger in her voice. 'I had to interrogate him myself.'

'You!' The guard was shocked. 'You are a Runner. You do not question people.'

'I questioned him because you failed to keep him secure.'

'The questioning of a prisoner is for Yeppuno or the Sanctuary Leaders,' said the guard.

'That may be so but when a prisoner arrives at the room of a

Runner and there is no security, she is left with little choice.'
Kaia could barely contain her anger. 'This Gizi has breached
our Shield and I seem to be the only one who is concerned
about it.'

'The Leaders are very concerned,' said the guard. 'That
is why—'

'—why you allowed him to escape,' she finished. 'You have
placed us all in danger.'

'We will secure him again now,' said the Yeppuno.

'Do that,' said Kaia. 'And when you have finished, tell
Instructor Vasila that I wish to see her.'

'But . . .' The Yeppuno looked at her in confusion. 'You
must spend the hours before your Run in contemplation.'

'If I can make the Run at all,' said Kaia. 'Because of your
incompetence in guarding Sanctuary he interrupted it.'

'His presence is not our fault.' The Yeppuno sounded
defensive. 'We have excellent security. It should be impossible
to breach.'

'Yet he did and because of that I did not achieve Gimalle.
And that is why I need to speak to Instructor Vasila. To assure
her and the Sanctuary Leaders that I would have completed my
course ahead of time if this stranger had not interrupted me.'

'I will tell her of your wish.'

'Thank you,' said Kaia.

The Yeppuno nodded. Then the two of them lifted Joe, still
in the chair, and carried him back to his room.

They left him sitting with the ribbons tied tightly around him.
One of the Yeppuno stood at the doorway watching. Joe had

writhed and wriggled but he couldn't loosen the ribbons, so he thought it was a bit over the top for the Carcassians to have left a guard with him. They had also put grilles over the high window.

He wondered if his mother had started to worry about him yet. If she'd reported him missing. If he was the subject of one of those searches for missing kids that sometimes led the news. Any time that happened, his mum's eyes would fill with tears and she'd murmur about how awful it was for the child's parents. Was it awful for her now? Or had she even noticed he was gone?

It was a long time before the door opened again. Joe turned and recognised the tall woman who had been with the group of Runners. She looked worried. Good, he thought. I'm glad they're worried about me. I hope they think I have some kind of super powers! Although that made him worry himself. If they believed he had super powers, maybe they'd try super means to try to keep him here. Or worse. He felt himself begin to sweat.

'*Akka.*' Vasila nodded at the guard, who walked out of the room and stood outside the open door.

She pulled up a chair and sat in front of Joe.

'I have spoken to Kaia Kukura,' she said.

Joe held his breath.

'She told me what you said to her. That you do not know how you got here.'

Joe didn't speak.

'It seems you were very persuasive,' said Vasila. 'She believes you. But then, young girls, even Runners like Kaia Kukura, can easily be persuaded by the words of a handsome boy.'

It was the first time in his life anyone had called Joe handsome. Even though he was tied up in a chair in a place he didn't know, and was scared about what might happen to him next, he couldn't help being pleased at Vasila's words. Handsome. Had Kaia said that he was handsome? he wondered.

'But I am an old woman and not turned by tall tales from strangers,' continued Vasila. 'So I want you to tell me the truth.' She glanced at the open door where the guard was still standing. 'I will know if you do not.'

Joe debated whether to stay silent. But it seemed to him that the more people he persuaded about how he'd arrived in Carcassia the better.

'Tell him to take these ribbons off me,' he said. 'Then I'll talk. Right now, I can hardly breathe.' He was proud at how defiant he sounded. As though he was in control of the situation when he very clearly wasn't.

Vasila thought about it for a moment, then nodded. She called the guard who waved at Joe. The ribbons fell from his chest and landed on the floor.

'You are free,' said Vasila. 'Free to talk.'

Once again, Joe recounted what had happened to him while Vasila listened, her expression attentive, her dark eyes never leaving his face.

'So your Earth found a way to send you to Carcassia?'

'Me being here has nothing to do with Earth,' said Joe. 'The furthest we've gone to is the moon, which isn't very far. And if scientists found a way of reaching another planet they wouldn't send someone like me.'

'You are strong and capable,' said Vasila. 'Why would they not send you?'

'Because . . . because . . .' Joe shrugged helplessly. 'They just wouldn't. I'm not important. I'm nobody. And I'm here by mistake.'

'In that case it is a bad mistake,' said Vasila. 'Because you are somebody here. Somebody we do not want.'

'So help me get home.'

'My priority is to help Kaia Kukura,' said Vasila. 'She is my charge. She is a Runner. And she must complete her task regardless of what has happened.'

'Have Runners ever been captured by Kanabians?' asked Joe suddenly.

Vasila shook her head. 'We cannot tell. It is impossible to track a Runner once they are far outside the Shield.'

'So they might have been? And they might have given information about the Shield that the Kanabians could use? Maybe something they did created a kind of portal on Earth and that's how I came through?'

'A Runner knows what to do if he or she is captured,' said Vasila. 'They do not give information. They release the Muqi.'

'Kaia told me about that. Basically, they commit suicide. That's barbaric.'

'It is our way.'

'And if they're successful they commit suicide too.'

'It is a small price to pay to keep their families and all of Carcassia safe.'

Joe wondered if everyone in Carcassia felt the same.

'Why did you interfere with Kaia Kukura's Gimalle?' asked Vasila.

'She could've been killed!' he cried. 'I had to try to help her.'

'If she had died it would have been because she was not good enough,' said Vasila.

'You're joking, right?' Joe was angry now. 'She's a young girl and you want her to do something incredibly dangerous and you prepare her by nearly killing her!'

'Being a Runner *is* dangerous. She will be on her own, away from her people, knowing that others want to stop her. The Kanabians will do anything to penetrate the Carcassian Shield. As you did.'

Vasila sat silently for a while. Her eyes were closed. There was no sound in the room. Not the tick of a clock, nor the buzz of an insect. The only thing Joe could hear was his own breathing.

'The Sanctuary Leaders want to question you,' she said, opening her eyes after Joe had begun to think she'd fallen asleep. 'They will get the answers they need.'

'I can't tell them what I don't know,' said Joe.

'But you will tell them everything you do.' Vasila stood up. 'Your story is strange but I do not believe that you are a Haaken terrorist. Well,' she laughed and it sounded like she was cracking stones, 'if I am wrong, you are the worst terrorist they ever had. And as for being a Kanabian – you are not Kanabi, that is obvious. But an alien from another world . . .' She sighed. 'This is something Carcassia does not need.'

'I'm sorry if I'm complicating things for you,' said Joe bitterly. 'But it's quite complicated for me too.'

'I will speak to the Sanctuary Leaders,' she said. 'They will decide what will happen to you.'

She left the room. A Yeppuno walked back in. He locked the door and stood in front of it.

Joe was under guard again.

9

It was almost dark by the time more Yeppuno came. Through the window Joe could see the arc of white light more clearly in the sky, as well as a small sliver of moon which shone close to the horizon.

Two Yeppuno grabbed him by the shoulders and escorted him along the tiled corridor, through a small passageway and down a short flight of steps. At the bottom of the steps, they opened a double door which led into what seemed to be a cellar. It had no windows and was lit only by faint egg-shaped lights around the walls. At the far end of the cellar was a big table, and behind the table sat five people. He couldn't tell if they were men or women, because they were identically dressed in dark robes and their faces were hidden by white masks with cut-outs for the eyes and mouth.

There was a chair in front of the table and the security guards pushed Joe on to it.

'So.' It was the person in the centre who spoke, and his voice was deep and booming. 'You are the Outsider who breached the Shield.'

'I'm Joe,' said Joe. 'I didn't do it deliberately. I've explained . . .'

'Instructor Vasila has spoken to us in detail about you,' the man said. 'We need to know how you came to be in Carcassia. And in Sanctuary.'

'If she's told you about me, she's told you that I don't know how.' Joe was feeling very anxious. The masks were freaking him out. The people behind them freaking him out even more. This isn't funny, he said to himself. I have to get out of here. I really do.

'It is not possible that you do not know.' The next voice that spoke was a woman's. It was sharp and severe.

'But it is,' said Joe. 'I was being chased. I was running. I couldn't escape.'

'Running?' The man spoke again. 'You run on your homeworld?'

'Well, yes. But not like it is here. We run for enjoyment. Or for a bus or something. I was running because I was being chased.'

'Who was chasing you? Kanabi?'

'I don't know any Kanabi,' said Joe. 'I don't know any Carcassians either.'

'If you deny being Kanabi or Carcassian, you must be Haaken. So what is your plan, traitor?'

'I'm not Haaken. I don't have a plan. Except to go back to Earth and forget all about this place.'

The five masks remained impassive but the people behind them spoke to each other again in hushed tones.

'We do not know this Earth.' The man spoke to Joe again.

55

'We think you are lying to us.'

'I'm not. I swear I'm not!'

'Where is the weakness in the Shield?'

'I don't know.'

'Have you been altered, Kanabi?'

'I'm not—'

But Joe didn't get to finish what he was saying because the questioner make a gesture and suddenly the Yeppuno guards moved forward and began to strip his clothes from him. He squirmed and wriggled but it was useless. After a moment he was standing in front of them, wearing only his boxers.

The five people whispered to each other while Joe shivered. He wasn't cold, but he was scared. As scared as he'd been when Niall and Greg started to chase him. More scared, in fact, because then all he'd been worried about was a beating. Now he didn't know how bad things could get.

The man and the woman got up from the table and stood in front of him. They looked at his palms and his wrists, and behind his ears. Then they looked over every inch of his body. Joe was embarrassed, especially when the woman started to pinch him around his stomach where he had a bit of fat, and then on his arms where he didn't, and where he was still bruised from Kaia's grasp of him earlier.

'You are not Kanabi.' She sounded disappointed. 'You are not Haaken. Yet you are here, in Carcassia. This has never happened before. You will be punished.'

'You can't punish me for something that isn't my fault!' cried Joe. 'I didn't ask to come here. I don't want to be here!'

'Silence!' The woman hit him on the side of his head with such force that the Joq fell from his ear and slid across the floor. Joe couldn't help his eyes filling with tears. His head was buzzing from the pain of the blow.

The Sanctuary Leaders began talking again, although without the Joq he hadn't a clue what they were saying. For the first time since he'd woken up here, Joe was really afraid. Their voices were angry and heated, a babel of incomprehensible noise as they argued about him.

He said nothing but rubbed his eyes and the side of his head.

After a few minutes, the door opened and Kaia, along with Vasila, walked into the room. They bowed in front of the Leaders and then sat on two large chairs that the Yeppuno placed in front of them.

Then the man spoke directly to him. 'Sho Hun-ter.' Joe understood that, at least. But nothing else of what was said to him. He pointed to his ears.

'I don't understand,' he said.

The woman handed another Joq to Vasila who gave it to Joe. He placed it in his ear. It was a relief to hear clearly again and to understand what they were saying.

'We are keeping you here at Sanctuary,' said the man. 'You will be taken and restrained. You will not be going anywhere again.'

'No!' Joe squirmed as the Yeppuno took hold of him. 'You can't keep me here. I've done nothing wrong. Kaia . . . tell them—'

But Kaia, still sitting on her chair, remained silent as

she watched him being dragged out of the Security Chamber by the guards.

Joe was brought to a different room, which was bigger than before but more secure as there were no windows at all. The Yeppuno had left his clothes in a pile on the table in the centre, so he got dressed again. He took the phone from the pocket of his jeans, relieved that they hadn't found it, although without any signal it wasn't much use either to him or to them. He messed around with the settings for a while, hoping that there might be some kind of WiFi instead, but without any luck.

Then he heard the key in the lock. He slid the phone back into his pocket as a woman he'd never seen before walked in. She was wearing a long white dress, and carrying a tray on which there were two bowls and a bottle of the juice that Kaia had given him earlier. She placed the tray on the table and looked at him.

'Food,' she said.

He walked over to the table and looked at the tray. In the first bowl was a gloopy green mixture. In the second were what looked like multicoloured grapes.

'Good food,' she said.

As he looked warily at it another woman walked into the room. She too was wearing a long white dress and in her hands she carried a bundle of clothes which she placed on the narrow bed alongside the inner wall.

'For you,' she said.

The two women bowed slightly and then walked out of the room again.

Joe looked at the tray. He suddenly realised that he was very hungry but he was afraid to eat or drink anything, even the Umqo juice. For all he knew they could have poisoned it.

But he changed into the clothes which were similar to Kaia's tunic and pants of the previous day, although in the green colour that made his blond hair seem even blonder. If he found a way out of here, it would be better to be wearing Carcassian clothes than his school uniform. The woman had also brought a pair of flat runners but Joe ignored them because he was comfortable in his Nikes.

He spent two hours going over every inch of the room, putting his fingers in the cracks between the stones, looking behind the furniture for any means of escape. But he couldn't find a way. Eventually, too exhausted to try any more, he lay down on the bed and fell asleep.

When he woke up again, it took Joe a few seconds to remember where he was, and to realise everything that had happened wasn't a dream. He got up and looked at the food that the two women had left the night before. He was really hungry now and very tempted to try the multicoloured grapes, but even as he was looking at them the door swung open.

One of the Yeppuno stepped inside. He totally ignored Joe as he waved a clear crystal in front of a wall and a door opened into another room. Joe was astonished and annoyed with himself. He hadn't seen a doorway in his examination of the room the previous night. What else might he have missed? The Yeppuno motioned him to go inside. Joe walked warily to the threshold and then he realised that the room was a bathroom, tiled in the same mosaics as in the passageway. The shower, which the guard showed him, consisted of four strong streams of water pouring through gaps in the ceiling. The toilet was a simple circular bowl in the opposite corner of the room.

Joe went into the bathroom and the Yeppuno stood at the doorway, his back to him. Another Yeppuno was at the opposite side of the room, facing him but not looking directly at him. Joe shrugged, then undressed and stepped under the shower. As he did, the water changed from clear to a rosy pink and a soft lather appeared on his body. He ran his hands over it and it became more and more foamy. After a couple of minutes, the colour of the water changed to a light blue and rinsed the lather away. Then it changed again, to a pale green which, Joe realised, was like a moisturising cream. He thought that this was far too girly for him but when he tried to step out of the shower it began to beep and the Yeppuno turned around. He gestured to Joe who, embarrassed at being seen naked, quickly got under it again.

To his surprise, because he hadn't noticed it happening, his skin was completely dry when the water stopped. It also felt different: stronger, tougher and more elastic. He pinched it a few times to test it and then, when he realised that the guard was getting impatient, he got dressed again.

Almost as soon as he was ready, Vasila came into the room and looked at him.

'Sho Hun-ter,' she said. 'You almost look like a Carcassian Runner.'

'Is that a good thing?'

'Of course,' she said. 'Come.'

He followed her out of the room, along a corridor, and across the courtyard. She opened the door to yet another room; this time it was more of a cell, but with a narrow opening to a huge hall. The hall was filled with trainee Runners all wearing white ribbons in their hair. There was a tiled stage at the front of the room, on which stood two glass jars which glittered and sparkled beneath the light which came in through a roof-top window. On the stage was a man Joe had never seen before, flanked by the boy and the girl who had been watching the trials of the day before. They were dressed in the green tunics. Kaia, also wearing green, was sitting beside them. Her dark hair was tied back and held in its plait by a ribbon of the same colour. She was staring straight ahead and looked completely focused.

'Sit and watch,' said Vasila.

Joe sat on the chair beside the opening and almost immediately he was bound by the Flagali again.

'What are you going to do now?' His heart was thumping.

Vasila didn't answer. She walked out, closing the door behind her. A moment later Joe saw her in the hall. She marched to the top of it and mounted the stage, facing the students. Immediately the hum of conversation stopped.

'We are here to wish good luck to our chosen Runners,' said Vasila. 'They have trained with you for many years and they are the ones that this year have achieved Gimalle, in the allotted time. I know that you wish them every success as they keep Carcassia safe.'

There was a round of applause from the trainees.

'They know that we all wish them well,' said Vasila. 'What

61

we must do now is to choose their routes.'

The trainees cheered.

'As you know, we send three Runners every cycle to maximise our chances of placing the Kerala safely. This cycle, our three runners are Mihai Dalca, Oani Lupei and Kaia Kukura.'

The trainees cheered again.

'Now our Selector Han will draw the routes.'

'Draw. Draw. Draw,' they cried.

The man stood up. He was short and stocky and only reached Vasila's shoulder. He put his hand into the jar and drew out a piece of paper which seemed to shimmer in front of Joe's eyes.

'Route One. The Great Plains Route,' he said. He put his hand into the other jar and pulled out another piece of shimmering paper. 'Oani Lupei.'

The girl, sitting beside Kaia, stood up. She pressed her palms together as though she were about to pray, then bowed in front of the crowd who clapped and cheered. When they stopped, Oani fell to her knees and bent over so that her head was touching the floor.

The Selector reached into the first jar again.

'Route Two. The Road to Lagat,' he announced. And then, taking out the second name. 'Mihai Dalca.'

The crowd applauded. Mihai stood up then did the same as Oani.

'Which means,' said the Selector reaching into both jars at the same time. 'That Route Three, the Mountains and the Rivers, will be Kaia Kukura.'

Joe watched as Kaia followed the lead of the other two

Runners. When the three of them were in a prostrate line, loud music began to play and dozens of flower petals fell from the roof on top of them. Joe grimaced at the noise of the music which seemed to him like nails on glass. But it didn't stop, and neither did the applause of the trainees, until the Runners were almost completely covered in petals. The three Runners stood up, then Vasila walked to the centre of the stage.

'We congratulate our Runners for this cycle who will place the Kerala and keep us safe. In the next cycle, if you work hard and train hard you may be the one to have that honour. Now you must bid farewell to the three who completed Gimalle.'

The students banged their feet on the ground in approval.

Vasila held up her hand for silence. 'Now and Always,' she said, when the noise died down. 'Carcassia will be safe!'

'Now and Always!' they cried. 'Carcassia will be safe.'

Vasila bowed to them.

The Selector bowed.

The Runners bowed.

Then they all walked from the stage.

Joe was trying hard to free himself from the Flagali. There were so many students standing around the big hall that he might be able to lose himself in the crowds if he could get free. But this time he couldn't reach them with his teeth so had no way of loosening them. By the time the students had left the hall, he'd succeeded only in rocking the chair he was tied to so much that it had fallen over. He was lying on the floor, the chair on top of him, when Vasila walked in.

63

She waved her hand over his body and the ribbons fell away from him.

'Come,' she said.

'Where?' He stood up.

'We are going to the Citadel,' she told him. 'This is where the Runners say their goodbyes.'

Joe was relieved to be untied, as Vasila led him along a narrow corridor. Being untied would make things easier. With the extra strength he had here, he'd have a better chance of taking an opportunity to escape.

Vasila stopped when they reached a small courtyard. Unlike the one Joe was familiar with, this didn't have a pool, but the centre was filled with brightly coloured flowers in equally brightly coloured pots. Vasila crossed the courtyard to a large wooden door covered in metal studs. She pressed one of the studs and the doors swung open.

Joe gasped. They were high up on a mountain and stretching below them was a green valley, through which a silver river flowed. Close to the horizon, he could see the spires and columns of buildings. Behind him, he could also see the buildings of Sanctuary which were surrounded by a high, rose-red wall.

'Wow,' he said.

Vasila didn't seem to be awed by the view. She stood outside the wall, waiting.

'What's going to happen now?' he asked.

'Transport,' she said.

A moment later, a red vehicle approached along the dusty track that surrounded Sanctuary and came to a stop in front of them, hovering very slightly over the ground. It was, Joe thought, a bit like a dodgem car but without the conducting rod at the back.

Vasila looked at Joe and nodded. There were no doors, so he clambered over the side. Vasila stepped in more elegantly and sat beside him.

'We depart,' she said and pressed a symbol.

The dodgem car (Joe couldn't think of it in any other way) moved along the track, gathering speed before suddenly shooting off the edge of the mountain. Oh my God, thought Joe, as the car tilted downwards. We're going to crash. This is how she plans to kill me. She probably has a parachute or something. He realised that he was screaming like someone on a roller-coaster.

'Stop yelling like a child,' said Vasila.

'I thought we were going to die.' Joe was gripping the bar in front of him tightly as the car levelled out, a few hundred metres above the ground.

'You do not have the use of a Zaal for transport on your world?' asked Vasila.

The Joq didn't translate Zaal.

'We have other transport,' said Joe. 'I have a bike. And mum and dad have cars. There are buses and trains and there are planes too, but nothing like this.'

Vasila glanced at him but said nothing. Joe continued to grip the metal bar as tightly as he could.

A few minutes later the Zaal descended to ground level and glided to a gentle stop. Then it proceeded along a paved track until it reached what was clearly an enormous parking zone filled with more of the vehicles. The Zaal automatically stopped in an empty space.

'And now for the Citadel,' said Vasila. 'And the leaving ceremony.'

10

Joe was surprised by the city. He'd expected it to be old and crumbling, but it was a maze of straight streets lined by very modern whitewashed buildings with big glass windows. Joe wondered how people knew where they were because everything looked the same to him. And there were crowds of people all hurrying along the streets, wearing brightly coloured robes (in the case of the women) and equally brightly coloured tunics (for the men).

'They have been invited to the Citadel for the Farewell Ceremony,' said Vasila. She led him through a deserted alleyway and then stopped at a sheer white wall. She pressed against it and a door slid open. Vasila beckoned them inside.

'The Citadel,' she said.

They walked through the doorway into a corridor. At the end of the corridor was another door. It was guarded, not by the Yeppuno guards Joe now recognised, but by taller, broader men dressed in red who held long staffs in their hands.

'Instructor Vasila,' she said.

The guards nodded. She walked up to the door and stopped. Then she pressed her face against the wall, which began to shimmer. Joe wondered if she was going to walk right through it. But it suddenly solidified again and gave off a pale blue light.

'Instructor Vasila,' said one of the guards. 'You are expected. Welcome to the Citadel.'

The door opened and Vasila walked through, motioning Joe to follow her. Now they were in a large open-air room, surrounded by white marble statues and unending tubs of multicoloured flowers. There was a marble fountain in the centre and, suspended from the high ceiling, hundreds of little glass balls. The sun was reflecting off them and casting coloured patterns on the white floor.

'What next?' asked Joe as he looked around him. 'What's going to happen to me?'

'Next you wait. But not here.'

Vasila crossed the room and Joe followed her. Once again she pressed a stone in the wall and once again a door opened. To yet another cell with a narrow opening.

'You can look out,' Vasila told them. 'You will not be seen.'

'You're not going to tie me down this time?' said Joe.

'There is no need.' Vasila left the cell and Joe looked around him. There was nothing inside, not even a chair. And the opening, which led on to a plaza reached by an enormous flight of steps, was far too narrow for him to squeeze through. Joe sat on the floor and leaned up against the wall.

He lost track of time but then he heard the sound of voices and laughter coming through the opening. He stood up and looked out. People were pouring into the plaza, finding benches to sit on before starting to share food and talk animatedly.

When the plaza was almost completely full, they stood up and began to look in his direction. Joe shrank back from the opening, afraid he'd be seen and worried about what a mob might do to him. Then he realised that they weren't looking at him at all – somewhere above him a man's voice was talking about the Run and saying Mihai, Oani and Kaia's names.

The crowd roared its approval, the people clapping and stamping their feet. There was more of the awful, scratchy music which set Joe's teeth on edge. And then the sky above suddenly turned inky black, lit only by the arc of light that crossed it. Joe heard a hissing noise before a barrage of fireworks were released upwards, exploding in a rainbow of colours. The crowd cheered and, as quickly as it had darkened, the sky resumed its original light blue again.

Almost immediately, people began to leave the plaza. Joe watched them go. Then he sat on the floor again and waited.

It was about half an hour later when Vasila walked in.

'Did you enjoy the farewell ceremony?' she asked.

'I'm a prisoner. I'm not enjoying anything.'

'You will not be a prisoner for much longer,' said Vasila.

'Why? What are you going to do with me.'

'You will be safe. Do not worry.'

Easy for her to say, thought Joe.

'It was a good ceremony,' Vasila told him. 'One of the best.'

'I'd want more than a good ceremony if someone was sending me my death,' said Joe.

'It is a noble sacrifice.'

'If you say so.' Joe snorted.

'Not me,' said Vasila. 'All of Sanctuary. The Leaders. The people of Carcassia. And the Runners themselves.'

Joe said nothing and Vasila sighed.

'You will leave us now,' she said.

'Great.' Joe was relieved. 'When do I go?'

'You will leave with the Runners,' she said. 'With Kaia Kukura.'

'But where will I go?'

'Kaia Kukura will bring you to her Loran, where she will place her Kerala. I think you may find a portal to your Earth world there.'

Joe was excited. Finally he was going to get out of here.

'It is an arduous journey,' said Vasila. 'You are strong. You will survive.'

'But Kaia dies.' Joe's excitement faded a little.

'Kaia Kukura has prepared for this ever since she came to Sanctuary,' said Vasila. 'It is our way.'

'I thought you were going to keep me here,' said Joe.

'You would prefer that I do?' Vasila raised an eyebrow. 'That can be arranged.'

'No!' Joe spoke quickly. 'It's just . . . you seem to have changed your mind about me.'

'We do not need the disruption of your presence,' said Vasila. 'Carcassia is a safe place, with safe cities. People are happy. They obey the law. Our ways keep us safe and keep the Shield in place and the Kanabians outside. The Carcassian Leaders make sure that this happens.'

'Do your leaders know I came through the Shield?' asked Joe.

Vasila said nothing.

'You didn't tell them! They don't even know I'm here, do they?'

'The fewer people who know about you the better,' said Vasila. 'I have made that decision along with the Sanctuary Leaders. The Carcassian Leaders . . .' she hesitated. 'I do not think Carcassia's best interests are served by you being a part of their questioning.'

'So you really are helping me.'

'If you think that being outside the Carcassian Shield is of help.'

A sudden realisation hit Joe. 'You think I'll die out there with Kaia and the others before I ever get the chance to go home.'

'I expect Kaia Kukura to reach her Loran,' said Vasila. 'She is an excellent Runner. That will be your opportunity to reach your homeworld. If you die before then, it will not be my problem.'

She took him by the arm and, before he could react, clicked a bracelet around his wrist.

'Ow!' he cried as he looked at it. It was made of a hard blue-green material, decorated with symbols and tiny jewels, one of which glowed green. 'What's that for?'

'It is your Link,' said Vasila. 'It connects you to Kaia Kukura. As she has already told you, the Runner lays down his or her life to protect Carcassia. For as long as Kaia is alive, and you are within calling distance of her, you are safe. But if you try to leave her the stone will turn black. The Link will release the Muqi poison inside and you will die. If Kaia Kukura dies, the toxin will be released and you will die too. But if you find a way home, you are safe. The Link will cease to function if you leave our world. All its functions are neutralised.'

Joe stared at her. 'You want me to die. You just don't want it to happen here in Carcassia.'

'If I wanted you to die senselessly I would have you killed without another thought,' said Vasila. 'I am giving you a chance because, strange as it is, I believe your story. I want you far away from here. But if that does not happen, yes, I want you dead.'

She turned away and walked out, locking the door behind her.

Joe felt sick. He sat silently in the cell knowing that there was no escape. And even if there was, where would he go? How far from Kaia was calling distance? How long before the Muqi began to release the toxin? And how long would it take him to die? He could feel himself breathing faster, his palms beginning to sweat and his mouth going dry. Maybe, he thought, it was already working. Maybe Vasila had never intended for him to leave Carcassia with Kaia. It could all be part of a plan . . .

Suddenly the room began to spin. And then he slid slowly off the chair.

When he opened his eyes again he was lying on a narrow bed. The room he was in was dark and cool but as soon as he swung his legs over the side of the bed he threw up. His vomit splattered the marble tiles of the floor and he groaned softly as the door opened and allowed in a shaft of light.

'You will feel better soon.'

He was relieved to recognise Kaia's voice, even though the

sudden brightness meant he couldn't see her properly.

'What happened?'

'This sometimes happens when the Link blends with your body,' said Kaia gently. 'It is a good sign.'

'It is?'

'It means you will make an excellent Runner.' She handed him a glass tumbler filled with Umqo juice. Then she began to clean around him.

'Vasila is sending me to my death,' said Joe. 'I haven't trained to be a Runner. I know nothing about Kanabia. And if I move away from you, I'll die. When you die, I'll die.'

'I will help you and we will reach the Loran. You will then return to your Eng-land. You will not die.'

'I wish I believed you.'

'Vasila has said this. And I have faith in her,' said Kaia. 'She has been an Instructor for a long time. She is very knowledgable. And you, Sho Hun-ter, you are strong and fast. I would prefer to do my Run alone, as is the custom. But I have the good wishes of all Carcassia behind me. Together we will succeed.'

'I saw the Farewell ceremony,' said Joe. 'It was extravagant.'

'It was the best moment of my life,' said Kaia.

'And did you all say goodbye to your families?' he asked.

'Yes. We had private time with them,' said Kaia. 'It was joyful for everyone.'

'Even though you'll never see each other again.'

'Especially because we will never see each other again,' she said. 'We make the most of every moment.'

Joe stood up. He still felt shaky but no longer wanted to be sick. Kaia put the cloth she'd used to clear up after him into a bowl which she then placed into an alcove in the wall. Both cloth and bowl disappeared.

'Where did they go?' asked Joe in astonishment.

'The power within the objects has been turned to energy by the Kerala,' said Kaia.

Joe frowned as he tried to get his head around it.

'If you are feeling well again we must prepare to depart,' said Kaia. 'The others have already left and that has never happened before. Runners always start together. But Vasila made me wait for you.'

Kaia pressed a section of the wall and revealed another small alcove. She took Joe's headphones from it and handed them to him. 'The Sanctuary Leaders have tested these,' she said. 'They have determined that they are useless.'

Joe was about to make a remark about music on the journey but he realised that she'd find out about his phone then. If they examined it with all his photographs and his music and his apps he was sure they'd think it was a secret weapon. So he wasn't going to say anything about it until they were well away from Carcassia. If he got near a portal or something to Earth, the phone might pick up a signal, although he was worried that it would run out of charge before that happened. But if he didn't use it for listening to music or playing games, then it would last a bit longer. And if it did pick up some kind of signal he was going to make a run for it. Maybe she would come with him.

Because that way neither of them would have to die.

Which seemed to Joe to be a much better plan than Vasila's.

11

Joe was feeling a lot better when Vasila walked into the room. In fact he'd never felt so well – the Umqo juice seemed to have given him boundless energy and made him more alert. His plan was to look for narrow alleyways with some kind of shining metal at the end. That was what had got him here, that would be what would get him back to Earth.

Vasila led Joe and Kaia through the long corridors of the Citadel until they arrived at a white door studded with transparent crystals. On the two hooks beside the door hung a pair of rucksacks and beside the rucksacks were two crystal staffs.

'You must hurry,' said Vasila. 'But you will reach the Shield in time. You are both fast.'

'In time for what?' asked Joe.

'It is only possible to leave from this side at the designated hour,' Vasila said. 'If you are late you will not be able to pass through.'

'If we pass through it at the wrong time the energy will surge through the Link,' explained Kaia. 'The power will transfer to our bodies and we will fry.'

'Fry? Literally?'

'Yes,' said Vasila.

'What happens if we can't place the Kerala on time?' asked Joe.

'Carcassia will be at war and there will be a great many deaths,' replied Vasila. 'Our lives are in the hands of the Runners.'

'We will not let you down,' said Kaia.

'I'm not a Runner,' Joe protested. 'And your life can't be in my hands.'

'You will not let us down, either,' said Kaia firmly.

Joe wasn't feeling hugely confident about that.

'Here.' Vasila gave them the rucksacks. 'Your supplies.'

Joe hoped there was lots of food in the supplies. Despite his anxiety, he was hungry again.

'And your Hizu.' She handed them the two crystal staffs he'd also seen.

Then she bowed towards Kaia. '*Kash*, Kaia Kukura. Good fortune and goodbye.'

She opened the door. Joe peered ahead of him. He'd expected it to lead into bright sunlight, but the way ahead was dim.

'This leads to the edge of the Shield,' explained Kaia.

'So we just walk out into the middle of a Kanabian army?' Joe was horrified.

Kaia shook her head. 'It is in a very remote place. They do not even know that we leave. Also, the Shield generates a noise.

Carcassians cannot hear it but it is painful for Kanabians. That means they cannot come too close, although they are always waiting for their opportunity.'

'The time for talking has ended,' said Vasila. 'Now it is time to depart.'

Kaia turned to the older woman. 'Thank you for making me into a good Runner,' she said.

'Thank you for training so hard.'

'Thank you for the lessons you have taught me.'

'Thank you for giving me your attention.'

'Thank you for protecting Carcassia.'

'Thank you for your sacrifice.'

Joe realised that the words between them were a ritual. As they finished speaking, Kaia and Vasila leaned towards each other. Their foreheads touched and they remained in that position for a moment.

'Be safe,' whispered Vasila. 'Be well.'

When they stood apart, Joe could see that there were tears in Vasila's eyes. For the first time he really believed that they were walking into danger. And he was frightened. For himself and for Kaia.

As well as being dimly lit, the passageway Joe stepped into with Kaia was damp and smelled slightly musty. The walls were irregular and although they didn't exactly sparkle, they were pale enough to reflect the light from the crystal staffs which had begun to glow as soon as Vasila closed the door behind them.

Kaia looked at her Link. It was a bigger and more complex

bracelet than Joe's and as well as the green jewel that showed their connection, a large red ruby glowed in the centre. Joe could see that the colour came from a network of tiny lights inside it.

'Half an orph from the edge of the Shield,' replied Kaia.

'How far is an orph?' asked Joe.

Kaia shrugged. 'One light fades for the time it takes to travel ten orphs.'

'So we haven't come ten orphs yet. But is the tunnel ten orphs long?'

'More,' said Kaia. 'I do not know the exact distance. I know we must leave Carcassia before two lights fade.'

'Right,' said Joe. 'Will we catch up with Oani and Mihai, d'you think? If we call them would they hear us?'

'They are far ahead by now,' said Kaia.

She kept walking. Joe followed.

'They could have waited for us,' he said after a few minutes.

'A Runner does not wait for anything.'

She strode along, surefooted despite the unevenness of the surface. Even with the light of the Hizu staffs and the reflection from the walls, Joe found it difficult to see what was ahead, but Kaia didn't seem to have the same problem. After he'd stumbled a couple of times she stopped and took a small stick from her rucksack. She tapped it against the wall and it glowed gently in the gloom. She handed it to him.

'I would not expect to have to use this in a place with as much light as this,' she said. 'But you are slowing me down.'

'What are you talking about?' said Joe. 'It's pretty dark down here. I don't know why you're not tripping up too.'

She looked at him and he gasped slightly. Her bright blue eyes were now almost green.

'My vision adapts,' she says. 'Like all Runners it has been modified.'

'Wow,' he said. 'You're like a cat in the dark.'

'A cat?'

'It's an animal on my planet,' said Joe. 'They can see better than humans in the dark. But it's natural to them.'

'They are obviously intelligent beings.'

Kaia began to walk again. Joe got the impression that she didn't want to talk, that she thought of him as a nuisance slowing her down. He continued behind her, holding the glowstick in front of him and using the Hizu to help keep his balance. Of course he could've turned on the torch on his phone (which he'd slipped into the rucksack just after they'd entered the tunnel) but he was sticking to his plan not to take it out while they were still in Carcassia.

Joe didn't know how long they'd been walking when they reached a wide cavern and Kaia stopped.

'It is time for nourishment,' she said. 'Sit.'

'Great,' said Joe. 'I'm starving.'

Both of them sat on the ledge that ran around the cavern. Kaia opened her rucksack and took out a packet containing what looked to Joe like oatmeal biscuits. She also removed a narrow bottle of a pale yellow liquid. Not Umqo juice, she told him. A stronger drink, Gira, for the additional energy which they would need as they continued on their mission. A single mouthful would quench a thirst and refresh a Runner. And the Cheebas would give him energy.

79

'Good?' she asked as he bit into one.

'Better than I expected.'

She nodded. 'My mother used to make them when I was small.'

'When did you leave to train as a Runner?' asked Joe as he uncapped the bottle and took a sip of the energy drink.

'After four cycles,' replied Kaia.

Joe assumed that a cycle was a year, but he didn't know if a year in Carcassia was the same as a year on Earth.

'How old – how many cycles – are you now?' he asked.

'I have completed fourteen,' she said.

So, more or less the same age as him which is what he'd thought. But that meant that she'd started training at four and she'd been doing it for ten years. Ten years away from home.

'That must have been hard,' he said. 'On you and your family.'

She shook her head. 'Having a Runner in the family brings blessings to your home.'

'Right.' Joe looked thoughtful.

'We must move,' she said.

Joe got up. He put the wrapper and the empty bottle in his rucksack and heaved it on his back again. He thought that Kaia was thawing a little in her attitude towards him. He hoped so. He needed her. And even if she didn't appreciate it yet, she might need him too.

12

He was trying to work out how far they'd gone when he felt the ground rumble beneath his feet. He stopped and so did Kaia.

'Dragons,' she said, sounding worried.

'What!!!!' Joe looked at her in astonishment. 'There are no such things as dragons. At least,' he added, 'not on Earth. Here, I suppose, there could be anything.'

'They are not on the surface,' said Kaia. 'They do not come into our cities. But they live below ground and when they fight the Earth shakes.'

'Are you sure about that?' asked Joe. 'Are you sure it's not just an earthquake?' Although he wasn't certain himself which would be worse.

'It is a dragon,' she said as the ground shifted beneath them. Stones fell from the roof. Joe pulled her closer and covered her head with his arm. The shaking grew worse and he could feel more and more stones raining down upon them. He was trying to protect his own head with his shoulder when Kaia broke free of him.

'Kaia! Don't. You could get hurt!'

She stood in the centre of the passageway, holding her Hizu which she then banged on the ground three times. It began to emit a sharp white light and Joe could sense more than see the force coming from it when the stones, which had become small rocks, were no longer falling on top of them but bouncing harmlessly away.

'What is that?' he asked. 'What have you done?'

'The Hizu has Kerala,' she told him. 'It protects us from dragons. Like the Shield.'

'Oh.' Joe looked at his own staff. 'I should have done that too.'

'You did not know.' She looked at him in surprise. 'Instead you tried to protect me with your body. That was foolish.'

'I didn't want you to get hurt.'

'It is I who will not allow you to get hurt, Sho Hun-ter.' She gave him a faint smile. 'I want you to get back to your Earth. And your Eng-land.'

'You do?'

'Of course,' said Kaia. 'Now, let us go on.' She tapped the Hizu gently on the ground again. The white light faded back to the original glow.

'What now?' asked Joe as they looked in front of them and realised that the stones and rocks had blocked the tunnel ahead of them. 'Do we go back?' He looked behind him where the way was still perfectly clear.

'We cannot go back,' said Kaia. 'We must clear a passage.'

'Can the Hizu do that for us?' asked Joe hopefully.

'Unfortunately not.' Kaia started shifting the stones

with her hands. Joe helped her.

It was hot, dusty work and – even with the extra energy he seemed to have gained from the Gira drink – it was very tiring. He could feel his arms and legs begin to ache and more than once he wondered what they would do if the tunnel was completely blocked and if they couldn't make their way through. Kaia was determined that they couldn't go back, but what if there was no alternative? They could hardly sit here and die! Although, he thought glumly, given the fact that Kaia was prepared to die anyway, maybe that was actually a possibility. The idea made him work even harder and eventually he began to see a chink of light through the rocks.

'Nearly there,' he told Kaia.

She didn't reply. Her face was streaked with dust and her hair had come loose from her complicated plait. Her tunic was dusty too, and there was a small tear in the shoulder where she'd been hit by one of the bigger rocks.

'Are you OK?' asked Joe.

Kaia nodded, still without speaking. She seemed to be focusing her entire energy on clearing the way. Joe could see that her fingers were bleeding.

'Stop,' he said, catching hold of her hands. 'You need to rest for a moment.'

'When we are through,' she told him.

They worked side by side for another half hour until finally there was a gap big enough for both of them to squeeze through. Joe pushed his rucksack through first, then went ahead of Kaia 'to make sure it's safe,' he told her, although she snorted at that. She followed him and the two of them stood side by side, panting slightly with the effort they'd made.

'I didn't realise that the problems in this trip would start so soon,' said Joe. 'I thought it would only happen when we got to Kanabia.'

'To be honest, so did I.' Kaia gave him a weak smile. 'Although the dragons sometimes make Carcassia shake it is never as bad as this.'

'You know deep down it's not dragons, don't you?' said Joe.

Kaia tossed her head and began to fix her hair.

'What about your hands and your shoulder?' asked Joe.

'They are fine.'

'But—'

'We need to move on,' said Kaia. 'We are still behind the others.'

'Will we catch them up? Does it matter?' asked Joe. 'After all, you take different routes, don't you? Wasn't that what was happening at the choosing ceremony at Sanctuary?'

'It is tradition to start out together although they will not wait for us,' said Kaia. 'Then we place our Kerala and move to the next Loran.'

'If you only need one Kerala to make the Shield work and you're not sure how much extra power and life the others add, then maybe you shouldn't bother going to the other Lorans,' remarked Joe.

'We cannot communicate outside the Shield,' Kaia told him. 'So one Runner does not know if the other was successful. Therefore it is necessary to continue to the next.'

Joe nodded.

'We are falling behind,' said Kaia. 'We must move faster.'

She picked up the pace. Once again, he followed her.

It surprised Joe that even though they'd been walking for hours he didn't feel tired. Walking wasn't something he normally did a whole lot of, but today it really wasn't a problem, despite the unevenness of the ground beneath him. It was as though his feet only barely touched the surface, as though he was wearing super-expensive trainers instead of his basic ones.

Nevertheless he was tired of the tunnel and following in Kaia's footsteps. She was ploughing on with a fixed determination, never slowing down or wavering for an instant. She didn't stop and chat from time to time, she just kept on going.

Until they reached another rock fall. This wasn't as bad as the one they'd had to dig themselves out of, but the shock that both Kaia and Joe received as they came upon it, was that Oani was still there. She was sitting on the ground, her knees drawn up to her chest, her head resting on them. She seemed to be sleeping.

'Oani?' Kaia knelt beside her. 'What has happened here?'

Oani jerked her head upright and her eyes snapped open. They opened even wider when they saw Joe standing behind Kaia. She reached for her Hizu but Kaia stopped her.

'This is Sho Hun-ter,' she said. 'He is with me.'

'A Hunter? A Hunter cannot run with us!' Oani was astonished.

'It is hard to explain,' said Kaia. 'Vasila has sent him. He is not a Hunter. He has come from another part of

Carcassia.' Kaia added, 'He has special skills.'

'Kaia Kukura, I have faith in you and in Instructor Vasila,' Oani said. 'I have faith in the Sanctuary Leaders. But I cannot understand why it is necessary to send this Outsider with us.'

'I only knew about him myself today,' said Kaia. 'I am as surprised as you.'

'Mihai and I questioned Vasila when we were sent ahead of you,' said Oani. 'She said nothing to us. We thought that there was a problem with you, Kaia. There had been rumours about your Gimalle. That you had received assistance. Was it from the Outsider?'

'No,' said Joe.

'Nevertheless . . .' Oani still looked doubtful.

'Nevertheless he is here and I am in charge of him,' said Kaia. 'But, Oani, more important than this is what happened to you? Why are you sitting here? Where is Mihai?'

'He has gone ahead because I cannot walk,' said Oani. 'I am sure you felt it when the dragons came. The walls started to shake and fall. I did not get my Hizu raised in time and I was hit by a rock. I stumbled and now I cannot walk.' A tear began to trickle down her face. 'I have failed Carcassia. I have not even started my Run and I am a failure. I will stay here and activate my Muqi.'

'It wasn't your fault,' said Joe sympathetically. 'We were nearly trapped by a rockfall ourselves. You can't possibly sit here and wait to die. Can you walk at all?'

She shook her head. 'Perhaps in some time,' she said. 'But that will be too late. I will not be able to get to the Shield in time to leave.'

'Oh, Oani.' Kaia was distressed. 'You will forfeit your Run.'

'At least you can try to make it back to Carcassia,' said Joe. 'They can patch you up, send someone else, and maybe you can be a Runner another time.'

Oani's expression was shocked. 'Where exactly do you come from, Sho Hun-ter, that you do not know it is impossible to return to Carcassia?'

'Of course you can,' said Joe. 'You haven't left yet so it's not like you're going to be zapped by the Shield, is it? It might take you some time but at least you'll be looked after.'

'You are Carcassian.' Oani stared at him. 'And yet you ask these questions?'

'He is from the . . . the . . . Nygat region,' said Kaia. 'They are remote. Backward. Too stupid to train as Runners. Too stupid to remember traditions.' She turned to Joe. 'You know that Oani would not be accepted back in Carcassia if she failed her Run.'

'What is it with you people!' cried Joe. 'You seem to think that it's perfectly OK to send each other to their deaths! And me to my death too.'

'I do not trust this Outsider, Kaia Kukura,' said Oani. 'I do not believe he is from Nygat. I think he is Haaken and has fooled you all.' Her fingers closed around her Hizu.

'Oani, no!' Kaia reached out for the other Runner's staff. 'I should have told you the truth at the start. It is . . . complicated.'

'Complicated?'

Kaia told her everything about Joe and Oani's eyes opened wider and wider.

'And so you will go with Kaia to the Loran of Zwemat?' she said, looking at him.

'That's the plan,' said Joe.

'I have never heard of such a thing.'

'Instructor Vasila thinks it is important to send Sho Hun-ter home,' said Kaia. 'And so that is part of my mission too.'

'And you are sure he is not a traitor? He is called Hun-ter after all.'

'That is just his name. He cannot hunt. But he may be useful. He is strong and . . .' she glanced at Joe. 'He is brave.'

'Thank you,' said Joe.

'I must resume my Run, Oani.' Kaia looked worried. 'I am already late. Perhaps your situation will improve.'

'It will not,' said Oani. 'I will die here. But it will be an honour.'

'That's just rubbish,' Joe told her. 'Let me see your leg.'

The girl hesitated, then stretched it out. Joe could see that her ankle was badly swollen.

'I cannot put my foot on the ground,' she said. 'It is very painful.' She looked at Kaia. 'I would be sent from Sanctuary with this injury.'

Joe looked at it and then gently eased her foot out of her light trainer. Oani cried out in pain but Joe continued what he was doing.

'I don't suppose we have ice?' he said.

'Ice?' asked Kaia.

'Frozen water.'

'We do not freeze water in Carcassia,' said Kaia.

'Probably a bit late for it anyway.' He opened his rucksack

and took out one of the rolls of black ribbon which he began to wrap around Oani's foot.

'What are you doing!' she exclaimed. 'These are Flagali restraints.'

'And they make pretty good compression bandages,' said Joe. 'I don't think you'll be able to walk, but at least this will help it to stop swelling any further. Really what you should've done was to elevate your foot to stop the blood flow and help keep the swelling down.'

Kaia and Oani stared at him.

'I did first aid at school,' he said. 'And I can't believe that with all the training you did at Sanctuary you don't know how to treat simple injuries. Though in fairness this is a bad sprain.'

'If you were injured at Sanctuary so that you could not walk or run, you had to leave,' said Kaia.

'That's crazy.'

'That is the rule. But I am pleased that you are here, Sho Hun-ter, to tend to Oani.'

Joe grimaced. 'I'm glad to be able to help.' He looked at Oani. 'You really shouldn't put any weight on this for a while but you can't stay here.'

'I must,' said Oani.

'I'm not leaving you to die,' Joe said.

'You have strange ways, Sho Hun-ter,' said Oani. 'If you and Kaia do not leave and you get blocked by the Shield, you will die too. And the only person left to Run will be Mihai. The odds are not good. Especially as he is the weakest of us.'

'You're coming with us,' said Joe. 'If we all get through

we at least have a chance, don't we? If you stay here, Oani, you've none.'

'Sho is right,' said Kaia. 'With his treatment you may recover more quickly and complete your Run. That would be a good thing.'

'I cannot walk,' protested Oani. 'I will not be able to Run.'

'Put your arms around my neck,' said Joe.

'What?'

'I'm going to carry you,' said Joe.

'You cannot.'

'Of course I can. Now put your arms around my neck.'

Oani looked doubtfully at Kaia. She nodded her agreement and Oani put her arms around him. He straightened up so that he was giving her a piggyback.

Kaia gave a sudden laugh. 'Now you are like a Mooni,' she said.

'What's a Mooni?'

'A kind of animal,' said Kaia. 'They had territories in the north and many Carcassians used them for transport. But they could not live under the Shield.'

'Pity,' said Joe. 'They might have been useful. You'll have to hold both our rucksacks,' he added to Oani.

'And I will hold your Hizu,' said Kaia. 'But this will slow us down, Sho.'

'No,' said Joe decisively. 'You've been slowing me down. You're supposed to be a Runner but we've been walking through the tunnel. I think the time has come to Run.'

'But we are supposed to walk through the tunnel,' said Oani. 'So that we arrive at the Shield at the correct time.'

'And we're late,' Joe reminded her. 'This is an emergency. So let's go. Keep those glowsticks in front of me.'

With Oani holding tightly on to him, the glowsticks and the two rucksacks, he began to run. Slowly at first and then picking up the pace. Not being at all worried about the uneven ground. Hardly aware of Kaia behind him, keeping up. He was enjoying it, he realised. He was enjoying the feeling of pushing his body and yet not pushing it too much because it really wasn't hard for him at all. He'd been thinking about it earlier and he'd decided that it was something to do with gravity. That here, on this planet – wherever it was – gravity was lighter and that was why he could jump and run so easily. He didn't know how long he was going to be here. He hoped it wouldn't be too long at all. But while he was here, he was going to enjoy the benefits that being here gave him. Because he'd never felt this strong in his life before.

After what seemed like an eternity of running with Oani on his back, Joe began to see a glimmer of light ahead of them. He hoped it was the end of the tunnel – they'd been underground for a long time now. He picked up his speed still further and suddenly there was an opening in front of him and he knew they'd reached the end.

The exit was a narrow gap, partly covered by dry yellow foliage. Joe stopped, still inside the tunnel, and Oani slid from his back. She still couldn't put any weight on her foot and she leaned against him for support.

'So – anything we should know before we go outside?' he asked Kaia. She took a moment to catch her breath and then shook her head.

'The Shield is only a few steps beyond the exit,' she said.

'Why did we have to come through this tunnel at all?' asked Joe. 'Why couldn't we just get one of those flying car things to take us here?'

'Because the Zaal do not travel to the edges of the Shield,' replied Kaia. 'Besides, if we did not leave in secret, the Carcassian people would want to watch us pass through. And maybe try to leave too, to fight the Kanabi.'

'Don't they ever want to leave anyway?' He turned to look at her. 'Don't they get bored with living in a place that's shielded from the rest of the world?'

'Carcassia is the best place on Charra to live,' said Kaia. 'Kanabia is our enemy. Karkasona is a region that was abandoned even before the war. And no Carcassian would want to live in Mooni territory.'

'I thought you said the Moonis died out.'

'Any of them that were in Carcassia did,' said Kaia. 'There may be others outside the Shield. They are harmless.'

'Famous last words,' muttered Joe. Then he looked at Oani. 'Are you sure you don't want to go back?'

She shook her head. 'I cannot.'

'In that case . . .' Joe pushed the dried grass out of the way and then stepped outside the tunnel. He blinked in the sudden glare of the sun as he looked around him. The land was flat and desolate, with occasional tired and parched bushes breaking dotted around. There were no other signs of life – no trees, no birds, no animals. Although, he thought with a shred of amusement, maybe a dragon would come hurtling along any minute and make toast of them all.

'This is not like Carcassia at all,' said Oani as she hobbled out to join him.

'Perhaps it is what Kanabia is like,' said Kaia. 'If so, it is no surprise that they want to take over our country.'

The two Runners nodded in agreement.

'So, where now?' asked Joe.

'The Shield is ten paces from the exit,' Kaia told him. 'We just walk straight ahead. You can see.'

And Joe did see. He couldn't understand how he hadn't before. Where he thought he'd been looking into the distance, he was actually looking at the land around them, reflected. And as they walked nearer to the Shield – both he and Kaia supporting Oani – he saw themselves reflected in it too.

When they were one step away they all stopped.

'Scared?' asked Joe.

'It is an important moment,' said Kaia. 'The fate of Carcassia is in our hands.'

'Will you be OK, Oani?' Joe glanced at her.

'I will stay outside the Shield and keep safe until my ankle is healed,' she replied. 'The Great Plains Run to Domote is the easiest. I will recover and make sure that I place my Kerala long before you get there.' She smiled at Kaia as she spoke.

'I am sure that I will have placed my Kerala first,' said Kaia. 'But I will be happy if you reach your goal.'

'Is it a sort of competition?' demanded Joe.

'Of course.' Oani smiled. 'Now, are we ready?'

She took Kaia's arm and then Joe's.

And the three of them stepped through the Shield.

PART TWO

THE CRYSTAL RUN

13

It was like being attacked by a swarm of mosquitos, thought Joe, as a prickling sensation ran through his body. At the same time, he felt as if he were being stretched like a piece of elastic. It was uncomfortable and scary and even though it only lasted a couple of seconds, he was relieved when he realised that they had come out the other side.

Almost at once he started to shiver, because although the temperature in Carcassia had been pleasantly warm, a hard, cold wind was now blowing and the sky was hidden by grey cloud. Nearby, a small copse of trees swayed and rustled. He turned to Kaia and Oani who were shivering too.

And then he saw Mihai. He was standing facing them, his Hizu in his hand.

'What are you doing here?' asked Kaia in surprise. 'You should have made progress by now.'

'Waiting for him.' Mihai nodded towards Joe.

'Why?'

Mihai tapped his Hizu once off the ground and the

tip began to glow.

'Because this is as far as you go,' he said. 'Haaken.'

'Huh?' Joe stared at him.

'We cannot have a Haaken terrorist reporting to Kanabi,' Mihai told him.

'What are you talking about?' Kaia stepped forward and stood in front of Mihai. 'Sho is not a terrorist. Instructor Vasila said—'

'Instructor Vasila!' Mihai snorted. 'Everyone knows that she has become soft. That she can be manipulated.'

'That is not true!' Kaia was angry.

'And that she keeps secrets.' Mihai looked from her to Joe. 'It is known that she kept the secret of your arrival from the Carcassian Leaders,' he said. 'And that she persuaded the Sanctuary Leaders you were no threat. And that she allowed Kaia Kukura to reach Gimalle even though you assisted her. It is believed that Instructor Vasila is now a traitor to Carcassia.'

'No!' cried Kaia. 'That is not true.'

'If she was not a traitor she would not have allowed a Haaken to accompany a Runner through the Shield,' said Mihai. 'But fortunately the Leaders found out about her plan and I have been charged with stopping him.'

'If he was the enemy we could have stopped him in Carcassia.' Oani, who was still holding Joe's arm, spoke up. 'But he has helped us. Helped me, when you left me behind.'

'I had to leave you,' said Mihai. 'You cannot run. You could be captured by the Kanabi. You are a liability.'

'Any of us could be captured by the Kanabi,' said Kaia. 'We know what to do if that is the case.'

'Sho carried me on his back,' said Oani. 'This is not the way a terrorist would behave.'

'It is exactly the way a terrorist would behave,' said Mihai. 'He wanted to get you here, injured, so that the Kanabi can capture you and question you.'

'If I am captured I will release the Muqi,' said Oani. 'I know what to do. Sho has been kind to me.'

'I have my orders.' Mihai pointed the Hizu at Joe.

'Orders from who?' asked Joe.

'The Leaders,' said Mihai. 'You think they did not know you were in Carcassia, Hun-ter? They know everything.'

'Mihai!' Kaia's eyes were wide and disbelieving. 'You cannot!'

'Yes, I can,' said Mihai. He jerked the Hizu and Joe leaped high into the air in just enough time to feel a hot glow as the light passed beneath him. Mihai cried out in anger. He pointed the Hizu at Joe again but Joe was faster and this time jumped behind Mihai. Before he could turn around Joe caught hold of his arm and tried to wrestle the Hizu away from him. Joe realised that although he was faster, Mihai was the stronger. It was taking a big effort just to keep hold of his arm. The two of them were wrestling on the ground while Kaia and Oani watched. Eventually, Mihai managed to shake himself free from Joe and raised the Hizu again.

'No!' Oani threw herself at him just as he fired. Mihai fell to the ground and the light missed Joe by inches. 'This is wrong, Mihai. You cannot kill someone like this.' She was sitting on his chest now, pinning him down.

'I will not let you harm Sho,' Kaia said. She opened her rucksack and took out another of the Flagali. She nodded at

Oani who rolled off Mihai's back and, as he sat up, she threw the ribbon towards him. It wrapped itself around him, pinning his arms to his side.

'What are you doing?' he demanded.

'The Flagali will release you in time,' said Kaia. 'You can then begin your Run. Meantime, Oani, Sho and I will run too.'

'You are betraying our country, Kaia Kukura,' cried Mihai. 'You should never have been awarded Gimalle. You will bring destruction upon us.'

'No I will not,' said Kaia. 'I believe in Sho. He has proved himself in the tunnel. With his help, I will place my Kerala and I will keep Carcassia safe.'

'But what about him?' Mihai's face was red with anger. 'What will he do?'

'He will help me,' said Kaia. 'And I will help him too. I will help him return to his Earth and his Eng-land.'

'And her?' He looked disdainfully at Oani who was now leaning against Joe for support.

'We will assist Oani until she can run.'

'You are leaving me defenceless against the Kanabi,' said Mihai. 'What happens if one comes upon me tied up like this.'

'You activate your Muqi and you die,' said Kaia. She picked up her rucksack and looked at Joe and Oani. 'Time to run,' she said.

'How do you know which way to go?' asked Joe a short time later when she stopped beneath the shade of an enormous tree.

'Maps, of course,' she replied.

She opened her rucksack and took out a sheet of paper.

Only it wasn't really paper, more like a thin, flexible plastic. She touched an egg-shaped icon in the top corner and the outline of a map appeared on it, followed a second later by more and more detail.

'This is Carcassia.' She pointed to the southern end of the map. 'Here is Sanctuary and the Citadel, and here is the boundary where we left the tunnel. And all this,' she added, drawing her finger over the centre and north of the map, 'is Kanabia.'

'So which way do we go?' asked Joe.

'This is the route of the Mountains and the Lakes,' she said, pointing to a broken red line. 'The three Loran are here, here and here.'

The locations were marked in gold on the map. The first was on the eastern side of the map, through what seemed to be a gap in the mountain range that was past a forest and a lake. The second was to the extreme north of the country, and part of another mountain range; and the third was on the west side of the land mass, near the coast.

'The last is the most dangerous,' said Kaia, 'because this is Lagat, the main city of Kanabia and the Kerala must be placed in the centre. I had hoped to draw Lagat as my first Loran but that honour fell to Mihai.'

Joe could hear a tone of disgust in her voice. Even if she hadn't defended him against Mihai earlier, Joe would have guessed she didn't like him much.

'So where exactly are these Loran?' he asked.

'The map will show us the precise location when we are close.' Kaia placed her fingers over the area where they currently were and swiped. Immediately the map zoomed in and gave a bird's eye view of the landscape.

'Just like Google Maps,' said Joe. He took his phone from the rucksack and was surprised to see that it was fully charged.

'What is that?' asked Oani, a hostile tone in her voice.

'It's a communication device—' Joe began, and the next thing he knew he was on the flat of his back with Kaia standing over him, her foot on his chest.

'Haaken Gizi!' she hissed. 'I should have let Mihai kill you when he had the chance. You are communicating with the Kanabians.'

'No, I'm not!' he cried. 'It doesn't work here. There's no signal. You can check it yourself.' He handed the phone to her.

Kaia took it.

'What are these symbols?' she asked as she scrolled through the apps.

'You use them for things,' said Joe. 'Like listening to music. And maps – but I guess that won't be much use here.'

'Show me.' She allowed him to stand up, but he saw that Oani now had her Hizu pointed at him.

He tapped Google Maps but got a 'location not available' message. So he opened his music instead. Almost as soon as it started playing Kaia knocked him down again.

'You are calling to the Kanabians with this terrible noise!' she exclaimed. 'Make it stop.'

'It's not noise. It's music. Like at your Farewell Ceremony,' he said.

'Liar! That was beautiful. This hurts my ears.'

'I guess we like different things,' he said. 'Honestly, Kaia, it's just a phone. It's like the Link.' He held up his wrist. 'But it doesn't work here. I need to be at home.'

'He may speak the truth,' said Oani. 'We cannot use the Link as a communication device outside the Shield. This phone could be the same.'

Kaia looked at Joe with narrowed eyes. 'I do not know if I should trust you or not,' she said. 'You could still be Haaken.'

'I'm really not,' he told her.

'He did not have to help me.' Oani lowered the Hizu. 'He could have let me die in the tunnel.'

Kaia continued to glare at him. 'You kept a secret from me.'

'I was afraid you'd think exactly what you're thinking now,' said Joe. 'I didn't want you or anyone in Carcassia taking it from me in case a message from home somehow comes through. That's all.'

She turned it over and over in her hand and then nodded. 'I will keep this device,' she said. 'If the Kanabians try to contact you I will know.'

'OK,' said Joe.

'We have wasted too much time.' Kaia looked at her Link. One of the lights in the ruby stone had faded to a rose pink. 'We must begin the Run,' she said. 'If all of the lights turn white before I complete my mission I will have failed and the Muqi will be released. So we cannot stand around here talking.'

'What about you, Oani? Are you coming with us for some of the way?' Joe asked.

'I cannot.' Oani looked at the ruby stone on her own Link, then took a similar map from her rucksack. She also tapped the icon in order to call up the map. This time the route to the three Loran began with the north location.

'You'll move in a giant triangle,' said Joe. 'The North is furthest, Oani. You have more distance to travel than anyone but you're injured. And Lagat is closer which means less of a Run for Mihai. Maybe you should have swapped.'

'You do not change a Run with another Runner.' Oani looked horrified. 'It must be done properly in accordance with the rules. I must go north, to Domote. Kaia goes east to Zwemat. And Mihai Dalca goes west to Lagat.'

'What difference does it make what order you go in, if you all die at the end?'

'It is our Rule. And we die with honour,' said Kaia.

'Yeah. That's the part I'm not looking forward to,' said Joe.

'We will talk of your future later, Sho,' said Kaia. 'I am sure you will not die.'

'Perhaps we could find a way to break the Link between us?' Joe tried and failed to move the bracelet on his arm before running his fingers over the symbols.

'Please do not press anything you do not understand,' Kaia said. 'You could release the Muqi.'

Joe snatched his hand away from the bracelet.

'You should go,' said Oani. 'I will find shelter and I will begin my Run when I can.'

Kaia nodded. She looked at Joe who reluctantly picked up his rucksack. And then, leaving Oani sitting beneath the tree, they started to run again.

* * *

Away from the cover of the trees, the wind became stronger and colder. As they continued to run the sky darkened and eventually Joe felt drops of rain hitting his face.

'Kaia!' he called. 'I think we should shelter for a bit.'

'We are behind our schedule thanks to Mihai Dalca.' Kaia didn't stop running as she shouted back at him. 'We must keep moving. There is a stop marked on the map thirty orphs from here.'

Joe picked up his pace to keep up with her.

He reckoned it was nearly two hours later before they arrived at a lake in the middle of a flat landscape. Joe pushed his wet hair out of his eyes and looked around him. The water of the lake was dark grey, and being pounded by the increasingly heavy rain.

'There should be shelter here.' Kaia looked around her. 'But I do not see anything.' Water streamed from her hair down her face. She shivered.

'Are you cold?' asked Joe.

'Of course I am cold,' she snapped. 'The wind is cold. It is raining. I do not know rain from the sky. It does not happen in Carcassia. Nor do we experience this wind. But it does not matter. We have trained for it.'

'That's why they tied you to the pole!' exclaimed Joe. 'So that you'd experience rain.'

'Yes.' She nodded. 'But this wind, this rain – and this cold – it is very different from training.'

'Real life is always different from training,' said Joe.

For the first time since he'd found himself in this world he felt superior to Kaia. He knew about life outside the Shield.

He knew about cold and rain. He could cope with them. Maybe he could help her cope too.

'However.' She stood tall and spoke before he could say a word. 'I will become accustomed to it. It is part of my Run.'

So is dying, thought Joe suddenly. But surely it doesn't have to be. There must be a way for us to survive. If I can find a way to get home I could take you with me. Oani too, if we meet her again. Because you can't simply kill yourselves. You're both too brave to die.

'Let us find our shelter,' said Kaia.

First things first, thought Joe, and nodded.

14

The two of them stood at the water's edge.

'There are trees and boulders on the other side,' said Joe. 'Is that where your shelter is supposed to be?'

'I do not think so.' Kaia looked at the map. 'The route takes us around the lake, not across it.' She started to pace along the shoreline and then she stopped.

'Look,' she said doubtfully. 'This must be the shelter.'

'It's not shelter, it's a rowing-boat,' said Joe. 'If we turn it the right way up we can use it to cross the lake.'

'I am not meant to cross the water here.' She held the map open for him. 'Look. Here is the mark. This is my shelter for today.'

'Kaia, we can't both fit under this boat,' objected Joe as he tried to turn it upright. 'It'd be much better to use it to get to the other side and find something among the trees.'

'The shelters were not designed with two people in mind.' Kaia eventually began to help him. She admitted, 'You are right. The trees are a better option.'

'Hopefully tomorrow's shelter will be bigger,' said Joe, breathless from the effort.

Between them they managed to right the boat and drag it over moss and shingle into the water, which made them wetter than ever. The driving rain, which was continuing to get even heavier, made it difficult to see very far ahead. In fact, as Joe fitted the oars into the locks, he could no longer see the opposite side of the lake.

'How does it work, this boat?' Kaia's teeth were chattering.

'You've never rowed one before?'

'No. There are no lakes or rivers in Sanctuary. And I did not have to learn for my Run.'

'The oars propel you through the water,' said Joe. He clambered inside. Although a puddle of rainwater was already forming in the bottom, it seemed solid and safe. 'Come on,' he said to Kaia. 'Get in.'

She followed him into the boat, leaving her rucksack on her back so that it didn't get wet.

He pushed the boat away from the lakeshore with one of the oars. Then he sat on the bench and grasped both of them. Rowing was much harder than he'd expected because the grey water seemed thick and gloopy.

'I will help,' said Kaia as she saw him struggle. 'Give me one of these moving sticks.'

At first Joe wasn't sure that her help would make any difference, but she was strong and steady and they eventually found a rhythm that began to move them more quickly across the water. The rain continued to beat down upon them and, as they reached the centre of the lake, the wind howled even more fiercely, causing the water to become very choppy and the boat to bob up and down almost uncontrollably.

'I do not like this,' said Kaia. 'Perhaps we should not have used this boat.'

Joe wasn't liking things much himself. He couldn't believe that the lake, which had been still when they'd first set out, was now as rough as the sea on a bad day. And he was feeling bad that he'd been so gung-ho about the boat when Kaia hadn't wanted to use it.

'Sho!' she suddenly screamed in alarm. 'What is that?'

He looked around. Behind him, coming out of the lake, was an enormous black – well, he thought, it looked like a whale. But it had a horn like a unicorn on the front, and a large fin behind which spun like a propellor. It was coming towards them, churning up the water and making it impossible to steer the boat.

'Sho. We must move. It will kill us!'

He pulled frantically at the oar while Kaia worked just as hard with hers. They were managing to keep barely ahead of the whale, but only because the waves that it was creating were also pushing them away from it. Every so often its entire body would leave the water and then crash down again with a tremendous splash. Eventually one of them sent a huge wave over the boat and washed the two Hizu overboard.

'No!' cried Kaia as she made a grab for one, but it disappeared beneath the water and she couldn't catch it.

'Forget about it. I need help here,' said Joe.

She abandoned her attempt to save the Hizu, and both of them struggled with the oars, but they knew it was a losing battle. Eventually, the long horn of the whale pierced through the wood and water started to flood in.

I'm going to drown, thought Joe. After everything that's happened to me since Greg and Niall chased me down the laneway, I'm going to drown on an alien planet and be eaten by a half-whale, half-unicorn. Which isn't how I imagined dying.

'We have to leave this boat.' Kaia's voice was suddenly calm. 'We cannot stay here.'

'I know.'

'Your rucksack,' she said. 'It is important. Do not forget it.'

He nodded and pulled it on to his shoulder. Then they dropped the oars, held hands and leaped out. The whale impaled the boat again with its horn as they jumped. The wood stuck to the horn and the whale thrashed around, trying to free itself.

'Come on!' yelled Joe. 'While it's occupied. Swim. Swim.'

He struck out towards the shore, Kaia beside him. The heaviness of the water made it difficult to move quickly but the whale was still struggling with the boat. Finally, it freed itself and began to come after them again. Joe was pushing hard for the shore, with Kaia a little behind him, when suddenly he felt ground beneath his feet. He grabbed Kaia by the hand and staggered upright just as the whale made another leap out of the water. It landed with a thud, half-in, half-out of the lake. Joe and Kaia stumbled on to dry land and stared at it. The whale stared back from two huge purple eyes.

'Back away,' said Kaia to Joe.

'Will it follow? Is it a land creature as well as a water creature?'

'I do not know,' she said. 'I have never seen anything like it in my life before.'

They took baby steps away from it. The whale shuddered and opened its mouth. Joe half expected it to leap forward again and swallow the two of them, but instead it let out a long, loud cry. And then it slid slowly back into the grey waters of the lake.

Joe and Kaia stood shaking, their arms around each other. Joe wasn't actually sure if he was shivering or trembling.

'Narrow escape,' he said through chattering teeth.

'Yes,' whispered Kaia. 'And we still have to find shelter.'

The rain seemed to be easing off a little. Joe looked around. There were boulders and rocks on this side of the lake, but the trees they'd seen from the other side were sparse close up. They weren't as good shelter as he'd hoped. And then Kaia pointed to one of the bigger boulders, set into a small hill.

'Look,' she said.

There was a narrow fissure in the boulder.

Joe walked towards it. The gap was barely wide enough for him to squeeze through, but once inside it opened into a warm, dry cave. He took a glowstick from his rucksack and looked around.

'This is better than the boat,' said Kaia. 'Although it is clear to me that I was never supposed to take it across the water.'

'I'm sorry, I'm sorry.' Joe held up his hands. 'I should've listened to you.'

'We have succeeded in the crossing,' said Kaia. 'Tomorrow we will resume my Run. But we will stick to the route.'

'OK.' Joe began to look in his rucksack for the Cheeba

cookies and the Gira drink. And for something to dry himself with.

'Here.' Kaia reached in and took out a small square of black material.

'A hanky?' He looked at her.

'For the water,' she said.

He took it and wiped his face and hair. Almost at once he was dry again. Kaia did the same with a square from her own rucksack.

'It is time to rest now,' she said. 'But first we must make the cave secure.' She opened her rucksack and removed a small round crystal. She tapped it once on the ground and it shone with a very faint creamy light. 'This Kerala will protect us,' she said.

Joe looked inside his own rucksack. He also had some of the miniature crystals, in different colours. He placed one at the back of the cave. 'Just in case,' he said to Kaia.

She nodded and the two of them sat down, leaning against the rugged wall of the cave. It wasn't very comfortable but Joe didn't care. He took a Cheeba out of his rucksack and ate it. His eyes started to close. He was asleep before he even realised it.

Once again, when he woke up, it took Joe a moment to figure out where he was. The light from the glowsticks had faded during the night, but now there was something else. Hundreds of little red dots danced in front of his eyes, and Joe jumped up with a cry. Because he realised that the tickling sensation was a large, furry spider walking across him and that the little red dots were the eyes of hundreds more, descending slowly from the ceiling.

'What! What is it?' His cry had woken Kaia and when she saw the spiders she yelped.

'We have to get out of here,' said Joe.

Kaia didn't say a word, just got her things together. Joe did the same and followed her out of the cave at the same time as the spiders reached the ground. They scurried after Kaia and Joe, but she turned and replaced the Kerala crystal at the entrance. About a dozen spiders had escaped with them but the rest were trapped behind the force field of the crystal.

'Hurry,' she said and set off at her fastest pace yet away from the lake and across a field of tall grasses which swayed in the breeze. The grey skies weren't as leaden as the day before and the rain had stopped, so their frantic run wasn't as uncomfortable as it might have been. After about half an hour they came to a clearing and Joe yelled at Kaia to slow down.

'We need to be sure where we're going,' he said. 'And we need to talk about what else we might encounter. I didn't expect whales with horns and red-eyed spiders.'

Kaia, who'd been about to plunge into another field of high grass, stopped.

'You are right,' she said. 'I need to be more thoughtful and organised. It was foolish going into that cave before I established that it was the correct shelter. It clearly was not. Now we have left two Kerala behind. As well as which I lost my Hizu.'

'I lost mine too. It wasn't our fault,' Joe pointed out. 'But we have more of those Kerala and the little glowsticks too. Plus . . .' he added. 'My phone has a torch. Although getting dunked in the lake won't have helped it.'

'Your communication device?' She took it from her rucksack.

Joe was surprised and pleased to find it was still working and still had a full charge too. He showed her the torch app.

'This is Kerala,' she said warily. 'You have power, Sho Hun-ter.'

'I have to keep charging it or it runs out of power,' he told her. 'But for some reason it's stayed fully charged here. Maybe it's the crystals,' he said suddenly. 'It could be picking up the charge from them. That's so cool.'

'I do not understand what you are saying,' she said. 'But I am not happy about this device.'

'Kaia, it won't communicate with Kanabians, I promise you. There's nothing it can do here that's particularly useful. The torch is handy but you already have glowsticks for light. Though the compass might help if it works here.'

'Compass?'

'For finding your way.' He opened the app. After a moment, the digital needle told him that they were facing north-east.

'Which is the direction we want to go,' he said happily. 'This can help us if we have to leave the route for any reason, Kaia.'

'We must stick to the route. But . . .' she nodded slowly. 'Although I can see well in the dark, I cannot see everything. You may keep this device. The light from it is brighter than the Kerala and the glowsticks. If there are spiders in caves, it will show them.'

'They might have been poisonous.' Joe shuddered as he put the phone into his own rucksack again. 'We were lucky to get out when we did.'

'Everything about Kanabia is dangerous,' said Kaia. 'Even their animals.'

'I suppose we were the ones invading their environment,' remarked Joe. 'They were just defending themselves.'

Kaia stared at him. 'So you think it is OK to be nearly killed by a whale?'

'Of course not. But I don't blame it for chasing us. And as for the spiders . . .' he shuddered again as he remembered the feel of it on his hand, 'well, they're entitled to their cave, I guess.'

'We will not get far if this is your attitude, Sho,' said Kaia. 'It will be necessary at some point for us to kill. You cannot always say "they were here first".'

Joe wasn't going to argue with her. He just hoped that they wouldn't run into other animals of any kind, ferocious, creepy or cute. And the way Kaia was talking, he hoped they wouldn't run into other people either. He thought again of Oani. He hoped she was all right. He hoped Mihai hadn't freed himself from the Flagali and gone after her. But surely he would put his Run first? That was the priority for all of them.

'Let's get a plan together,' he said, putting them out of his mind. 'How are we going to continue?'

The two of them sat down and Kaia opened the map again. Joe saw that the route they had travelled was now marked in blue. The point where they had escaped from the lake differed from the already marked route, and they were off course by a few miles. But they were still heading in the right direction.

'If we stick to the route it'll probably be safer,' he mused.

'Of course it is safer,' agreed Kaia. 'From now on I will

follow my training and we will do the Run as it is supposed to be done.'

'Agreed,' said Joe.

'It will be a problem for the next Runner.' Kaia looked anxious. 'They will seek shelter and there will be none.'

'It's a pity you can't get information back to them,' said Joe. 'And a pity the last Runner couldn't get information back to you about that whale.'

'The last Runner was Kizan Maal. I am certain he took shelter beneath the boat and ran around the lake as he was supposed to. He would not have encountered the whale.'

She was blaming him, Joe thought. He could see why. But he could also see why the Carcassians sent three Runners to place the Kerala. The way things were going, he and Kaia would be lucky to make it to the first Loran alive.

15

They continued to run in silence for the rest of the morning, then Kaia signalled for them to stop.

'This is a rest point,' she said, pointing at the map. 'It should be safe.'

'It was safe when the map was drawn up,' said Joe. 'Who knows what it's like now?'

But nothing and nobody disturbed them as they had another meal of Gira juice and Cheeba cookies. Despite their energy-giving qualities, Joe was starting to get tired of the cookies. He wouldn't have minded something else to drink either. All the same, he said nothing, not wanting Kaia to think that he was forever criticising the Carcassians.

They spent more time studying the map before they set off again. More of the lights on Kaia's Link had faded but she told Joe that they were making good time. And, she added, despite their encounter with the whale and the spiders, the Mountains and Lakes route was mainly uninhabited so they didn't have to worry too much about hostile Kanabians. However, she also said that they would make some adjustments to their appearances so that they would look more like the enemy as soon as they reached their next shelter.

'Does the map tell you if the others have succeeded?' asked Joe as she folded it up. 'Does the icon next to the Loran light up or something?'

Kaia shook her head. 'No. And it is better that way. It means a Runner concentrates on their own job and does not think of anyone else.'

'And takes the Muqi at the end,' said Joe. 'About that . . . isn't there some way you can avoid it?'

'Why would I do that?' asked Kaia. 'I would not be able to live in Kanabia.'

'Perhaps not in Kanabia,' Joe said. 'But—'

'We have been talking for too long.' Kaia interrupted him. 'Now it is time to run again.'

She was bossy, thought Joe. But brave. He hefted the rucksack on to his back and followed her.

It was a much pleasanter run than the previous day. The wind had died down completely and the air was warm. The sky was pale blue, without the grey clouds, and the arc of white light that crossed it was clearly visible. Joe wondered if the brightness of the arc had something to do with the strength of the Shield. Maybe it actually *was* the Shield, he thought, as he followed in Kaia's footsteps. Whatever it was, it was beautiful. As was the countryside he was running through. The grass was lush and green and the hills were covered with pink and purple flowers. The mountains, in the distance, shone with a copper light. Joe ran easily along the trail that Kaia was following.

She'd set a fast but steady pace and he was keeping up with her easily enough. In fact, he thought, if he put more effort into it he could probably run straight past her. But perhaps that wouldn't be a great idea. So he held back, allowing her to take the lead as the mountains which had been in the distance earlier in the day grew closer and closer.

At the base of the mountains, close to a small stream, they stopped for a rest. Joe opened his rucksack to take out the Cheebas and Gira again, but Kaia shook her head. She cupped her hands and took the water from the river, gulping it down.

'Are you sure that's safe?' asked Joe. 'Wouldn't we be better drinking the stuff we've got?'

'No,' she said impatiently. 'This river is safe and pure. The map says so.'

'And the map is always right,' said Joe.

She caught the cynical tone in his face. 'You think there is a problem with the map?'

'It's out of date.'

'It has served us well for generations.'

'More by luck than anything else,' said Joe.

'It is not luck that the Shield has been maintained all that time.'

'How do you know the Kanabians haven't poisoned this river since the last Runner came by?' He didn't really believe that they had but he wanted to rattle her.

'Do not be so childish,' she said. 'First of all, there are no Kanabians in this region. Secondly, if there were, they would need the water for themselves.'

She drank the water which she'd scooped into a small

container, then shrugged her rucksack on to her back and said that it was time to go again.

'But we've hardly stopped at all,' protested Joe.

She held up her arm to show him the red stone in the Link. It was a shade lighter. Joe shivered.

It was harder going now. The trail was getting steeper and steeper as it twisted through the mountains. Joe felt the backs of his legs beginning to ache and he wondered if Kaia was getting tired too. He still felt as though he had plenty of energy, but he was sure it was leaking away from him more and more quickly. He tried to push on but it was difficult. In fact, he realised, he was beginning to fall behind Kaia, who was maintaining her original pace. She hadn't looked behind once to see how he was doing. For all she knew, Joe thought, he could have broken his leg or something. Not that she'd care if he had. All that mattered to her was putting the Kerala in place.

It was getting cooler the higher up they went. Joe just concentrated on putting one foot in front of the other. He suddenly began to wonder about the trail. Because of the map, Kaia believed that this was a deserted area of Kanabia, but the fact that there was still a trail must mean that some people used it, mustn't it? Joe looked up anxiously, as though he would see an army of Kanabians waiting to attack. But there was nothing, only the steep sides of the mountains, half covered by trees and scrub.

When he finally fell, it was almost a relief. The ground beneath them had become stony and a little slippery. Joe had been looking around again when his feet went from under him and he felt himself begin to slide. He yelled out as he tumbled over and he wondered how far he'd fall before Kaia would help him. To his surprise though, he stopped much more quickly than he'd expected. And then he found out why. He hadn't stopped of his own accord. He'd been stopped. By a large net. Which had now closed around him and was lifting him high into the air.

He was trapped.

16

The more he twisted and turned as he tried to free himself, the more he seemed to stick to the net itself, which was coated in a type of gel. And the more he came into contact with the gel, the less he was able to move.

'Kaia!' he called. 'Help me.'

She didn't reply. He tried to sit upright in the net so that he could look around him but he was now more firmly stuck to it than ever and the only thing he could see was the top of the mountain and the white arc in the pale blue sky above it.

'Kaia!' he called again. 'I'm stuck. I can't get out.'

There was still silence. It suddenly occurred to Joe that she had left him. That she was continuing her Run and leaving him behind. Because that was what she was trained to do. Run alone. Now he was even more worried. Without Kaia nearby, the Link would be broken, the Muqi would be released into his veins, and he'd die. Although if he'd been trapped by the Kanabians he was going to die anyway.

He wondered what their torture would be like. Or if they

didn't bother with torture, if they just killed their victims. Maybe that would be better. He didn't know. He didn't want to wait to find out. He tried desperately to turn himself around so that at least he was looking at the ground below. But by now he was now completely stuck to the net. He thought of a fly caught in a spider's web and he wondered if the net had actually been spun by the furry spiders they'd seen in the cave. He felt sick at the thought.

There was a strong smell from the net, a bit like creosote, and it was making his eyes sting. He could feel them beginning to water and there was a part of him that thought perhaps he was actually crying. Because right now he felt like crying. He was in an unknown place, alone. Nobody knew where he was and nobody cared about him. He might die here and he'd never have the chance to tell his parents that he loved them. Or to say to his sister Susan that he was sorry for deleting all her playlists from her MP3 player in a fit of annoyance. Or to go to a football match at Wembley with his older brother, George, which they were always planning to do but they'd never got around to. There were loads of other things that he'd planned for the future – a part-time job, college, plucking up the courage to talk to Ashley Jones, the prettiest girl in the school – anyway, it didn't matter what those things were, the point was he was never going to do them now. He was going to die at the hands of the Kanabi.

His eyes were watering more than ever. And the rest of him was feeling very itchy. In fact, he realised, he was itching all over and he desperately needed to scratch. Only he couldn't move his arms. He couldn't move at all. Whatever the sticky stuff on the net was, it had paralysed him. He closed his eyes. He had to. The light was making them sting more than ever and he could feel that his lids were puffy and swollen. His ears were hurting too. He wanted to take out the Joq but he wasn't able to move his hand. He felt tired. There was no point in fighting it. He should just sleep. Maybe the Kanabi would kill him in his sleep. Maybe that would be for the best.

'Sho!'

At first he didn't recognise her voice.

'Sho!'

He opened his eyes, slowly and painfully. The light was almost too bright to bear.

'Kaia?' His own voice was scratchy.

'Sho, are you all right?'

Her words seemed to be coming from a huge distance.

'Sleepy,' croaked Joe. 'Can't move.'

'Sho, you have been caught in a Kanabi trap.'

Try telling me something I don't already know, he thought. But he was relieved to hear her voice.

'I am going to help you. But we must be quick. The Kanabi will be here soon. They always know when a trap has caught something.'

I don't care, he thought.

'Sho, can you hear me?' Kaia's voice was urgent.

It was getting harder to hear too. And harder to understand her.

'I am going *go xug wodn* the net. You will *uzoo*,' she said. 'Try to *ozpe bofihep zh happ* as possible, OK?'

124

What? What was she going to do, what was going to happen to him and what did she want him to do? He groaned softly. It didn't matter any more. It really didn't.

'Sho!'

'I can't hear you,' he said. 'I can't . . .'

'Be strong.'

He couldn't really be strong. He couldn't be anything. But he'd pretend, just to keep her happy. And so that she didn't leave him.

Suddenly he felt the net sway and then, before he had time to register what was happening, the net, with him still in it, was falling towards the ground. He landed with a bump which jerked his eyes open.

'Oh, Sho!' Kaia looked at him anxiously. 'We need to get you out of there.'

But he couldn't help her as she used one of the glowsticks to hack at the sticky filament of the net. Every so often she made a whimpering sound as though it was beginning to make her itch too, but after what seemed like an age she finally pulled him by the hand and hauled him to his feet.

'Come on,' she said. 'We must move. They are on the way.'

He staggered after her, off the trail and towards the opposite mountain. He couldn't see properly and he could hardly keep his balance but she supported him until they were crouching in a crevasse of a rock together.

'Keep quiet,' she whispered.

He was glad that at least he could understand her again. And there was no chance of him being anything other than quiet. His throat was so sore and itchy now that he couldn't speak.

'The Kanabi are coming,' she warned.

Joe wished he could see the dreaded Kanabi. He wished he could see what was going on.

'*Torro!*'

It was a group cry, more than one voice and it was fearsome.

'*Torro!*'

Joe felt himself shrink further into the crevasse. Kaia was in front of him, protecting him.

The voices of the Kanabi were closer and now they were talking. It took a moment before the Joq started to translate what they were saying. They were arguing about the net. About what they'd caught and how it had escaped.

'Perhaps it was a Porra,' said one.

There was a loud discussion about how it couldn't have been a Porra, how Porras lived in the woods and never came along the trail. Joe didn't know what the animal was, but from what the Kanabians were saying it seemed to be big and fearsome.

'Perhaps someone from Thalia took our catch,' said another Kanabian. 'We should go and check. Make them sorry.'

There was joint agreement that this was probably what had happened, that a different band of Kanabian hunters had come upon the catch suspended in the net and had taken it for themselves. The group was decided. They would go to Thalia and demand the return of their prey. After all, said one man loudly, it was known everywhere that these nets belonged to the Mboli. The voices began to recede and Joe released the breath he'd been holding.

'I do not know where Thalia is,' said Kaia. 'There is no Thalia on the map. Or Mboli. But it is clear that the Kanabians not only fight Carcassia, they fight among themselves.'

Another time, Joe might have cared. But right now his only concern was trying to scratch himself.

'No!' warned Kaia as he attempted to raise his arm to his face. 'You will spread the poison.'

'Poison?'

'The Kanabian nets are made of poisonous thread,' she explained. 'They were used extensively against the Carcassians in the war. Many people died.'

'Am I going to die?' asked Joe.

'Hopefully not.' She took a small vial of rose-pink liquid from her rucksack. 'Drink this.'

He didn't hesitate but swallowed it down. Almost immediately the itch began to ease and after five minutes his eyes had stopped streaming and the puffiness had gone. His throat felt immeasurably better too, although his body still itched like crazy.

'What is that stuff?' he asked as he scratched the back of his neck. 'It's fantastic.'

'An antidote,' Kaia told him. 'When it was developed in Carcassia it made a big difference to the war.'

'Do we have a lot of it with us?' asked Joe who had moved to scratching his arms which were covered in huge red spots.

'Two vials,' she told him. 'Stop scratching.'

He did as she said but the itch was still driving him mad. 'Is my face spotty too?'

'Yes.'

'I don't know what happened,' he told her. 'One minute I was walking along and the next I was falling and trapped.'

'It is my fault,' she said. 'I should have been more alert to the possibility of Kanabian nets. They place traps on the road. You step in one, lose your balance and then the net scoops you up. The poison paralyses you.'

Joe shuddered. 'I felt that happen. My eyes, my throat – and I couldn't move.'

'They say it is very painful.'

He scratched at his face.

She reached into her rucksack again and took out a damp tissue.

'This will help a little,' she said. 'It is just cooling paper.'

Joe took it and began to dab it over his face. It was icy cold and almost at once the itching eased.

'Thank you,' he said. 'For this and for rescuing me. I thought you'd left me.'

'Of course I did not leave you. When I saw what had happened I ran to the top of the hill to see if the Kanabians were nearby. Then I came back.'

'Thank you,' he said again.

'There is no need to thank me. We are working together, yes?'

'Yes.' He gave her a weak smile. 'We're a team.'

'We will wait here for a while,' she said. 'To be certain that the Kanabians are gone and to give you time to recover your strength.'

Joe was happy to fall in with the plan. Although he felt a lot better he knew that he was weak and he didn't think he could run yet. And he needed to be able to run, just in case there were any more Kanabians out there.

The rest of the mountain climb was uneventful. They didn't see any more Kanabians or fall into any new traps, although Kaia pointed out another one to Joe who gave it a wide berth. By the time they reached the summit the spots on his face had grown smaller and his itching had almost stopped. He knew that he hadn't been as light on his feet during the climb as usual. He'd felt weighed down by his rucksack instead of hardly noticing it. Nevertheless, he thought, as they stopped and looked down into the valley below, he had escaped a Kanabi poison net which was a result.

'It is pretty.' Kaia waved her arm towards the valley, which was yellow and green.

'That looks like cultivated farm land to me. Which means there will be people around.'

'We will have to be careful,' said Kaia. 'We will have to be as Kanabians.'

'And how is that?'

'I will show you when we find shelter.'

They'd walked a little further down the mountain when Kaia nudged him.

'Look,' she said.

It was a hut. Small, made of wood, with a sloping roof and a single window in the side. A bit like their garden shed at home, thought Joe, although it was bigger and looked considerably older.

'Shelter,' said Kaia.

It was certainly better than a cave full of spiders but Joe worried that it might belong to one of the Kanabian hunters. He said this to Kaia.

'Perhaps,' she agreed. 'But it looks abandoned to me and it would be a good place to stop. Maybe even clean up a little.'

It was only then that Joe realised how long it was since they'd been able to wash. He supposed he looked a mess, especially since the incident with the net. Kaia, on the other hand, was still pretty, although now that he thought about it, her complicated plait had loosened and she had streaks of mud on her cheeks and a few scratches on her arms.

'Well . . .'

'Please, Sho. We can check this place out. If nobody is around we could spend some time here. We could sleep.'

He looked at her. Her eyes were bright and he thought that perhaps she was going to cry. But she was too tough to cry.

'I am tired,' she explained. 'I have not slept properly since we left the Citadel.'

'All right then.' He nodded. 'Let's check it out.'

They approached the hut cautiously. It seemed deserted but neither of them were taking any chances. They sidled up to the window, wiped the dirt from it, and peered inside. There was no sign of life. Joe could see a small stove, a chair and a table in one corner. There was nothing on it. Everything about the hut said that the owner had left some time ago.

They walked around to the front and tried the door. It was locked.

'This must belong to a Kanabi hunter,' she said. 'But this door has not been opened in a long time. We will have to break it,' she added as she examined the big old-fashioned keyhole.

'Maybe not.' Joe lifted up a large stone near the front of the hut to reveal a big black key. He picked it up, put it into the lock, turned it and then opened the door to the hut.

'Why would someone leave the key to be found so easily?' asked Kaia.

'My mum is always asking questions like that,' said Joe. 'When we watch those crime programmes and intruders find keys hidden in flowerpots and stuff. She says it's incredible how daft people can be.'

'Crime programmes?' asked Kaia. 'Flowerpots?'

'Not important.' Joe walked into the hut.

Although the stove was unlit, the hut itself it was warm and cosy. As well as chair and table, there was a more comfortable sofa beneath the window and a tall dresser with crockery and pots to one side. At the back of the hut was a small staircase leading to a platform. There was a mattress on the platform, covered in blankets. Downstairs again, a door led to a tiny bathroom with a shower.

'Oh, a water shower!' Kaia beamed at Joe. 'It is a long time since I had a water shower. I really want one!'

He laughed. 'Go ahead,' he said. 'I'll check out the contents of the dresser.'

'OK.' Kaia left her rucksack on the sofa and disappeared into the bathroom.

Joe walked around the hut, every so often glancing out of the window to check that nobody was coming. There wasn't much in the hut although there were fabric packets containing an assortment of dried food on the dresser, and a sheet of paper printed with symbols that meant nothing to Joe. There were no electronic devices – well, Joe thought, given there was nothing in the hut to power them that was hardly surprising. He wasn't sure how the Kanabians powered things generally. Kaia had said that they didn't have the same Kerala as Carcassia, but he supposed they must have something.

He flopped down on the sofa and closed his eyes. They still stung a bit from the poison of earlier. He'd had a narrow escape.

'Sho.' It was Kaia who woke him and he realised that he must have been asleep for a long time because it was dark outside. He blinked a couple of times at the sky. It was the first time it had been cloudless since they'd started the Run. Now it was sparkling with thousands of stars and the arc, which had been a faint, dusky light during the day, was bright and vibrant. He realised that it was made up of individual bands of light. He frowned as he tried to recall where he'd seen something like it before and then remembered. It was like looking at pictures of the rings of Saturn from the planet itself. But they couldn't be on Saturn. Joe knew from what he'd learned at school that it was a gas planet. It didn't sustain life, at least not like on Earth. But its rings were breathtaking. And so were the ones he was looking at now.

'It's amazing,' he said.

'What is?' asked Kaia.

He turned to look at her and forgot what he was going to say. She stood beside him, wearing a slightly too-long blue robe which she'd obviously found upstairs, her dark hair was loose down her back. Her blue eyes were sparkling. She looked completely different.

'What is amazing?' she asked again.

He pulled his look away from her and pointed at the arc.

'But you have seen the Qaan already,' she said.

'Not like that,' he told her. 'It's lovely.'

'Perhaps. You have been sleeping, Sho, and that is a good thing,' she said briskly. 'But I am very tired now and I cannot stay awake to keep guard any longer.'

She was keeping guard like that? thought Joe. They had no chance! He didn't say this. He apologised for having slept for so long and told her that of course it was her turn for some rest. She smiled at him in thanks. Her lips were rosy pink. Stop it, he said to himself. Stop noticing her. She's not Ashley Jones, after all.

'I will go upstairs,' she said. 'You can remain here.'

'Sure,' he said.

'This will help you.' She handed him a blue Kerala crystal. 'You keep it in your hand. It vibrates when someone is within an orph.'

'If we have this we can both sleep,' said Joe. 'It will wake us.'

'I know,' she said. 'But we would lose time and I am afraid for us.'

He stared at her. She had never admitted to being afraid before.

'It is harder than I expected,' she said. 'This Run. There are obstacles I did not foresee. The map is not exactly correct, I believe now. I was careless in allowing you to be trapped because

I did not think there would be people living in the mountains.'

'Things never work out the way you expect,' said Joe. 'It's like the rain and the wind. The theory isn't the same as when something actually happens to you. And your Run . . . well, the rules were made by people who aren't running.'

'But the other Runners succeeded,' she said.

'Who knows what they had to do,' said Joe. 'We need to be flexible.'

'You are right,' she said. 'I can be flexible for the sake of Carcassia.' She yawned suddenly.

'Go and get some sleep,' said Joe. 'I'll keep watch.'

'And afterwards we will be Kanabian,' she told him.

'Whatever you say,' he agreed.

When she went upstairs he checked the time on his phone. He'd been asleep for four hours. All that time, he thought, and she'd just sat and waited for him. He'd do the same for her.

17

Joe woke Kaia as the light of the sun was beginning to creep over the horizon. Dawn on the planet was very beautiful. The air was crisp and clear and the sky a palette of pink and gold. The Qaan was a band of soft white light halfway up from the horizon. During the night, while Kaia had slept, Joe had stood outside the hut, looking up at it, and then at the rest of the night sky. He'd been overwhelmed by the number of stars that had pierced the darkness. Thousands and thousands of them. Far more than he'd ever seen in his life before. And, as well as the stars, and the Qaan, two moons, both faint, but still very clear. It had been seeing the sky at night that made him really and truly believe he was somewhere else in the universe. It was both exciting and terrifying. It was exciting to know that other places existed. Terrifying to realise that he was millions of miles from home. And to be reminded that he might never find a way back.

When he went upstairs to wake her, Kaia was lying on the bed, her arm flung across the narrow pillow and her long hair fanned out around her. He touched her shoulder and she sat bolt upright, immediately alert.

'What is it?' she asked.

'Morning,' he told her.

'Already?' She looked aghast. 'We must go.'

'If it's OK, I'll have a shower while you get dressed,' he said. 'I didn't want to have it when you were sleeping.'

She nodded and he went into the bathroom. The water was cold but very refreshing. He wished he had toothpaste, although the Gira drink in their rucksacks left a minty aftertaste which was very much like cleaning your teeth.

Kaia was already sitting at the table of the hut by the time he was finished and there was an array of what looked like coloured pens in front of her. Joe looked at her in surprise.

'Now we become Kanabian,' she said.

'How?'

'Like this.' She took up one of the pens and rolled up the sleeve of her robe. 'They have marks on their arms,' she told him. 'We will draw them now.'

'Like tattoos?'

She thought about it, processing the word. 'Yes, but they are born with these marks,' she said as she began to draw three parallel lines in dark blue ink around her wrist, another three, this time in orange, across the palms of her hands. Then, using a mirror to see what she was doing, she added three small circles behind her right ear.

'This is what the Sanctuary Leaders were looking for on me,' said Joe. 'This is what made you all know I wasn't Kanabian.'

'You could have camouflaged them,' said Kaia as she assessed

136

her handiwork. 'Before the Shield, the Kanabians hid their markings so that they could infiltrate Carcassia.'

'Why didn't we do this before leaving?' asked Joe.

'It is a crime to have Kanabian markings in Carcassia,' said Kaia.

'We were on the way out,' objected Joe. 'What difference would it have made?'

'It is a crime,' she repeated as she began to draw his markings.

The lines were in black and purple. She also added two small circles on his temples.

'The symbol of a Kanabian warrior,' she said.

He grinned at her.

'It is not funny,' she said.

'I know. But there's something cool about being a warrior, even if I'm pretending and even if I'm the enemy.'

'Sometimes you can be very silly, Sho,' she said.

'What about food?' he asked. 'Do you think we can eat some of their stuff, save our Cheebas and Gira?'

She nodded. 'But we will take the containers with us.'

'Of course,' agreed Joe. 'Let's try not to leave any sign we were here.'

She took a couple of wooden containers from the cupboard and prised them open. Joe looked inside. It was a sort of semi-solid rice pudding, something he normally never ate. But he stuck his finger in and tasted it. The flavour was like smokey apples. He finished it quickly and asked if she thought they'd notice another few packets missing.

'You are still hungry?'

'I've been eating biscuits for days!' cried Joe. 'Of course I'm hungry.'

Kaia laughed. While Joe was eating the second rice pudding she began to braid her hair, although not in the complicated style she'd worn before. Now she simply worked it into one simple plait at the back of her head.

'Kanabian,' she explained to Joe. 'Their women are not warriors. They do not need the style of a warrior.'

Joe nodded. He didn't say anything. Girls were notoriously sensitive about their hairstyles. If he was going to say anything, though, he would've said that he liked it.

Suddenly, the small Kerala began to vibrate. Joe and Kaia looked at each other.

'We must go,' she said.

The Kerala was vibrating even more vigorously by the time they'd made sure the hut was totally spotless. They let themselves out and Joe locked the door. He replaced the key carefully beneath the rock. By the time the Kanabians reached the hut, he and Kaia were running under cover of the trees, even though they now had the Kanabian markings on their faces and hands.

18

Kaia kept up a fierce pace as they followed the map towards Zwemat. It was easier running through the valley where the only creatures they encountered were small animals like hedgehogs trundling along and, high in the skies, large birds with enormous, almost circular, wings. At night they slept in rock crevasses or beneath one of the spreading trees that dotted the landscape. Joe wasn't keen on sleeping under the trees because the rustle of the leaves kept him awake and worried about what might be out there. But they were undisturbed.

Every morning Kaia checked her Link. It was impossible to tell how many lights had faded, but now there was a small pink patch in the centre of the ruby stone. As the days on Charra were shorter than on Earth, Joe found it difficult to keep to a time he understood. But when he said this, Kaia told him that the only thing he needed to understand was the importance of reaching the first Loran while there was still plenty of red light in the stone.

Eventually, the landscape changed and Joe could see that

the green meadows were divided into fields and that there were roads – or at least dirt tracks – leading in different directions. Some of the fields had small houses in their centre. The houses were A-shaped, like triangles, the roofs reaching right down to the ground, but Joe and Kaia didn't see any people around them. They did, however, see a signpost with two signs on it. Joe couldn't read what was written on it because the letters were completely unfamiliar to him, but Kaia said that they pointed to the towns of Thalia and Zwemat.

'Thalia. That's the place those Kanabians talked about,' said Joe. 'They were a long way from home.'

'According to the map there is no such place as Thalia,' said Kaia. 'In fact our route seems to go straight through it.'

'Even if it takes us a bit longer I think we should avoid towns,' said Joe.

'I agree.' Kaia folded the map and put it away again.

'I can't believe we're nearly there,' said Joe. 'We seem to have been running for ever. I hope . . .'

'What?'

'Well, that you place your Kerala and save Carcassia and . . . and that I find a way home.'

'If you cannot find a way from the Loran at Zwemat, there may be a way from the Domote Loran in the north,' said Kaia. 'And if not there, definitely Lagat.' She grimaced. 'I would have preferred to start my Run there.'

'Why?'

'The best Runner should always go to Lagat first.'

'But it was a draw,' objected Joe.

Kaia shrugged.

140

'You think it was fixed?'

'It is possible that the Sanctuary Leaders make choices in this matter and do not tell us. I think . . .'

'What?'

'I think it is possible that I would have been given Lagat if you had not interrupted my Gimalle.'

'I saved you!' cried Joe. 'Those spikes—'

'I have told you before that I had a plan.' Kaia reminded him. 'I would have freed myself.'

'How?'

'There is a sequence to the spikes,' she said. 'And to the water spray. It is not easy to work it out and untie yourself at the same time but I was ready to do it. Although,' she added with a sudden grin, 'if I had known it was possible to eat the Flagali . . .'

Joe grinned too. 'They taste disgusting. I wouldn't recommend it.'

'Anyway,' said Kaia. 'The Leaders were not happy with what happened and they wanted Instructor Vasila to demerit me – I begged her not to.'

'Maybe she wanted to save your life,' said Joe. 'Just like I thought I was doing.'

'My life would have no honour if I did not make my Run,' said Kaia as she hitched up her rucksack. 'This does not matter now. I have my mission and I will complete it.'

Joe ran alongside her as she struck out across the fields and away from the narrow road that led towards Thalia.

'I have to confess that it is perhaps more . . . it is good to have someone with me,' she said suddenly.

'Even though I'm getting in the way.'

'You make me think differently.' She turned and gave him a short smile. 'You make me be flexible.'

Although not flexible enough to consider an alternative to taking the Muqi, thought Joe. He wondered how he could possibly save her. Always provided he could save himself. Somehow he had to find a way to do both.

It was becoming too hot to run. The sun was beating down on them now and they were both beginning to perspire. The only shade was from the occasional spindly tree dotted around. Kaia didn't want to stop. Better to keep going, she told Joe, and put Thalia safely behind them. They'd almost done that when they heard a cry.

Both of them stopped and looked in the direction of the sound. It seemed to come from the far end of the field they were crossing.

'It is probably an animal,' decided Kaia.

Joe nodded agreement. And then both of them heard it together.

'*Svok!*' yelled a voice. '*Svok.*'

'Help?' Joe looked at Kaia as the Joq translated it for him.

'That is a Kanabian shouting,' said Kaia. 'It is a trap. We will not stop.' She began to stride forward again.

'Kaia – it sounds like a kid.' Joe put his hand on her arm.

'Yes, the Kanabians often use their children as warriors,' she said. 'That is probably a Kanabian boy.'

'*Svok!*' The word trembled on the air. Joe thought that the kid was probably crying.

'He doesn't sound much like a warrior to me,' said Joe. 'He sounds in trouble.'

'In that case his parents can help him,' she said.

'Maybe his parents can't hear him,' protested Joe.

'We can,' she retorted. 'I am sure everyone else can too.'

'We can because we're nearby,' Joe pointed out. 'The village is a good distance from here.'

'I will not fall into another Kanabian trap,' said Kaia.

'It's not a trap,' said Joe. 'And we can't leave him in trouble.'

He began to run across the field away from her. She yelled at him to stop but he didn't listen. And then he suddenly felt the Link tighten around his wrist and a sensation like pins and needles shoot through his arms and legs. He stumbled and nearly fell.

It was becoming difficult to walk. He could see that the green jewel was now pulsating. He should go back to Kaia straight away. But if he did, what would happen to the boy?

Suddenly the pressure from the Link eased. He looked around and saw her walking towards him.

'You must stay with me, Sho,' she said when she got closer.

'I know,' he gasped. 'But I also have to help this kid. Come with me. Please.'

He started running again. This time, though, he heard her behind him. She was calling after him to stop. And then he saw the boy. He was about ten years of age. He was lying in the field and his foot was caught in a bright red circular trap which was chained into the ground.

His first thought was that he and Kaia had been lucky not to have stepped on to one of these traps themselves. And his second was that at least it wasn't the steel jaw type that he'd often seen on TV programmes at home. It was smooth and round and it had closed around the boy's ankle. It was rather like the bracelet on Joe's arm, only broader.

'Are you OK?' called Joe before realising that the boy probably wouldn't understand him.

'I can't move,' he replied.

'I can see that,' said Joe, wondering if the boy had a Joq too. 'But are you hurt?'

The boy shook his head. 'I can't get it off,' he said. 'Chai Loshi will have to do it. We're on his land.' His face crumpled. 'I'm not supposed to be here. He will tell my mother and she will be angry.'

'I guess that's what happens when you disobey your parents.' Wow, thought Joe as he spoke. I sound like my mum now! The kid was just playing. I should cut him some slack. 'I'm sure she'll forgive you,' he added.

'She may,' said the boy. 'But Chai Loshi will not. And he will fine my mother even more because this is the second time.' A tear rolled down his cheek. 'And he will beat me too and lock me away. I didn't really mean to be on the land. I was trying to catch Bobie.'

'Bobie?'

'My Pashwa. He ran away from me.'

Just as Joe was about to ask what a Pashwa was, a small animal, like a dog but with a rabbit's tail, and paws that were invisible under a ball of curly fur, came running across the field.

'Be careful, Bobie,' cried the boy. 'Don't get caught in one of Chai Loshi's traps too!'

The Pashwa was luckier than his owner. He sat down beside him and pushed his head into his chest. The boy began to stroke him.

'So how do you get this off?' asked Joe, looking at the trap.

'I can't,' said the boy. 'I must wait for Chai Loshi who'll be here soon. He will have seen the alarm.'

Only now did Joe see that a small white light on the side of the trap was blinking slowly.

'So why did you call for help?' asked Joe.

'I hoped . . . sometimes I play with Chai Loshi's son. I hoped he would come and free me, even though he's not supposed to.'

'How long will it take for this Chai Loshi person to get here?' Joe was examining the trap. It was perfectly smooth. He couldn't see a visible way of opening it.

'Not long,' said the boy. 'He is with Chai Malin working his fields.'

Joe looked at Kaia who was standing a few metres away, watching them.

'Kaia!' he called. 'I need some help here.'

'This is a Kanabi matter,' she said coldly. 'We will not interfere. The child is not in danger. We will go.'

'C'mon, Kaia,' said Joe. 'He's just a kid who made a mistake.'

'A Kanabian child who disobeyed Kanabian rules,' said Kaia. 'This is not our affair.'

'Kaia, his mother is going to be fined and he's going to be locked up and beaten!'

'A just punishment for his disobedience,' she said.

'Oh, for crying out loud!' He left the boy and walked over to her. 'What's wrong with you? He's a kid. He's caught in a trap. Can we help him or not?'

'And if we do?' she asked. 'He tells his mother that two strangers assisted him? The Kanabians learn of our presence here? You think that will help us? Do you?'

The boy gave a squeal and Joe turned to him. 'Are you OK?'

'The trap is tightening,' he said. 'That's what it does. Until Chai Loshi comes to beat me. Or my leg breaks. He might let it break this time because he has beaten me before.'

'Kaia!' Joe looked at her in horror. 'We have to help him.'

'We do not,' she said.

'Well, if you won't I will.' Joe looked at her angrily. 'I'm not going to let him have his leg broken or be beaten and have his mother fined, when all he was doing was running after his dog!'

'Dog?'

'Oh, Padwa, Pshaw, whatever the hell it's called.'

Joe walked away from her again and knelt down beside the boy.

'What's your name?' he asked.

'Kho,' said the boy.

'Hey, that's like my name.' Joe grinned at him. 'I'm Joe.'

'Sho.'

'Everyone here calls me Sho,' he said. 'So how does Chai Loshi open the trap?'

The light was blinking more quickly now and Joe felt anxious. Even though he was furious with Kaia for not helping, he knew she had a point. And if he was caught – well, he wasn't sure what would happen. Despite having Kanabi marks on his arm, he wasn't sure how good he'd be at talking his way out of the situation. And he was worried that somehow they'd find out about Kaia. He couldn't let that happen.

'He has a key,' said Kho.

'But not like at the hut,' murmured Joe. 'Not an old-fashioned key. This is an electronic device. Which means that the Kanabi aren't as behind the times as the Carcassians might like to think.'

He studied it for a moment and then opened his rucksack. He took out one of the small Kerala crystals. He wasn't exactly sure how he was going to use it. However, given that it possessed Kerala energy he might be able to crack the trap open with it. Problem was, he thought as he sorted his way through the different colours, if he picked the wrong strength he might damage the boy's leg even more.

The blinking speeded up further.

'Oh, crap,' thought Joe as he picked up a black crystal. 'I've got to try something.'

He pointed it at the trap and was about to shake it as he'd seen Kaia do when he felt her hand grab his arm.

'Stop,' she said.

'I told you.' Joe looked angrily at her. 'I'm helping.'

'Not by killing him, though.' She picked up the pale pink crystal and held it to the white light. There was a sudden crack and the trap flew open. The boy jumped up and so did his pet.

'Thank you!' he cried. 'Thank you very much.'

'Kho!' It was Joe who stopped him before he ran across the field again. 'Two things. Stay away from the fields and be careful of traps. And don't tell anyone about us. Nobody at all.'

'That's three things,' said Kho.

'Yes, it is. But it's very important.'

'Are you in trouble too?' he asked.

'Maybe a little,' said Joe.

'Chai Loshi will be angry with you for breaking his trap.'

'I know. And he'll be angry with you if he finds out you were in it. So go home and be good and don't say a word to anyone. Not even your mother.'

'OK,' said Kho. 'I won't. Come on, Bobie.'

He and the animal ran back across the field. Joe waited anxiously, worried that another trap would snap around the boy's leg. When Kho ran on to the track, he waved and then disappeared down the road.

'That was incredibly foolish,' said Kaia, who had severed the trap from its chain and put it into her rucksack. 'He will not stay silent.'

'I'm sure he will,' said Joe. 'He was really scared. And he promised not to say anything.'

'A Kanabi promise is worthless.' She snorted.

'How come he understood me?' asked Joe suddenly.

'It is a Kanabi thing.' She tossed her head impatiently. 'They have a Joq in their ear from birth.'

'Really? How do you know?'

'It is not a man-made Joq,' she said. 'It is the way they are born. They understand everything. It took the Carcassians a long time to discover it. And then we copied them and made the Joq.'

'That must have been very difficult,' said Joe. 'It's one thing to have something natural in you, it's something else to make it.'

'They used Kanabi ears to figure it out,' said Kaia.

Joe stared at her. 'Ears? From real people?' He put his hand to his head and took out the Joq.

'*Du szw jo ovzim*,' said Kaia.

Joe wasn't sure he wanted to put the Joq into his ear again but he didn't really have a choice.

'We had to find a way to understand them,' said Kaia. 'It was research.'

Joe said nothing. He felt slightly sick.

'We are in danger here,' Kai said as she covered the trap's chain with grass and dirt. 'We need to go.'

'And we need to be careful in case we get caught in those traps too,' said Joe, even though he was still thinking of the Carcassians experimenting with the Kanabians' ears.

'That is why I think we should go this way.' Kaia pointed towards a dip in the field, where a dusky pink hedge was growing. 'A farmer would not put traps near Roxana.'

'Roxana?'

'That hedge. It is poisonous.'

The two of them made their way to the hedge. The grass was slightly longer near it too which helped to hide them. Which was a good thing. Because they'd only barely reached it when they heard the voices of two men. They were talking about the trap and what had sprung it. And they were arguing because they couldn't find it. Joe and Kaia crouched low to stay out of sight.

Suddenly Joe's phone began to vibrate in his rucksack. He felt Kaia stiffen beside him as he hauled it from his back and reached in, frantically switching it off before the men could hear its insistent buzz.

'The signal was from here,' they heard one voice say.

'Perhaps it was a false signal.'

'Chai Gemmel sold me these traps. They have worked before. I caught Kho Khristi, little brat. Thinks he can go where he likes just because he's in the same school as my boy. Perhaps I should pay the Khristi house a visit.' He laughed suddenly. 'The mother is a fine woman.'

'You do not have time to be playing with fine women,' said the second man. 'You have crops to grow and weapons to make.'

'It is to keep my crops safe that I bought those damn traps,' said Chai Loshi. 'I will speak to Chai Gemmel about them.'

'You should.'

The voices faded. Kaia and Joe remained where they were. When everything was completely silent, Kaia turned to Joe. She was holding the black crystal in her hand. Her expression was fierce.

'Prove to me that you are not a Haaken terrorist,' she said. 'Prove to me that you have no links with Kanabi. Prove to me that you are not here to sabotage my Run.'

'Kaia!' Joe was astonished. 'Why would you think this? We've been running together for days now. We've helped each other so many times. And you saved me from the Kanabi nets.'

'Yes, I did,' she said. 'But I wonder if it was not a mistake.'

'Why are you saying these things?' asked Joe.

'How is it that the Kanabi boy cried out just as we approached? Why did he speak to you so pleasantly? Why did you run from me even though you knew the Link would stop you? Did you think the Kanabi would save you? What signal did they send you to your communication device?'

'It wasn't a signal, it was a reminder on my phone that made it beep.' Joe went to take it out of his rucksack again but Kaia shook her head.

'Give it to me,' she said.

He passed the rucksack to her and she removed the phone.

'The clock is still working,' said Joe. 'I have a reminder set for my hearing appointment. The clock thinks it's today. That's why the alarm went off.'

Kaia looked at the phone and then at Joe. Then she took the Flagali from her rucksack and threw them at him. They wrapped around him, pinning his arms tight to his body.

'I began to trust you,' she said as she did up her bag again. 'Maybe I would have kept trusting you. But you betrayed yourself by wanting to free that boy. No Carcassian would do that.'

'I'm not Carcassian,' he reminded her. 'I'm English. And most English people would help a child who was trapped.'

'In that case most English people are fools, like Kanabians.' Her voice was hard and cold. 'Goodbye, Sho. You will die when the link is broken.'

She hefted the rucksack on to her back. Joe wriggled again but he knew that it would be impossible to free himself from the Flagali.

'You cannot eat them,' she said. 'I have made sure of that.'

'Kaia, please believe me. I know nothing about your world. Nothing at all. But I'm on your side in this war with the Kanabians. Listen to me – you could have persuaded Vasila

151

and the Sanctuary Leaders to have me killed at Sanctuary. But you didn't. Why?'

She said nothing.

'Was it because you believed me? That you knew I was telling the truth?'

'I cannot judge if you are telling the truth or not,' she said.

'And yet you didn't object to me coming on this Run with you.'

'It was not my place,' said Kaia. 'Vasila decided.'

'And you rescued me from the Kanabi net.'

'I did not want Kanabians to find you. I knew you would not resist their torture.'

'Kaia, you can't really believe I would do anything to betray you. I'm sorry about the boy but . . . but I couldn't let him get beaten.'

'It would have been a just punishment.'

'No,' said Joe. 'It wouldn't. He should have been grounded or something but no kid should ever be beaten.'

She sighed and turned away from him. He stayed perfectly still and didn't try to free himself. After what seemed like an age she turned around and slowly began to peel the ribbons from his body. When he was eventually free he put his arms around her and hugged her.

Immediately she pushed out with her arms, caught him and threw him to the ground.

'What the hell are you doing now?' he gasped as he tried to sit up.

'You attacked me!'

'No I didn't.' He scrambled to his feet. 'Not at all. I was

just . . . on Earth we do this when we want to thank someone. Or when we care about them.'

'You try to crush them?' Her eyes were glittering.

'No. It's a hug. That's all.'

'I do not know this hug.'

'I know. I know. I'm sorry.'

'Do not hug me again, Sho Hun-ter.'

'No.'

'Or do any other touching customs of your world.'

'I won't.'

'We have wasted valuable time,' she told him. 'With talking and with hugs. So we will have to Run through the night.'

Of course we will, he muttered to himself as he followed her. Why did I ever think any different?

19

Night-time running was eerie. As well as the sound of his own breathing, which seemed extra loud, Joe could hear other new noises – quiet rustlings in the grass and the occasional startled croak – which he guessed were from animals hunting. Once he saw pinpricks of green light moving rapidly towards them and he caught Kaia by the arm.

'Do not worry,' she said. 'They are Oxyls. They fly by night.'

And then he heard the beating of their wings and felt a rush of air as the big black birds flew over them.

It wasn't completely dark because the Qaan's silver light lit a ghostly trail for them to follow. But they were both careful to watch out for traps as well as stray rocks or tree roots that could trip them up.

As dawn broke, Kaia finally held up her hand and stopped running.

'Settlements,' she said. 'Everywhere.'

She was right. The landscape ahead of them was dotted with clusters of houses in the middle of large fields.

'Is any of this on the map?' asked Joe.

She shook her head, a worried expression in her eyes.

'D'you think there are traps on all of the land?'

'I do not know.' She finally turned to look at him. 'I did not know about the trap the Kanabi boy was in. We had no information about the development of Kanabi traps.'

'Let's just try to steer clear of them,' said Joe.

'That would be good.' She glanced at the stone in her Link. 'We do not have time for rescuing anybody now.'

'Thank you again for rescuing me before.'

'I had to,' she said. 'You might have given them information about me.'

'No chance. I could hardly speak.'

'They would have given you an antidote,' she said. 'And they would have made you talk. It made sense to rescue you before that happened.'

'I don't think so,' he said. 'Once the link between us was broken, I would have died anyway.'

She was silent. She looked down at her feet and then across the countryside which was slowly being bathed in golden light. Finally she looked at Joe.

'I did not want to leave you, Sho,' she said. 'I did not want you to die.'

'I don't want you to die either, Kaia,' he said.

'I promise you I will not die before I complete my mission,' said Kaia.

'Even afterwards . . .' Joe looked at her.

'Afterwards I must,' she said. 'I cannot live in Kanabia.'

'What if there was another way?'

'There is no other way,' said Kaia.

'If I find a portal back to Earth . . . you could come with me.'

'If there is a portal at Zwemat – and I hope for you that there is, Sho Hun-ter – you will take it and I will carry on with my Run. That is what will happen.'

'But—'

'There is no but,' said Kaia. 'There is only what must be.'

He said nothing, then suddenly leaned towards her and kissed her lightly on the cheek.

'I know you said no touching but on Earth we kiss people when we want to show someone we care about them. Or sometimes to thank them. I care about you, Kaia Kukura. And I want to thank you for everything you've done for me.'

'You have strange customs,' she said. 'The hug is dangerous. And touching faces with lips . . . it makes no sense to me.'

'When you really like someone you kiss them on the lips,' said Joe. 'That means lips against lips.'

'That is a very strange way of expressing affection,' said Kaia.

He grinned. 'What's the Carcassian way?'

'For thanking . . .' She placed her palms one on top of the other and brought her hands up to rest against her forehead. 'And for showing we care . . .' She reached out and touched Joe's temples with the tips of her middle fingers. Then she tilted her head close to his. 'And if you do the same it is further affection,' she added.

He copied her. Their foreheads touched. He could feel a sudden surge of heat run through this fingers, along his arms and then his body, growing hotter and hotter as it took over every part of him.

'Wow,' he whispered.

'Someone is coming!' Kaia took her hands away and he felt himself stumble. She motioned him to move behind a crop of boulders. For a moment he couldn't see anything through the small gap in the rocks, and then two girls around the same age as Kaia, and two older women walked across the field. They were wearing brightly coloured mid-length dresses, and were carrying large baskets which they swung between them as they laughed and chattered, talking so quickly that Joe couldn't understand what they were saying.

'I do not know either,' said Kaia. 'This is not the Kanabian we learned. It will take time for the Joq to work it out.'

The women and girls started to sing. Their voices were clear and the tune was catchy.

'It is about caring for your family,' said Kaia, after a while. 'They are talking about building happy homes.'

'That doesn't sound like the objective of a crack fighting force,' remarked Joe.

'All Kanabians are fighters,' Kaia said. 'I have studied them at Sanctuary. I have seen the papers and the messages sent by the Kanabians to Carcassia. There can be no doubt.'

'Perhaps so much time has gone by they've decided it's not worth fighting any more.'

'They have had to accept that the Shield thwarts their aims,' said Kaia. 'However, they are ready to fight the moment it fails.'

'You're probably right,' conceded Joe. 'I suppose I wanted them to be different. I liked Kho. I don't want to think of him as a future warrior. And those women seem so . . . normal.'

'That is the Kanabian way,' Kaia said. 'They pretend to be friends and then they slaughter you. This happened during the war. My people wanted to negotiate for peace. And while they were doing this the Kanabians launched a weapon against us, powered by Kerala that we had given them. It killed many Carcassians and wounded many more. So please do not feel sorry for them. They are dark-hearted people.'

Joe nodded and said nothing. He knew that wars happened between countries. He'd seen pictures of the conflicts in the Middle East. He'd watched movies about the two World Wars. He knew that sometimes it was impossible to sort things out. But it was depressing that the Kanabians and the Carcassians couldn't have found a way to share the Kerala peacefully instead of being perpetually at war. However, they hadn't and it wasn't up to him to try to change anything.

He didn't need to remember Carcassian or Kanabian, he thought, but it would be really cool if, when he finally got home, he was still as fast and as strong as he was now. With his current speed, he never would have been a target for Niall or Greg.

'Come,' said Kaia, breaking into his thoughts. 'Let us walk carefully.'

They moved forward again, keeping to the edges of the fields, watching out for traps and trying to stay out of the view of anyone who might be looking from one of the houses. But it was becoming more and more difficult to keep away from the roads, which were now wider and paved, not the dirt tracks through the mountains.

'We'll be in trouble if people see us,' observed Joe. 'We're wearing the wrong clothes.'

'I know.' Kaia glanced at her tunic and leggings. 'It was not possible for the Leaders to provide Kanabi clothing. We will have to get some ourselves.'

'How?' asked Joe.

'By taking what we need,' said Kaia. 'These clothes are best for our Run, they keep us warm when it is cold and help cool us when it is warm. Not enough,' she added as she wiped the sweat that glistened on her forehead, because the sun was high and the temperature was climbing again, 'but nearly. However, if all of the land between here and Zwemat is populated we need other clothes to wear in case we meet people.'

'I don't suppose you have Kanabian money,' said Joe.

'Money?'

'You give it to someone in exchange for something else,' said Joe.

'We do not do this in Carcassia.'

'How do you get the things you want?' asked Joe.

'I do not know.' Kaia looked confused. 'I had everything I wanted in Sanctuary.'

'Of course you did.' He sighed. 'In that case no, you don't have money. And maybe the Kanabians don't use it either, although if those women were going shopping they must manage somehow . . .'

'We will find Kanabian clothes and take them,' decided Kaia.

'I had a horrible feeling you were going to say that,' Joe said. 'Just let's not get caught while we do it.'

It took them about half an hour to get close to a Kanabian house where, just as on Earth, a woman had hung clothes on a washing line to dry. Kaia and Joe had watched her from the distance as she'd carried a big basket of different coloured clothes into the field behind her house and then proceeded to hang up her washing.

It must be a big family, Kaia murmured, as the woman hung up shirts and trousers, skirts and blouses, as well as other unidentifiable bits and pieces. Joe agreed. And he reckoned that they would be able to take something to fit them from the washing line, although at the thought of robbing someone's clothes his heart was pounding in his chest.

When her basket was empty, the woman walked back into the house.

'The clothes will be wet,' Joe reminded Kaia. 'So we need to leave them out for a while to dry first.'

He didn't know if he was saying this because he had no desire to put on someone else's wet trousers, or if it was because he wanted to put off the time when they had to steal them in the first place.

From their vantage point behind another Roxana hedge, Joe and Kaia could watch the woman inside the house. The entire back of it was made of a transparent material, like glass. They could see the layout of the house inside. Downstairs, at the widest part, was a kitchen and a living room. Upstairs seemed to be bedrooms, although there were screens across the windows there. But their eyes followed the woman as she cleaned the downstairs rooms, putting pots and pans into their proper places in the kitchen and plumping up cushions in the living room. Joe couldn't make out any gadgets – no televisions or phones or computers – but there were lots of papers and books lying around which the woman put into neat piles. Eventually, her chores finished, she left the house and walked down the path.

'This is our opportunity,' said Kaia.

Before Joe could stop her, she'd raced towards the washing line, unpegged a dress, a shirt and a pair of trousers and sped back to their hidey-hole near the hedge.

'Disguises,' she said. 'Although it pains me to wear the enemy's clothes.'

'Hope they fit.' Joe was eying the trousers dubiously. 'They look a bit big for me.'

'They will be perfectly adequate for your needs.' Kaia was already taking off her tunic. Joe quickly turned away as she folded it and put it in her rucksack. He didn't want to see her in her underwear. He got undressed and dressed in the Kanabian clothes as fast as he could because he didn't want her to see him in his underwear either. As he feared, both the shirt and the trousers were still a little damp, and although the trousers were a bit big for him around the waist, they were also too short. When she turned to look at him, Kaia giggled.

'What?' His tone was defensive.

'You look funny, Sho. Like a Kanabian but . . . not.'

'Gee, thanks.' He made a face at her. 'You look . . .' He wasn't sure what to say. The dress was a soft, rose-pink fabric with a low-cut round neck. It fell in loose pleats to just below her knees. The cut and colour suited her. For the first time Joe thought that she looked like any other girl. Only not any girl, any other pretty girl. 'You look Kanabian too,' he said eventually.

'I do not wish to look Kanabian,' she said. 'But it is a necessity. Let us go, before the woman returns.'

They began walking. Kaia said that they would draw too much attention to themselves if they ran, and Joe agreed with her. As they travelled along the road, they were passed by cars. The cars were similar to the Zaals that the Carcassians used, but they didn't fly, they just trundled along the road on wheels. And not very fast either – more or less the same speed as a bicycle. Joe tried to look at each one that passed by, and eventually he concluded that they actually were bikes, because the drivers were pedalling furiously.

'That must be tiring,' he said.

'They are very backward,' remarked Kaia.

'If they don't have the same kind of Kerala that you do, what d'you expect?' he asked.

She shot him a curious look but said nothing.

There were more and more people walking on the road too now. Every so often, someone would nod at Kaia and Joe in greeting. Joe thought that they all seemed very friendly, but he knew better than to say this to Kaia who, he was sure, would just have some other cutting comment to make. And he had to accept that she had lived on Charra all of her life and knew far more about what went on in her homeworld than he did.

They reached the centre of the village, which was a large

circle surrounded by the A-shaped houses. Here, the buildings were clearly small shops and cafés. Some of them had displays of fruits or vegetables piled up in the windows. Others had types of meat. A couple had open boxes containing herbs and spices. Joe got a strong smell of apple and cinnamon coming from what seemed to be a bakery. It made him suddenly think of the days he would go to the local shopping centre with his Mum. She would always buy him coffee and an apple and cinnamon muffin after they did the shopping together. He hoped she wasn't worrying about him.

'Oh, excuse me!' A woman, her golden hair pulled into a plait similar to Kaia's, had bumped into them with a bag full of shopping.

Beside him, Joe sensed the tension in Kaia's body.

'No problem,' he said pleasantly. 'It is a busy day.'

'Yes.' She smiled. 'We are lucky to celebrate the Valla today. It is good to have a successful season with lots of crops and food.'

'Sure is,' said Joe.

The woman's brow wrinkled slightly. 'You are from Thalia?' she asked.

'No,' said Kaia. 'From Zwemat.'

'Really!' The woman looked surprised. 'We do not often get people from the city here. And your friend . . .' she looked at Joe.

'We're not from Zwemat itself,' said Joe quickly. 'A village outside. We were told that this place is particularly nice so we thought we'd travel.'

This time the woman smiled. 'You were told well,' she said.

'And are you travelling because it is your Time?'

'I – yes, it is.' Joe hoped he wasn't making a big mistake by saying yes.

'Well, many congratulations,' said the woman. 'I hope you have a large family together.'

Kaia gasped.

'Thank you,' said Joe after a moment's hesitation. 'I hope we do too.'

The woman crossed the circle and went into a shop. Kaia turned to Joe.

'What was all that about? Our Time? It is not our Time. I am a Runner. I do not bind myself to a man.'

'But she doesn't know that,' said Joe. 'I guessed she thought we were married and so . . .'

'Of course,' she snapped. 'However, I do not want to be married to you.'

'I don't want to be married to you either,' said Joe. 'But I want to be captured by the Kanabians even less.'

Kaia sighed. 'I suppose you have a point.'

'Yes,' said Joe. 'I do. Now why don't we try one of those cafés and have something to eat and drink like a happily married couple.'

It did occur to him, as they sat at a table outside a café, that the Kanabians got married very young. And then, after the waitress brought them Xlov (which was a pale pink soft drink) and Yvir (a plate of berries) he wondered how they were going to pay. They could be in big trouble here just because he'd wanted to calm Kaia down. And, he admitted, he wanted to rest and just behave like a normal person for a while.

He felt almost normal as he sipped the Xlov, which was cool and refreshing. The berries were lovely too. And it was nice to sit down and be among other people, even if they were supposed to be his deadly enemy. Right now, though, they were just walking through the village, popping in and out of the shops, talking to each other in a very ordinary way. If Joe could put the fact that he was on another planet out of his head, it was like being on holiday in a place where people didn't have access to the latest fashions or mobile phones, and where everyone seemed to know everyone else.

A man and a woman, older than Joe and Kaia, sat at a nearby table. They started talking about the harvest and the price of some kind of grain, and then the man congratulated her on how well her eldest boy was doing in school.

'I wish Kho would study as hard, my brother,' said the woman. 'But without a father to discipline him, it is sometimes difficult. It was much easier with the other children.'

Joe and Kaia exchanged glances. They had come a long way since freeing Kho. Could the the man and woman possibly be talking about the young boy?

'I will discipline him for you,' said her brother. 'I can teach him to feel a stick across his back.'

'Ryal, there is no need for that sort of punishment,' she protested. 'It is simply that he is young and he has so much energy. I do not think he will ever be an academic.'

'Better an academic than joining the military,' said the man. 'Which will happen to him if he fails to get the highest of grades. Damn soldiers.'

Joe and Kaia exchanged glances again. And then a boy, with a Pashwa on a lead, ran up to the couple and they saw that it was indeed Kho. He saw them too and he looked at them in amazement.

'Kho!' his mother said. 'Stop staring at those people.'

'I wasn't staring.'

'You were.' She looked apologetically at Joe and Kaia. 'I am trying to teach him manners. I apologise for his rudeness.'

Kaia gave the woman a brief smile and took a sip of Xlov, leaving about a third of it still in the glass.

'We should go,' she said to Joe.

He nodded, but before he had the chance to get up from the chair, Bobie, the Pashwa, jumped at him. The dog's leap knocked the chair sideways and knocked Joe to the ground. The table flipped over, sending the remaining Yvir berries into the air and spilling the Xlov.

'Kho Khristi!' cried his uncle. 'How many times have I told you to keep control of that damned animal. Now look what you have done!'

'I am sorry.' Kho was frantically pulling on the Pashwa's collar, trying to stop him from both eating the berries and licking Joe.

'He should not be acting like that,' said the man. 'With complete strangers! What the hell sort of Pashwa is he?'

'A very silly one.' Joe got up and patted the animal on the head. Both the man and woman stared at him.

'You can tame a strange Pashwa?' she asked.

'No animal is strange to me,' said Joe.

'You have a gift,' said Kho's mother. 'It is extraordinary.

I always thought a Pashwa had to be introduced slowly to a new person.'

'Some people have a talent,' said Joe as he righted the chair.

'Well, in that case Kho was lucky it was you his animal attacked and not anybody else,' said his uncle. 'We are most sorry.'

'That's OK,' said Joe.

'Kho, you must apologise to these people. And you must whip that animal later.'

'Oh, no!' cried Kaia. 'That is not necessary.'

Kho's uncle stared at her. 'It is the only way to train it,' he said. 'And Kho is the one that must do it.'

'You are right of course,' said Kaia quickly. 'It is just that my husband is so good with these animals I am not accustomed to the other ways of training them.'

'You are very gracious,' said Kho's mother. 'And as our thanks we would like that you allow us to pay for your refreshments.'

'That would be kind,' said Joe.

'Then it is done.' Kho's mother smiled at them and they thanked her again while her brother apologised on Kho's behalf. The boy didn't say anything. And, for half an hour, until they were clear of the village, neither did Joe or Kaia.

20

'Let's try to avoid towns and cities in future,' said Joe as they changed back into their running clothes.

'Agreed,' she replied. 'If the boy had betrayed us we would be in one of their prisons now.'

'Kho doesn't know we're from Carcassia,' Joe reminded her. 'He just thought we were strangers. And I didn't think those people were too keen on the military.'

'Nevertheless, if he had started talking about us they would have asked questions.' Kaia was rapidly replaiting her hair in the Kanabian style.

'He wouldn't have said anything,' Joe said. 'Otherwise he would've had to admit where he'd seen us.'

'I suppose you are right.' She put her rucksack on her back. 'That feels a lot better.'

Joe was equally glad to be out of the too loose and too short trousers, although he couldn't help thinking that the Carcassian clothes could do with a bit of a wash now. The shirt had been fresh and clean, with a subtle fragrance of herbs. The

Carcassian top and trousers reeked a bit of lake-water, undergrowth and sweat.

'We should be close to Zwemat by nightfall,' said Kaia, as she checked the map. 'Unfortunately, the shelter is on the other side, but no matter. Tomorrow we will reach the Loran.' Her voice lifted. 'I will have completed the first part of my Run and helped to defend Carcassia.'

Joe could hardly wait to see the Loran at last. And if there was a portal back to Earth there, it meant that by this time tomorrow he could be home. He wouldn't have to worry any more about running through hostile territory and looking out for Kanabian spies or traps. Everything would be back to normal for him. But Kaia would still be running. She still had a mission to complete.

Joe hated to think of her doing the Run on her own. It had been hard enough so far with two of them. Maybe he had slowed her down a bit. Maybe he had caused her some problems. But they were doing well now as a team. He couldn't simply leave her. He couldn't. If there was a portal at Zwemat there would be one at Domote and Lagat too. He was going to stay with her until the end. And then he was going to try to persuade her to come back to Earth with him. He couldn't bear to think that she would die.

He ran quickly and quietly alongside her. And, as the sky turned a golden pink, they saw the tall grey buildings of the city ahead of them. They seemed to be clustered tightly together and their long narrow windows reflected the setting sun.

It didn't look welcoming.

'The route takes us right through it,' said Kaia, as she

consulted the map. 'We will have to be careful. We should change into the Kanabi clothes again.'

'Does the map have a shelter marked on it?' he asked as they entered the city.

She nodded. 'An orph from here.'

They walked quickly through deserted streets to the designated location. When they arrived there, Joe groaned. A wooden crane with a wrecking ball was parked on the spot where the building should have been.

'Great,' he said. 'They knew we were coming so they knocked it down.'

'They could not have known!' Kaia looked horrified.

'That was a joke. Sorry.'

'We will have to find an empty building and stay there instead,' decided Kaia. 'This is a quiet area. It should be easy.'

'We have to be careful,' Joe warned. 'We don't want to be caught by Kanabian security.'

'Of course we will be careful.' Kaia shot him an impatient look as she took the blue Kerala crystal from her rucksack.

'This will tell us if there are people in the houses,' she said.

'I thought it was to warn you of people approaching.'

'It does,' said Kaia. 'But also it glows when they are nearby.'

'It's glowing now,' said Joe.

'And vibrating,' added Kaia. 'Somebody is coming.' She slipped the crystal into the pocket of her dress. Almost immediately a group of young Kanabians walked into the square. They were arguing loudly and two of them – tall, well-built young men – were pushing each other aggressively.

They stopped when they saw Kaia and Joe but then started to walk towards them.

'Let's get out of here.' Joe stood up and began to walk in the opposite direction.

'Hey!' called one of the men.

'Just keep walking,' said Joe. 'That's the best thing to do.'

Kaia said nothing but fell into step beside him.

'Hey!' The man's voice was fainter.

Joe and Kaia kept moving and soon they'd managed to lose him in the maze of streets.

'This is becoming nerve-wracking,' said Joe as he leaned against a wall. 'Most ordinary Kanabians seem OK but—'

'Get down!' Kaia cried and Joe instinctively ducked. Which was just as well as she launched herself into a jump kick exactly where his left shoulder had been. Joe heard her connect with something or someone, and then a thud as whatever had been behind him slumped to the ground.

He turned around. It was an older, male Kanabian, poorly dressed and now unconscious. He had a knife in his hand.

'There are no ordinary Kanabians,' said Kaia as she took the knife from the unconscious man. 'Only murdering Chan.'

'Perhaps we're just in a bad part of town,' said Joe.

'You would have preferred I did not stop him?' She put the knife in her rucksack. 'He was going to kill you. To take things belonging to you.'

'Thank you for stopping him,' said Joe. 'But *you* haven't killed *him*, have you?'

'Not yet,' said Kaia. She nudged the man with her foot.

171

'Please don't,' begged Joe. 'I don't want to have his death on my conscience.'

'What do you mean?' asked Kaia. 'He is a thief and probably a murderer himself. He is Kanabian, he deserves to die.'

'But it's not up to us to judge.'

'You are weak, Sho,' said Kaia. 'It will be the death of us.'

'Sorry,' said Joe. 'It's an Earth thing.'

'We will dispose of him here.' Kaia lifted the lid on what looked like a big refuse bin.

'What's that for?' asked Joe peering inside. It was empty.

'I do not know,' said Kaia. 'Nor do I care. I will make sure that he does not wake for a long time.' She took out another crystal and tapped him on the side of the head with it.

'What did you do?' asked Joe anxiously.

'He is sleeping,' Kaia said. 'He will sleep until we are long gone from this horrible place. Help me place him inside.'

The man was heavy, but with his extra strength, Joe was able to lift him and slide him into the bin. The man didn't move, but he was now snoring loudly. Joe closed the lid. The snores echoed faintly inside.

'That's that,' said Joe. 'Now we need to find somewhere to sleep ourselves. Preferably somewhere safe.'

They walked away from the bin and the unconscious man, cutting through the narrow city streets until they saw a large building which, according to Kaia's crystal, was unoccupied. Joe wished he could read Kanabian writing. He was at a big disadvantage not to know what anything said.

'It is a school,' she said. 'So nobody will disturb us.'

'Can we get in?' asked Joe.

'It is locked, of course,' said Kaia as she tried it. 'And I do not think that there will be a key under a stone this time.'

'Maybe we can find another way.'

They walked around the school slowly and it was Kaia who spotted the small horizontal window just out of reach, but slightly ajar.

'I could try to jump,' said Joe.

Kaia gave him a scornful look. 'And if you did and you reached it, would you be able to climb through?' she asked. 'You are too big, Sho Hun-ter.'

'Can you jump that high?' he asked.

'No,' said Kaia. 'But I can climb on to your shoulders and reach it that way.'

'We could try, I suppose,' said Joe doubtfully.

He cupped his hands and Kaia stepped into them, then on to his shoulders. She couldn't reach the window itself, but her fingers closed around the narrow sill beneath it.

'Now push me higher,' she told Joe.

He put his hands beneath her feet and pushed her from his shoulders, turning at the same time so that he could see her. There wasn't much room for her to work with but she pulled herself steadily upwards until she was balancing precariously on the sill. Then she opened the window a little more.

She'd been right about him being too big to fit through it, thought Joe. He wasn't sure that she'd manage to fit either. He watched as she put her head through the opening and then squirmed and wriggled her body through. Halfway through she stopped. Joe didn't know if it was because she was stuck or if something else had happened. But then she began again until she was finally inside the building.

A couple of minutes later the door opened.

'Are you OK?' asked Joe. 'Why did you stop?'

'Because there was a bowl of Kinzi beneath the window,' explained Kaia. 'They are small fish,' she added as he looked at her enquiringly. 'Children keep them as pets.'

'In Carcassia too?' asked Joe.

Kaia nodded. 'I did not have one,' she said, 'because I was in Sanctuary. But nearly all Carcassian children do. Come, Sho, we do not want anyone to notice our presence here.'

Joe walked inside the school. It was like almost every other school he knew – low tables, small chairs, kids' paintings tacked to the walls and various jars, containers and books lining the shelves.

Joe studied the paintings. Lots of them were clearly representations of families, with parents and groups of children doing things like having picnics, sitting around a table together, or standing outside a house. Some of the paintings were of animals. Joe recognised a Pashwa, although he hoped that a painting of a horse with a spiked back was of an imaginary creature. There was one of the whale with the unicorn horn too. But what made him stop and stare were the pictures of a green landscape with a huge silver dome in the centre. Outside the dome, people were standing and pointing. And above the dome was a jagged bolt of lightning.

'Look,' he said to Kaia. 'Do you think this is what Carcassia looks like to them?'

She stared at the pictures too. 'It is a weapon,' she told

him, aghast. 'The Kanabians are trying to create a weapon against us.'

'What do you mean?'

'A power strike over Carcassia.'

'Oh.' Joe hadn't thought of that. He'd imagined that the drawing was of a natural bolt of lightning but Kaia could be right. The Kanabians were trying to break through Carcassia's Shield with everything they had. And if they did, how badly would they treat the Carcassians?

He thought of Kho Khristi, the boy in the trap, and how he was to have been punished. And he remembered the way Chai Loshi had laughed when he talked about Kho's mother. He hadn't wanted to believe the Kanabians were bad people. But he was wrong.

He looked at Kaia. Her face was fierce and determined.

'We will not let the Shield be penetrated,' she said. 'Tomorrow we will place the first Kerala and protect Carcassia from these animals.'

He nodded. If the Kanabians were teaching young children about attacking Carcassia, they deserved everything she said about them.

21

They slept in the staffroom. It was at the end of a long corridor and had soft chairs and comfortable sofas. It was warm too and as Joe stretched out on one of the sofas he felt himself become sleepy almost at once.

'I will keep watch,' said Kaia. 'And then you.'

'There's hardly any need to keep watch,' protested Joe. 'Nobody's going to come into a closed school and we have the motion sensor Kerala to warn us if they do.'

'We will need to leave early in the morning,' said Kaia. 'Someone will have to be awake.'

'I'll set the alarm on my phone,' Joe told her. 'For five hours from now. That'll be plenty of time.'

'It is useful, your communication device,' she admitted.

'It'd be more useful if I could communicate with someone at home,' said Joe. 'Although to be honest, I'm not sure what I'd tell them.'

'You will find a way home at the Loran,' Kaia told him. 'I am sure of it.'

Joe didn't say anything about his decision to stay with her. He thought she might argue with him and he didn't want to argue. So he just nodded.

'I am tired,' said Kaia.

'Then sleep,' Joe said. 'I promise the alarm will go off.'

She set the Kerala motion sensor alarm just in case, and then lay down on another sofa.

Joe was so tired that he thought he'd fall asleep straight away, but his mind was still buzzing. Home was never this exciting. But there was a lot to be said for the fact that his only worries there were Niall, Greg and double English on Fridays. He should get Kaia to teach him some of her fighting moves, he thought as he drifted off to sleep. They'd be useful back on Earth.

In his dream, she was there with him. They walked to school together and everyone envied him because she was pretty and clever and so damn good at beating up people who needed it. Nobody picked on him any more and he didn't care that it was because she was a better fighter than him.

Joe murmured happily as he slept. He was still dreaming when the phone alarm went off five hours later. He was awake immediately and shot upright on the sofa. He looked around him. There was no sign of Kaia. He felt his mouth go dry and then the door opened and she walked back into the staffroom.

'I woke earlier,' she explained. 'So I went to see if there was somewhere I could wash. There is, if you want to.'

Memories of his dream came back to Joe as she spoke. He'd been thinking about kissing her when the alarm had gone off. He told himself it was just as well it had.

Before leaving, they looked at Kaia's map. Although it zoned in on the area where they were, it didn't have street view or anything half as helpful. When it came to plotting a route out of Zwemat it was practically useless, because very few streets appeared on it.

'I guess it was made a long time ago,' said Joe. 'Possibly none of them existed back then.'

'Nevertheless, it makes things more difficult.' Kaia sighed as she studied the map. 'The Kerala is this way. But when we walk into the street I am not sure if we will go in the right direction.'

'We can use my compass.' He orientated himself in the room and then checked the map. 'OK, according to your map the Loran is north-east of here. So if we keep following the arrow we should get through the city and rejoin the route we were supposed to take.'

'Are you sure?'

'Nearly sure.'

'OK.' She rolled up the map and put it back into her rucksack. Then both of them walked quietly out of the school and into the still-dark streets of the city. Joe was glad they'd had some unbroken sleep. He was feeling much more alert now and he was conscious of everything around him. When a small animal scurried across the street he was ready to react, but Kaia put her arm on his and told him it was a Chium, a type of domestic pet which liked to roam at night.

'A sort of cat,' said Joe, which was about right, although the Chiums had curly tails and an extra ear on the top of their heads.

The only living creatures that he and Kaia saw for most of their walk through the city were Chiums, a few Pashwas, and occasional flying insects which moved in swarms high above their heads. Kaia didn't know what the insects were called and Joe kept his fingers crossed that they weren't the biting sort. But they didn't seem to be because they stayed above the level of the buildings and didn't come near them.

Joe was finding it all a little spooky because the street lighting was limited to the flickering torches on the corners but nothing else. Some of the buildings were faintly lit too, but most were in darkness. That was partly why he nearly fell over an obstacle on the path ahead of him.

The obstacle was a sack and the contents spilled on to the pavement.

'Chillos!' exclaimed Kaia as she picked up one of the round objects.

'Chillos?'

'It is a fruit. Very, very nutritious,' said Kaia. 'And rare in Carcassia because it needs a particular type of soil to grow.'

'Does it taste good?' asked Joe.

'It is the nicest fruit in the world,' Kaia told him. 'It was always a big treat when we got some at Sanctuary.'

Joe looked around him. The street was deserted. He took a deep breath.

'Would it be a crime to take some?' he asked. 'After all—'

'How could it be a crime?' Kaia was already stuffing the fruit into her rucksack. 'They have been grown by Kanabians!'

'It's not our fruit.' But Joe didn't sound convincing and Kaia gave him a withering look.

179

He stuffed his bag with them too, and then they closed over the top of the sack again.

'They will not even miss them,' said Kaia.

'Hopefully not,' said Joe. 'Given what we're here to do, it would be ironic to end up in a Kanabian prison for stealing fruit.'

The sky was beginning to lighten as the streets thinned out and they reached the outskirts of the city. Now there were occasional people but nobody took any notice of Joe and Kaia. They walked purposefully, keeping their heads close together as though in conversation, trying to appear busy and caught up in their own affairs.

And then, finally, they'd left the city behind and they were once again in the countryside. The wide, paved roads petered out too and became narrow tracks. Eventually, as the sun rose higher in the sky, Kaia decided that they could change out of the Kanabian clothes, sit in the shade of a tree and eat a Chillo.

'Oh my God,' said Joe as he bit into the fruit. 'It's . . . amazing.'

'I know.' Kaia was beaming.

'It's somewhere between strawberry and chocolate fudge,' said Joe.

'I do not know this strawberry and chocolate fudge.' Kaia wiped some juice from her chin. 'But in Carcassia it is called the Dessert of the Gods.'

'I'm not surprised,' said Joe. 'It's the best thing I've eaten since I arrived here. And I know you said they were your favourite food, but I was getting tired of those Cheeba cookies.'

'Me too,' admitted Kaia. She looked at the Link on her wrist. The ruby stone was now a shade of deep pink. 'OK, enough rest. We should go.' She looked at him with an excited expression. 'We are close, Sho. So close.'

'I can't believe we've almost made it,' said Joe.

He crammed another Chillo into his mouth and they set off again.

22

'Shouldn't we have found it by now?' Joe asked after they had been running for a couple of hours. 'What exactly are we looking for?'

Kaia frowned. 'I am not sure. The Loran will be well hidden. The map lights up when we are close.' She pointed to the little egg-shaped icon on the map which indicated the position of the Loran. 'I thought it would be illuminated by now.'

'Maybe we have to be right beside it,' said Joe. 'It can't be far.'

Kaia nodded. They started to walk, but not run, looking around them as they went. There were no trails, just hilly grassland, dotted with trees, bushes and the occasional boulder. Joe reckoned the Loran would be at one of the boulders. He thought there would probably be some kind of hidden entrance. And had a candidate for the spot – a big rock formation five minutes away.

He should have been right. The map led them directly to it. Yet the icon didn't light up and Kaia was worried.

'We cannot be wrong,' she said. 'We must have found it.'

'I think so too.' Joe walked around the boulders and the rocks. 'Kaia, look!' He pointed to a boulder on which a mark had been scratched. The mark was faded but it was a square with two lines crossing it diagonally.

'Oh!' Kaia stared at it.

'What's the matter?'

'It is Carcassian,' she said. 'It is a symbol of . . .'

'Of what?'

She looked anxious. 'Of the Haaken,' she said.

'Haaken!' Joe was taken aback. 'How could the Haaken have got here?'

'I do not know,' said Kaia. 'And I do not know why they would write on this rock.'

'Weird.' Joe clambered past the rock and then whistled. 'Over here!'

She followed him. Behind the rock were two more boulders leaning against each other and forming an entrance, although it seemed to be blocked by a variety of roots and other vegetation.

'This is it,' said Kaia. 'I know it is.' She looked at the map again, but the icon remained unlit.

'Let me.' Joe began pulling at the roots until he'd managed to open a gap large enough for them to squeeze through.

Kaia pushed her way in front of him and manoeuvred through the gap. Joe followed her. They were in a narrow passageway. Kaia took a glowstick from her rucksack and used the light from it to guide them along the passageway, which twisted and turned as it led them further underground.

'You're sure this is safe?' Joe was feeling claustrophobic. The roof was low and the walls seemed to be made of dry mud and stone. He remembered the earthquake in the Carcassian tunnel and shuddered.

'Of course,' said Kaia. 'There are no dragons in Kanabia and my people made it to be safe. Do not worry, Sho.'

He shrugged and continued to follow her. It was another five minutes before the passageway widened into a chamber. He and Kaia stood side by side as they looked at it.

In the centre of the chamber was a stone altar. On the altar were three large Kerala crystals. None of them was glowing. On the floor beside the altar were pieces of shattered crystal. Kaia picked up a shard of the crystal and turned it over in her hand.

'This should not happen,' she said, her voice trembling. 'The Kerala do not break. How can it be?'

'Maybe that can tell us?' Joe pointed to the writing on the wall. He couldn't read it, but he recognised the same symbol they'd seen on the boulder etched above it.

Kaia looked at the writing, then whirled around to the altar again where each crystal sat in an individually carved slot. She took the first of her own large Kerala crystals from her rucksack and placed it into a slot. It remained unlit. She moved the different crystals into other positions on the altar. Nothing happened. She changed them around again. Then she took the other two crystals from her rucksack and placed them so that all of the crystals on the altar were new. Still none of them glowed.

'Kaia?' Joe's voice was full of concern.

She stood in front of the wall again, a frightened expression on her face.

'There is something terribly wrong here,' she said.

'Obviously they're not connecting properly to the altar,' said Joe.

She nodded. 'Which means that Zwemat has failed us for a number of cycles. But why? And how did a Kerala break? And . . .' She turned and looked at the wall again. 'These names trouble me deeply.'

'Why?'

'This is a list of previous Runners,' she said.

'Makes sense.' Joe nodded. 'Someone comes, places the Kerala and writes their name. That shouldn't worry you, Kaia.'

'Bo Anka,' she said softly as she ran her fingers over the writing. 'He was ahead of me at Sanctuary. He was part of the last Run. Lila Dopla was before him. But . . .'

'What?'

'It says "We Are Defeated."' She turned to Joe. 'How can we be defeated when we know that the Shield is working?'

'Maybe they just mean that this Loran isn't working,' said Joe. 'What does this say?' He pointed to a large engraving.

'Resting place.'

'Like the shelters?' he asked.

'She shook her head. 'No. This is more . . . permanent.'

'You mean like a crypt?' Joe's voice was shaky. 'For dead people?' He looked around as though there should be bodies on the ground.

Kaia nodded. 'For the Runners who came here last,' she said. 'There would be nowhere else to go.'

Joe hadn't thought about where Carcassian Runners went to die at the end of their mission. Now he knew. They didn't go anywhere. They simply sat down and waited for the Muqi to take effect.

'Let's try moving the Kerala on the altar again,' he said. 'Maybe we didn't get it right the first time.'

'I tried all of the combinations,' said Kaia.

'Let's try them again.'

'There is no point. Something terrible has happened. None of the Kerala I brought will glow. Other Kerala have shattered, Sho. And Runners do not write their names beneath the symbol of the Haaken!'

Joe ignored her and went back to the altar. He moved both the new and the old Kerala again and again but nothing happened.

'We Are Defeated,' repeated Kaia. 'Perhaps the Kanabi and the Haaken have laid a trap.'

'I don't like the sound of that.' Joe looked around him anxiously. 'What d'you think we should do?'

'I cannot leave the Kerala here,' said Kaia as she replaced them in her rucksack. 'And there is no way for you to reach your home. So I think we must move on. I am sorry, Sho Hun-ter.'

'It's OK. You're right. Let's get out of here.'

'But first I must find the Resting Place and pay my respects to the other Runners,' said Kaia.

'Perhaps you should write your name on the wall instead,' suggested Joe. 'Maybe Runners do that at every Loran.'

'I will not write beneath a Haaken symbol,' she said. 'I cannot understand why someone like Bo would have . . .'

186

'OK, don't write your name but please – don't go into the burial chamber,' he begged.

'Why not?'

'It's just . . . I'm getting a very bad feeling about this place.'

'I also have a bad feeling, Sho,' said Kaia. 'But I must pay respect to those who came ahead of me.'

She knelt down in front of the wall of names. Then she touched her head off the ground and murmured softly to herself.

'It is a prayer for the dead,' she explained when she'd finished. 'We learn it at Sanctuary.'

Joe remained silent as they began to walk back. It was slightly uphill and he could feel himself starting to sweat a little as he followed her. He wasn't sure if it was because of the effort or because he was feeling claustrophobic again.

He was relieved when they finally reached the entrance. But Kaia held up her hand.

'We should be careful,' she said. She took one of the small motion sensor crystals from her rucksack and looked at it. It wasn't glowing or vibrating so she headed towards the gap in the rocks. And then there was a momentary flash of light and she was propelled backwards into the tunnel, straight into Joe, knocking him to the ground.

'Kaia! Are you all right?'

It took Joe a minute to catch his breath. Then he sat up and looked at the Carcassian girl who was rubbing her shoulder.

'Yes,' she said. 'I am stunned, that is all.'

'What happened?' Joe's voice was anxious. 'Were there Kanabians? Haaken?'

'No, Sho,' said Kaia. 'It was a shield. The entrance is guarded by a shield from the inside.' She dusted herself down. Then she looked around and finally cried out.

'*What?*' Joe stood beside her. 'What have you found?'

She pointed to a tiny yellow light in the rocks which was blinking slowly. 'It is a sensor. When we crossed it, it set up the Shield.'

'But who put it there and why?' asked Joe. 'I can understand that the Shield was there to stop people getting in, but not to stop people getting out. Unless . . .' He shivered suddenly.

'Unless what?'

'The Runners. Perhaps it's simply to keep them here to die,' said Joe.

Kaia stared at him, a horrified expression on her face. 'That is not possible.'

'In the end all Runners die,' Joe said. 'Maybe this is to make sure you do. Maybe they don't want you to go to different Lorans after all. Maybe once you're here, that's it.'

'You mean, a Runner is supposed to place the Kerala here but not go to the next Loran?' Kaia shook her head. 'That cannot be so. Vasila would have told me if that was the case.'

'Would she? Really?'

'It is more likely that the Kanabi found out about this Loran and set the trap to keep Runners here. Who knows, Sho, it may be like the trap that Kho Khristi found himself in. It will alert the Kanabians to our presence. They will come and . . .'

'We have to find a way to turn it off,' said Joe, even as he was thinking that some of the dead Runners must have tried to turn it off too. And they'd failed.

'I do not know how.' Kaia ran her fingers over the stones and mud of the walls. 'There is nothing here.'

'The same way as you turned off the other trap. With a crystal against the light.'

She nodded. 'But we cannot reach. It is too high.'

'I'll lift you like I did at the school,' said Joe. 'Good job I've been keeping my strength up with Cheeba cookies.'

'I still cannot reach,' she said as he held her up.

'Stand on my hands and I'll push you up with my arms.' As he raised her higher, Joe thought that this was something he'd never have been able to do at home. He heard Kaia grunt as she steadied herself and then tapped the Kerala close to the sensor.

Just as before, there was a flash of light, this time accompanied by a loud bang. Joe's arms wobbled as Kaia lost her balance. He stumbled backwards and ended up lying on the ground, Kaia on top of him once more. He felt something sting his cheek and he cried out.

'Sho, Sho, are you all right?' Kaia rolled from him and looked at him anxiously.

'I . . . think so.' He put his hand to his face and brought it back. Even in the dim light of the tunnel he knew he was bleeding.

'The Kerala shattered,' said Kaia. 'That is what must have happened to the other one we saw too.'

'If we can't turn it off we'll have to find another way out,' said Joe.

'There is no other way,' Kaia told him. 'We will die here, like the others.'

'I've survived being chased by Niall and Greg. I've survived turning up on another planet. I've survived the attentions of the Yeppuno. I've survived a Kanabi net. And together we've survived earthquakes, dangerous animals, encounters with the Kanabians and God knows what else. I am not going to die trapped in a tunnel, Kaia. I'm not.' Joe stood up and steadied himself against the wall because his legs were shaking.

'Your face, Sho!' said Kaia. 'You are injured.'

'I think a piece of the Kerala cut it.' He touched it. It was still bleeding.

'Wait.' Kaia took a small jar from her rucksack and opened it. She smeared a paste over Joe's cheek.

'Ouch,' he gasped.

'It will stop the bleeding,' she said.

'Thank you.' He gave her a faint smile.

'The only other way out must be past the Resting Place,' said Kaia. 'We will have to try.'

Joe didn't reply. He put his own rucksack on his back and followed her.

They walked to the chamber and past the altar with the useless Kerala crystals. Besides the way they'd come, there was only one other passageway.

She began to walk and Joe followed her reluctantly. He hoped it would bypass the so-called Resting Place. He'd never seen a dead body before and he didn't want to see one now. Although they'd be skeletons, he supposed. He'd seen a skeleton in his biology class. That hadn't been too bad. But it hadn't seemed like a person either.

A couple of minutes later Kaia stopped abruptly and Joe nearly walked into her.

'Are you – oh, God!'

He put his arms around her again as she turned away from the sight in front of her. And Joe himself found it very hard not to scream. Because there weren't skeletons in front of them. Sitting side-by-side on benches carved from the rocky walls were a dozen Carcassian Runners. Their faces were pale and they were staring at Kaia and at Joe from glassy, unwavering eyes. It took him a moment to realise that they were dead.

They were all wearing the same green tunic as he and Kaia, although the fabric on some of them was beginning to rot away. The women's hair was braided in the Kanabian style. The men wore theirs in a single plait. They looked as though they were sitting in judgement on the two young people in front of them. Joe shivered.

'I knew . . . but I did not expect . . .' Kaia was close to tears as she looked up at him. 'That is Kizan Maal at the end, the Runner who came before me. I thought I was following in his footsteps . . .' This time she couldn't stop the tears. 'He should not be here. He should have continued to run.'

'But some of the others . . . this is their last stop, isn't it?'

She turned her tear-streaked face to him. 'In Sanctuary, we talk about the sacrifice. We talk about the Muqi. It seems brave and honourable. But this . . .' She wiped her eyes with the back of her hand. 'This is sad. So many great people. Kizan, and Bo Anka and . . .' Her voice caught in her throat. '. . . And next to him is Shara Na. She was so quick and so clever. But here she is . . .' She couldn't speak any more.

'Let's go,' said Joe. 'C'mon, Kaia.'

But she didn't move.

'Come on,' he repeated.

'They stayed together,' she said. 'They did not flee.'

'Nobody's fleeing,' said Joe. 'We're trying to find a way out. We're trying to save Carcassia.'

But Kaia didn't move and Joe didn't know what to do. He was freaked out by the dead bodies, and by the fact that, except for the fact that the faces were a grey-white colour, they seemed perfectly preserved. Skeletons would have been easier to see than these shells of people who'd died in vain. All he wanted to do was to leave, but he wasn't going anywhere without Kaia.

Joe watched as she knelt on the floor in front of the seated bodies and pressed her head against the ground. She began chanting the prayer for the dead again. All the time, the eyes of the last Carcassians seemed to watch both of them.

'I'm sorry,' said Joe when she stood up again.

'I should not be sad,' said Kaia. 'The Runners were doing their duty. But there is something wrong with what has happened here.'

'We'll find out,' Joe promised, even though he didn't know how.

'Thank you.' She slipped her hand into his.

'One of the boys in my school died,' said Joe suddenly. 'He had a brain tumour.'

Kaia looked puzzled.

'It doesn't matter,' said Joe. 'Point is, he died. It was a terrible shock. He was younger than me. I couldn't sleep for weeks afterwards. So I know how you must feel.'

'I feel sad,' said Kaia. 'I did not expect to feel sadness on my Run. But that is how I feel.'

'We have to feel sadness to feel joy,' said Joe. 'That's what my mum says.'

'She is a wise woman, your mother.'

As he and Kaia walked slowly through the Resting Place, Joe wondered if his mum would have any wise words for this situation. She might tell him to keep calm, that everything would be all right. She often said that. And usually things worked out. But that was on Earth. This was different.

'Here.' Kaia's voice was just above a whisper. 'There is a way out here, Sho.'

He looked doubtfully at the narrow slit in the wall that Kaia was pointing to.

'Will we fit?'

'We must.'

'I'll try first.' He turned sideways to slide through the gap and sighed with relief when he realised it was a little wider on the other side. It was also very dark. When he switched on his torch app he could see that the walls were much rougher here and the stones more jagged.

'Be careful,' he said as Kaia joined him.

They moved forward cautiously, not speaking, both hoping that they'd find a way out as quickly as possible. It was hard going and more than once either Joe or Kaia stumbled. But they didn't stop until they came to a dead end.

'Oh no,' muttered Joe. 'Don't tell me this is it.'

Kaia shook her head and pointed upwards. The tunnel had turned into a shaft.

'You've got to be kidding me,' he said. 'How are we going to get up there?'

'We must climb,' said Kaia.

She took off her rucksack and turned it around so that it was at her front and only the straps were at her back. Then she pressed her back against one part of the shaft and her feet against the other. Slowly she edged her way up.

'Be careful,' said Joe. 'You might fall.'

'I will not,' she said. 'I have practised this many, many times in Sanctuary.'

Joe hoped that she had. Because, he thought, as he began to follow her up, if she did fall she was going to fall directly on to him. And that would mean him being flat on his back with Kaia on top of him for the third time that day.

23

He had no idea how long it took them to get to the top, only that by the time Kaia stopped, his legs were screaming with the pain.

'What can you see?' he asked.

'Something is covering the way out,' she replied.

Joe groaned, although he supposed it was inevitable that getting out wouldn't be easy.

'Can you open it?' He tried to sound more confident than he felt.

'It is stuck.'

He heard her pushing at it. She was panting hard and he knew that she must be as tired as he was. He wished he could help her but it was impossible. This was something she'd have to do on her own.

She thumped and pushed and panted a bit more and then she gave a satisfied grunt and told him that she'd opened it. As she scrambled out of the top he could feel loose clay and pebbles fall back through the shaft on top of him and he began to cough.

'Come on, Sho,' she said.

He looked up. She was peering down the shaft at him. The sky above her was dark, although the light from the Qaan was bright enough to see her clearly.

'Come on,' she repeated.

He made a big effort to push himself higher. Then Kaia grabbed him by the tops of his arms and rolled him on to the grass where she collapsed beside him.

'Thank you,' he gasped.

They lay on their backs looking upwards. Away from the Qaan, thousands of stars sparkled in the black sky. It was beautiful, thought Joe, but right now all he wanted was to rest.

'We cannot stay here, Sho,' said Kaia eventually. 'We must move.'

'I'm thinking we *can* stay,' he told her. 'Obviously nobody has been around in a long time. Otherwise they would have opened the entrance to the shaft before now. If it was a trap, it's a trap that nobody knows about any more.' He sat up slowly and looked around.

They were on the side of a rocky hill. There was nothing to see, only rough grass and boulders.

'I can't go any further,' he told Kaia. 'This rock will give us some protection.'

'I agree.'

They curled close to each other so that they were completely hidden by the rock and then, without either of them saying another word, they fell asleep.

* * *

They slept until the sun rose over the horizon and the sound of birds singing in the trees woke them. Kaia immediately rolled away from Joe and stood up, wiping her hands on her tunic. Then she checked her Link. All of the lights in the ruby stone were now rose pink.

'Look,' she said, in a worried voice, as she held her arm out to Joe. 'We have not travelled far enough to change it this much. Being in the Loran seems to have drained it. That means we have even less time than before.'

'In that case we should get moving right away,' said Joe. 'Plus, unlikely though it seems, we can't hang around if that sensor sent a signal to someone.'

Kaia was running even before she'd pulled her rucksack on to her back. Joe ran just behind her, checking their direction with his compass because she hadn't bothered to look at the map. She was covering the ground beneath them faster than she ever had before. He concentrated on maintaining a steady pace, and at the same time puzzling about the Shield that had been set up when they stepped into the Loran and the mystery of the shattered crystals. And the significance of the Haaken symbol too.

When Kaia eventually stopped, in the shelter of some trees, he was relieved, both because his legs were aching and because they hadn't had anything to eat. He took a Chillo he'd been saving out of his rucksack and took a bite.

'Eat quickly,' advised Kaia as she unwrapped a Cheeba cookie. 'We will start again in a moment.'

Joe nodded. Neither of them spoke while they ate. When Kaia had finished the cookie she immediately got up and started to run again. The sun was high in the sky and Joe was getting uncomfortably hot when she stopped at the top of another hill. Below them, glittering in the light of the sun and the Qaan, was a small lake.

'We will stop there,' she said. 'We can refresh ourselves in the water.'

'We haven't had a great experience with lakes so far,' said Joe. 'Are you sure?'

'I am not sure at all,' she said. 'But I need to be clean, Sho. I need to wash everything away.'

He understood. They hurried down the hill together and stood beside the lake.

'It looks safe—' Joe began. But he was talking to himself because Kaia had already removed her tunic and trousers and, wearing only her vest and shorts, plunged into the water.

'It is so good,' she told him. 'Come in, Sho. It will be fine.'

He hesitated and then, a little self-consciously, stripped to his pants before getting in.

Kaia was right. It was very good. He felt a million times better as he washed the dirt and dust of the tunnel from his skin. Then he lay on his back and floated on the surface.

'Hey, Sho!' He felt the splash on his face and immediately he righted himself and looked around him.

'What?' he asked Kaia who was treading water nearby.

'Nothing.' She gave him a half smile. 'You looked like you were a million miles away. I was waking you up.'

'I suppose I was a million miles away,' he said wryly. 'I was thinking about home.'

Kaia's eyes were suddenly full of sympathy. 'I am sorry that you are here, Sho,' she said. 'I am sorry that the Loran at Zwemat failed us. Perhaps at Domote . . .'

'Why didn't that guy, Kizan Maal, go to Domote?' asked Joe.

'The Haaken trap,' said Kaia. 'He could not.'

'Was there anyone there from Lagat?' asked Joe. 'Zwemat would be the next Loran for anyone who went to Lagat first, wouldn't it?'

'Yes. Lila Dopla came from Lagat.'

'Yet she didn't try to leave either. Knowing that Zwemat had failed she would have wanted to go on, wouldn't she?'

Kaia nodded.

'Was anyone from Domote there?'

'Bo Anka,' whispered Kaia.

'Zwemat would have been the third Loran for him. So you'd expect him to die. But the others should have at least tried to leave. I'm wondering about the writing on the wall too. If it was for another reason. A reason that Bo knew.'

'We are defeated,' said Kaia.

'Or betrayed. Perhaps none of the Loran is working and they realised that.'

'It cannot be so,' said Kaia. 'These are Runners from a number of cycles. They know that the Shield has not failed.'

'If only you guys allowed Runners back in, you'd know for sure what the situation was,' said Joe. 'You'd be able to plan for the future. You'd know what had happened there. But as it is, you're running blind.'

'I am not blind,' said Kaia. 'I have perfect vision.'

'It's another expression,' said Joe. 'It means you don't have all the information.'

'You are right about that.' Kaia turned in the water to look at him again. 'It is a flaw that there is no way to be in contact. But the thing is, we cannot afford to lower the Shield even for a moment.'

'I'm not talking about lowering it,' said Joe. 'I'm talking about sending a message through it. It's another thing I was thinking about when we were running.'

'But you know we cannot do that.'

'What about the Link.' He raised his wrist out of the water and looked at the green jewel on his bracelet.

'You know already that it does not work as a communication device outside the Shield,' she reminded him.

'Not between the Runners,' he agreed. 'Maybe because like with my phone, there's no signal. But there must be a signal in Carcassia itself. That's how it works when you're there. If you could penetrate the Shield you might be able to get a message back.'

'The Shield blocks everything from outside.'

'What if we could boost the power to the Link?' asked Joe. 'Enough so it could get through.'

'There is no way to do that,' said Kaia.

'Remember when we were coming through the Shield? You said that if we went through at full strength the power would surge through the Link and we'd fry.'

Kaia nodded.

'If we could somehow increase the power without frying it and killing ourselves, maybe we could get a message through. Or perhaps we could boost the power again and recharge the stone to give ourselves more time.'

'I do not know if that would be possible, Sho. This is not something we talked about at Sanctuary.'

'I'm not an IT expert,' said Joe, 'but I know you can make technology do almost anything. Kaia, the small Kerala crystals have kept my phone charged even though I've no idea how they're doing it. Maybe we could use those crystals, or the big one itself, to boost the power to the Link.'

'We cannot,' she said. 'We need the crystals to protect us. And the big Kerala needs all its power for the Loran.'

'If the Kerala we're replacing has some power left could we use that instead?'

'Perhaps.' She looked doubtful.

'We should keep it in mind,' said Joe. 'And how about having a try at breaking the connection between us now?'

'Why?'

'In case we need to separate,' he said.

'You would leave me?'

'No!' His answer was quick. 'Just . . . if we get into trouble. We might need to go our separate ways and meet up again.'

'Please do not interfere with the Link,' said Kaia. 'I do not care what trouble occurs. We will stay together, Sho. We will be safe that way.'

He nodded. He'd leave it for now. But not for ever.

24

Because so much time seemed to have been drained from Kaia's Link they ran by day and by night again. They made good progress as the countryside around them was flat and grassy.

Kaia's pace didn't falter but as they were running by the edge of a forest, where the branches of the trees drooped so low that they were like leafy umbrellas, she suddenly stopped and sank to her knees.

'Kaia.' Joe was beside her almost immediately. 'Are you all right?'

'I do not know,' she said. 'I feel . . .' And then she closed her eyes and tumbled on to her side.

The Run that day had been without any stops but, as usual, Kaia hadn't given any indication of tiredness. And now she had collapsed. It was a moment before he saw it, a fat pink and green caterpillar on her ankle.

'Oh, crap!' he breathed.

The caterpillar wasn't moving but Joe could see that it was stuck to Kaia's skin and he was sure that it had bitten her –

maybe it was still biting her! He grimaced and tried to flick it away, but it was holding on tightly. Even poking at it with a twig didn't dislodge it so eventually Joe took a deep breath and plucked it from her. He threw it as far away as he could and then looked at her ankle. There were six puncture holes where the creature had pierced her skin and her ankle was already swelling.

'Kaia.' He tried to pull her upright but she was a dead weight in his arms. 'Kaia,' he repeated.

She didn't reply. Eventually Joe hauled her into a seated position, propped against the trunk of the nearest tree, with her head bent forward. He opened her rucksack and rummaged around inside it although he didn't really know what he was looking for. Most of what was in the bag was Cheebas, Gira and crystals, although there was a small ampoule of multicoloured powder with no indication of what it might be. Joe wasn't prepared to waft it under her nose in case it was some kind of toxic drug, and he certainly wasn't going to make her swallow it for the same reason. So he simply uncapped one of the slim Gira bottles and held it to Kaia's lips.

'Here,' he whispered. 'Drink this.'

In the movies, giving someone something to drink always worked. They would splutter and cough and wake up a little upset, but usually none the worse for wear. He managed to get some of the liquid into Kaia's mouth, but she didn't open her eyes. He could see now that her lips were unnaturally dry. And that although her face was pale her cheeks were flushed. Obviously she'd reacted badly to the caterpillar's bite. But would she recover by herself? And if not, what the hell was he supposed to do to help her?

He put the back of his hand to her forehead as his mother did when she was checking to see if anyone had a temperature. Kaia's forehead was burning.

He tried to make a more comfortable area for her, using his rucksack as a pillow, and stretching her out on the soft springy ground beneath the tree. She groaned slightly. He placed a Kerala in front of them which he hoped would keep any other creepy-crawlies away. Then he sat beside her, so that her head rested on his lap.

It grew dark. Joe put his arm around her. He didn't know if he was comforting her, or if she was comforting him, because the woods were eerie. Every so often he heard snuffling noises but he didn't know where they came from. He kept a crystal in his hand, just in case. Later, he heard a trickling noise and realised that it was raining. They were perfectly dry beneath the leaves of the tree, but Joe took the wooden containers that Kaia had brought from the hut they'd broken into before, and used them to gather rainwater. He dabbed the water on her forehead to try to keep her cool. She was still burning up, even though the air temperature was low enough to make him shiver.

Joe was glad when the sun rose, although it was hard to tell how bright it was beneath the dark green canopy of the trees. Kaia had mumbled a little during the night, but she hadn't woken up.

He took the map from her rucksack to check it. But although he tapped the arrow icon, nothing appeared. He clenched his jaw. He needed to be able to see the map. He needed to know where they were supposed to be going. He tapped the icon again. And a third time. Then he had an idea. He picked up Kaia's hand and tapped the map with her finger. Immediately, the images of the route started to appear. He heaved a sigh of relief as he studied it. He wasn't sure how well he'd be able to run carrying her. He wasn't even sure if he should run at all. But there was no point in staying in the wood, and perhaps being out in the open would help Kaia's fever. He poured some more Gira water between her lips and she seemed to swallow it. But she still didn't wake.

He picked up the rucksacks and then Kaia. He moved cautiously out from beneath the tree and towards the open land again. Then he froze. Spreading across the land for as far as he could see were what looked like pink flowers open on wide green leaves. He and Kaia had noticed them the previous day. She'd even remarked on how pretty they were. But now he realised that they weren't flowers at all. They were the caterpillars. And there were thousands of them.

Even as he stood there he could see them move. They seemed to be coming closer to him. He looked around uncertainly. The nearest wave of caterpillars were almost at the woodland now. They stopped a couple of metres from Joe's feet.

He moved backwards into the wood. The caterpillars stayed where they were. Joe moved further back. The caterpillars didn't budge.

OK, he thought. I'm going to have to go through this forest. Which will be sending me in the wrong direction. But I can't get past those caterpillars. And we won't be going anywhere at all if they bite me too.

The noise, when he heard it, made him jump almost a foot into the air. It was a deep grunting sound and Joe's first thought was of bears. He'd never seen a live bear before and he didn't want to see one now. Unless it was the kind of bear that ate caterpillars and not people. Its huge brown eyes were fixed on Joe and Kaia. The creature seemed vaguely familiar to Joe and then he realised that he'd seen it in the mosaics on the Sanctuary walls, among the winged tigers and exotic birds.

It sniffed the air and grunted again.

'Hello,' said Joe softly. 'I won't hurt you.' Even as he spoke he thought it was a stupid thing to say. He couldn't hurt this creature, but it could certainly hurt him.

Although right now all it was doing was staring at him. And at Kaia.

'*Mooooni*.' The grunt was different this time. '*Mooooni*.'

Kaia had talked about Moonis. Carcassians had used them for transport. But they'd died under the Shield. Was this creature a Mooni?

'*Mooooni*,' grunted the creature again.

It waved its head from side to side. And then it sank down, so that its legs were curled up beneath it. Its eyes were still fixed on Joe and Kaia, and there was an enormous hollow in its back. Was that how the Carcassians had ridden them? wondered Joe. Would he and Kaia be able to ride it now? Would it take them away from the caterpillars?

He hesitated for a moment. Then he placed Kaia on to the creature's back. He got on beside her, keeping the rucksacks nearby.

'*Mooooni!*' The Mooni got to its feet again and ambled slowly out of the forest. It stopped when it saw the caterpillars. Then it started to walk again, with slow, ponderous steps. The caterpillars moved away in a pink and green swirl, leaving a passage for the Mooni to pass through. Every so often it stopped and grunted 'Mooooni,' again. Each time it did that Joe tightened his grip on Kaia, who was still unconscious.

The Mooni kept walking at the same pace. Joe didn't try to steer it or stop it. He was watching for the caterpillars but eventually they were left far behind. The Mooni continued to walk. Joe sat in the hollow of its back and cradled Kaia in his arms.

It was hours later when the Mooni stopped at a deep ravine. It slid to its knees again. Joe got off its back and looked into its enormous eyes.

'Thank you,' he said.

The Mooni stared at him and snuffled slightly.

Joe lifted Kaia down. He laid her carefully on the ground. Her entire leg was swollen now, and there was a thin gold thread running up the side of it, from the puncture wounds left by the caterpillar. The Mooni looked at her. It waved its head from side to side again. And then, before Joe could do anything, it extended the longest tongue Joe had ever seen and licked the golden thread.

Joe's heart was hammering in his chest. Was the Mooni tasting Kaia ready to take a bite out of her? Had it brought them here to eat them? It licked her again. The golden thread was broken now and a purple liquid gushed out of the puncture wounds on her ankle.

'Mooooni.' It was a softer, gentler grunt this time.

Quite suddenly, Kaia's eyes opened. Joe immediately took a vial of Gira from the rucksack. 'Drink this.'

She coughed and spluttered as she swallowed it. But after a moment her eyes began to clear. Her face lost its red glow and when Joe put his hand on her forehead, her temperature seemed normal again.

'Oh, Kaia. I was so worried.'

The Mooni grunted and snuffled. It bent its head towards her leg and sniffed it. She gasped.

'Is that a Mooni?' She reached out and touched it. 'I do not believe it. A Mooni. I have seen pictures but I never thought I would see the real thing.'

'*Mooooni*,' it said.

'I was afraid it was going to eat us,' said Joe. 'But instead it brought us here. It rescued us.'

She smiled faintly. 'Moonis are vegetarian,' she said. 'It would not have eaten us.'

'Oh.' Joe felt silly.

'What happened?' she asked.

'Gosekkas,' she said, when he explained. 'The things you call caterpillar. They are poisonous to Carcassians. When there were Mooni beneath the Shield we kept them because the Gosekkas spin a honeycomb of golden threads and the Mooni like to eat it. But Mooni also like to wander and they kept going as far as the Shield and trying to walk through it. Eventually they died out. And we got rid of the Gosekkas. I have only seen drawings of them until now. I did not realise they would look the way they did.'

'*Mooooni*,' said the Mooni and licked her leg again.

'Obviously it was the gold thread on your leg that it wanted,' said Joe.

'And licking it off allowed the poison to escape.' Kaia reached out and stroked the Mooni again. 'Thank you, Mooni,' she said. 'Thank you very much.'

'Does it eat Cheeba cookies?' asked Joe.

'I do not know,' replied Kaia.

Joe took some out of his rucksack and held them out to the Mooni. It swallowed them in a single gulp. Then, quite suddenly, it turned around and began to amble back in the direction they'd come from.

'So,' said Kaia, when it had disappeared out of sight. 'We must continue.'

'You were unconscious for a day,' said Joe. 'We're not going anywhere until you're OK.'

She reached inside her rucksack and took out the ampoule of multicoloured powder. She broke the top and sprinkled the powder on her tongue. Almost at once the colour in her cheeks improved.

'Vay,' she told Joe. 'It is for the worst injuries. It replenishes the body's strength.'

'We should have had more of that,' said Joe.

'Unfortunately it may only be consumed sparingly otherwise it is lethal,' she said as she slid the ampoule into the pocket of her tunic. 'Hopefully I will not need it again.'

'It's good stuff,' said Joe. 'You look so much better.'

'I feel fine,' she said.

'I was worried.' Joe's words came in a rush. 'You were so ill and I didn't know what to do. I thought you were going to die.'

Kaia looked at him.

'But I did not.'

'No.'

'Thanks to you.'

'Thanks to the Mooni,' said Joe.

'Thanks to you, Sho Hun-ter,' said Kaia again. She leaned towards him and kissed him on the cheek. 'Thank you for saving me.'

He felt himself blush. 'It was nothing,' he said.

But he felt as though it was everything.

25

When they consulted the map, they realised that they were supposed to cross the ravine. But the Mooni had taken them off course and they were a good distance away from the point where the crossing was marked.

'There is probably a bridge in that location,' said Kaia. 'We must run there.'

'Are you sure you can run?' asked Joe.

'To be honest, no,' she admitted. 'I am still very tired. But we must continue. We must reach Domote as soon as possible.'

Joe nodded and they started to run, but Kaia's pace was significantly slower than usual and it took them half a day to reach the crossing point.

'Oh no,' said Kaia when they arrived.

The bridge which was marked on the map was no longer there. There were posts each side of the ravine which had clearly held it in place, but the bridge itself had either collapsed or been destroyed.

'I cannot see any other place to cross,' said Kaia as she studied the map.

'Neither can I,' said Joe.

'So it has to be here.'

'We can't scramble all the way down there,' he said. 'It must be thousands of feet to the bottom. And even if we did, we'd never be able to get up again on the other side.'

'We do not need to do that,' said Kaia. 'We will jump.'

'Jump!' Joe looked at her in horror. 'We can't jump that far.'

'You could,' she said. 'You jumped up to the window of your room in Sanctuary.'

'That was different,' said Joe. 'If I fell I would've landed on the floor. If I fall here I've no idea where I'll land. Or if I'll be alive when I do.'

'It is the only way, Sho Hun-ter,' said Kaia.

'And if I jump . . .' He looked at her. 'What about you?'

She reached into her rucksack and took out the last of her Flagali ribbons.

'You will hold one end of the Flagali when you jump,' she said. 'I will hold the other. When you are on the other side you will tie it around the post. I will then jump and use the Flagali to climb up.'

'You've got to be kidding me,' said Joe.

'There is no other way.'

He tried to think of one, but she was right. They couldn't walk around. They couldn't climb down.

'But what if I don't make it?' he asked.

'You will,' she said.

Joe wanted to believe her. But all he could think of was

falling into the ravine.

'You are strong, Sho. You are a great Runner. You can do it.'

She believed in him. She really did. Joe wrapped the Flagali around his waist and took a deep breath. He tried not to picture himself at the bottom of the ravine. He walked back from the edge and looked to the other side.

He took another deep breath. He rocked back and forwards on his heels for a few minutes and then started to run as fast as he possibly could. He was at the very edge of the ravine before he launched himself into the air and yelled 'Let's go!' He could feel himself soaring over the gap. Then his body slammed into the earth and rock a little below the edge at the other side. He scrabbled frantically to get a handhold. He found a piece of root protruding from the sandy soil and grabbed it. He used the root to haul himself upwards and when he made it, he lay on the ground for a moment. He didn't quite believe he'd done it.

'Sho!'

He heard Kaia calling and he pulled himself upright. She was waving at him from the other side. 'Well done, Sho!' she cried.

'Your turn,' he said as he tied the Flagali as tightly as he could to the post.

She nodded and walked back from the edge. As Joe had done, she tied the Flagali around her waist and tested it. Then she started to run faster than he'd ever seen her run before. But even so, she didn't make it. Joe saw her body disappearing into the ravine.

He ran to the edge. She was suspended by the Flagali, about five metres below.

'Climb, Kaia!' he called. 'Come on.'

He watched as she used the Flagali as a rope to haul herself up. He pulled on it too, to help her. Eventually, her head appeared at the top and she clambered up beside him.

'That was not as easy as I expected,' she confessed breathlessly.

'It was brilliant.' Joe grinned at her. 'Flying through the air like that! I loved it.'

'You have the heart and soul of a Runner, Sho Hun-ter,' she said. 'Maybe that is why Vasila sent you with me. Maybe she knew I would need your help.'

'I'm glad I was here,' said Joe.

'I am too,' Kaia told him.

Kaia untied the Flagali from the post, rolled it up and put it in her rucksack. She said it might be useful to keep it, even though it lost its ability to simply wrap itself around a person after it had been used.

'We have lost more time with my illness,' she said, looking at her Link. 'The stone is beginning to turn white sooner than I expected.'

Even as they started to run again, Joe could feel the air around them growing colder. It was as though someone had flicked a switch and turned summer into winter. The days were shorter and the nights were longer. Even though the tunics were good at keeping them warm, Joe had noticed that his breath was forming little clouds in front of him and that the tips of his nose and ears were freezing. The sky above them had turned a leaden grey and he could feel the biting wind in his face.

'I have never experienced this before,' said Kaia when they stopped for shelter after another day when they'd run without a break. 'The temperature in Carcassia is always pleasant. This . . . this is not.'

'I think it could snow later,' said Joe. 'Do they have snow in Domote?'

'I do not understand snow.'

'It lies on the ground. It's white.'

Kaia shook her head. 'I have not seen it.'

'You won't see it yet,' said Joe as he glanced up at the clear sky. The Qaan was closer to the horizon than it had been before, but it was still there, still shining its light down on them. 'But if it stays this cold you probably will. I hope we find somewhere warm to stop soon.'

'Here,' said Kaia, pointing to a rock formation. 'This is good shelter.'

Joe was getting tired of sleeping under trees and rocks. But Kaia was right, the rocks made a warm and comfortable cave and they settled themselves in. They used the torch on his phone to check it for spiders and other creepy-crawlies then Kaia placed a Kerala at the entrance while Joe propped their rucksacks in a corner as makeshift pillows.

'I will be glad to reach the Loran,' said Kaia after they'd shared water and cookies. 'This is not a pleasant region.'

'On the plus side there aren't many people here,' said Joe. 'So hopefully that means we don't have to worry about being set upon by Kanabi warriors.' He stretched his hands out in front of him and looked at the lines that Kaia had drawn on them in the Kanabian hunters' hut. 'How long does this last?' he asked.

'It is supposed to last long enough to visit each Loran,' said Kaia. 'You do not need to worry, Sho.'

Kaia shivered suddenly.

'You cold now?' asked Joe.

'Just a little,' she admitted.

'Come closer,' said Joe. 'In the books I read they always say that you should share your warmth if you're trapped somewhere cold.'

Kaia gave him a sceptical glance but she shuffled across the dusty ground and allowed him to put his arms around her.

'Sho!'

'What?' he asked.

'Your face,' she said as she reached up and touched his cheek. The cut from the broken Kerala crystal had healed but that wasn't what interested her. 'There is hair growing there.'

'I know.' He gave a self-conscious shrug. 'I need to shave, that's all.'

'Shave?'

'It must happen to men in Carcassia too,' said Joe. 'You grow a beard if you don't shave. My skin is sort of smooth so I don't need to do it very often.'

'A beard?'

'Facial hair,' said Joe. 'On Earth, some men have them. But some men shave off the hair so they don't. My dad has one.' He took his phone from the rucksack. 'I should have shown you these before,' he said. 'But we've been too busy.'

He opened his photo app and held the phone in front of her. The first photo was one of him and his dad, standing outside the family home.

'Sho!' Kaia looked at it in astonishment. 'You have had these images all the time. Without letting me see . . .'

He shrugged. 'I didn't think. That's my dad,' he added. 'Complete with beard.'

'This is you on Earth?' Her voice was full of astonishment. 'These are Earth people?'

'Yes.' He swiped through the roll. There were about thirty photos, some of his family and others at a party he'd been to the previous year. 'Loads of people my age take photos of everything but I don't.'

'We do not have this in Carcassia,' said Kaia. 'If we had . . . if we had, then we could give our likenesses to our families. And keep them in the Citadel. And nobody would be forgotten.'

'Before the camera was invented, people on Earth had paintings of themselves,' said Joe. 'Don't you do that? I saw mosaics of animals in Sanctuary. And there were lots of drawings in the school.'

'We make representations of animals,' she agreed. 'But only children make likenesses of people.'

'Well, we have paintings of everything,' said Joe. 'And pictures of everything too. Oh, and look, Kaia. This is snow.'

Kaia touched the photo of Joe's garden covered in snow.

'It is not cold,' she said.

'The pictures only show you things. You can't feel them.'

'I like snow,' she said. 'It is very beautiful.' She began swiping as she'd seen him do. 'Who is this person?'

'My sister,' said Joe.

'And these?'

'Friends from school. Mike and Ralph and Danno and Jim,' said Joe.

'And this?' Kaia stopped at a blurry photograph. 'There is a flaw in this one.'

It was blurred because he'd taken a snap of Ashley Jones when she wasn't looking. It caught her sideways on, her head thrown back and her blonde hair tumbling over her shoulders.

'A girl in school,' said Joe.

'She is your friend?' asked Kaia.

'Not really,' said Joe.

'She is very pretty,' said Kaia.

'She's OK.'

Kaia looked at him through narrowed eyes. 'You are not friends but you have kept her likeness?'

Joe shrugged.

'Is she . . . is she someone you will be married to?'

'Of course not!'

'Why do you keep her likeness in that case?' asked Kaia.

'I just do, that's all.' Joe took the phone from her. 'But not any more.' He pressed the delete button and the picture of Ashley disappeared.

'Where has she gone?' Kaia looked shocked.

'Into the trash,' said Joe.

'Trash?'

'I've got rid of the photo,' said Joe. 'I don't need it any more. Smile, Kaia.'

She looked at him in puzzlement and then shrieked as the camera flashed.

'What have you done!' she cried, blinking in the light. 'What is this thing?'

'Look,' he said, handing her the phone.

She stared at the photo of herself. Her expression was startled, but also wary.

'This is me,' she said. 'You have captured me.'

'Just your photo,' he said.

She looked at it again.

'I have never seen myself like this before,' she said. 'I look . . .'

'. . . brave,' he finished when she didn't say any more.

She continued to stare at it.

'You will keep this?' she said. 'This memory of me?'

'Of course I will,' said Joe.

'And I will be in your phone as a friend? In place of the girl in your school?'

'Yes, you will.'

'That is good.' She smiled at him. Then she closed her eyes and settled down to sleep.

While she was sleeping Joe looked again at the photos on his camera. Then, quietly so as not to disturb her, he turned off the flash and took a selfie of them together. It didn't matter that the flash was off. There was enough light from the glowstick to capture them perfectly.

* * *

A biting wind howled around them the following morning and made it difficult to keep a steady pace. The ground was hard underfoot. The grey clouds on the horizon looked menacing. But they kept going, not speaking, just running. One step in front of the other. Not looking around them. Just moving forward.

It started to snow. The flakes were light at first but then grew heavier and heavier. Kaia stopped and turned to Joe.

'This is snow?' There was a note of wonder in her voice. 'It is not as I expected.' She held out her hand and watch the flakes melt. 'It is very strange.'

'It can be great fun,' agreed Joe. 'But it's going to slow us down.'

'We cannot afford to keep losing time.' Kaia glanced at the jewel on her Link.

'We'd better keep going,' said Joe. 'There's no shelter anywhere near.'

'There is never any shelter.' Kaia's voice was resigned. 'If we find a way to send information back to Carcassia, Sho, the first thing we will tell them is that there is not enough shelter.'

'Good idea,' said Joe. 'And you could tell them that although those Cheeba cookies are nice, it would be good to have some variety. Chocolate chip would be awesome. Or Chillo flavour,' he suggested, which made her laugh.

The snow was falling even more heavily as they got closer and closer to the position marked on the map. They made their way through a wooded area, which muffled the sounds of big black birds which had begun to circle overhead. Joe didn't like the birds, but Kaia ignored them. All of her attention was focused on the map. As they reached the edge of the woods, she stopped and looked around her.

In the distance were six wooden houses. They had steeply sloping roofs, laden with snow, and snow covered verandas to the front. Icicles hung from the wooden slats of the rails that ran the length of the verandas. In the murky, late-afternoon light, the houses appeared dark and unwelcoming.

'It looks deserted,' said Joe.

'This is the Loran,' said Kaia as she looked at her map. 'I have to place my Kerala here.'

'I wonder if Oani made it?' said Joe.

'We will have to see,' said Kaia, and began to walk to the nearest house.

26

They walked forward slowly and warily. Joe was conscious that they were leaving footprints in the pristine snow and he worried that a Kanabian or a Haaken or another unknown enemy might follow them. But they didn't have any choice so he gritted his teeth and followed Kaia across the open space. The snow was thick and walking was difficult, but eventually they arrived at the first house.

Joe and Kaia stepped on to the snow-covered veranda and looked around. Narrow threads, like cobwebs, laced the gaps between the wooden posts and sparkled with ice and snow. The icicles that hung from the rails were long and narrow. The windows of the house were coated with a thick covering of frost, making it impossible to see inside.

'What d'you think?' asked Joe.

'At least there are no signs of the Haaken,' she said as she looked at the outside of the house.

'Hopefully it stays that way.' Joe blew on the tips of his fingers to warm them, but it was futile. They were freezing and so was he.

Kaia consulted her map. 'The Loran could be any of these houses,' she said. 'There is no signal on the map.'

'In that case, no point in hanging around out here.' Joe reached for the handle of the door. He turned it gently and pushed at the door but nothing happened. The ice and snow were preventing it from opening.

'There can't be anyone in there,' he said to Kaia. 'They wouldn't have let it get into such a state.' He pushed the door harder with no success. Then, like he'd seen in so many movies in his life, he stood back from the door, made a slight run at it and kicked it as hard as he could.

It flew open, banging against the inside wall. Kaia immediately stepped over the threshold and Joe followed her.

The room was dark and cold, the floor half-covered with dried leaves. A long seat, made of the bark of trees, was placed in front of the empty grate of a fire. There was a small table to the side of it, on which was a carved wooden bowl, along with a wooden cup. The cup was half full of frozen water. More of the frozen cobwebs linked the roof and the walls.

'This doesn't look like a Loran,' said Joe. 'In fact I'd guess it's years since anyone has been here.'

Kaia nodded. Apart from the bowl and the cup there was nothing to suggest that the house had ever been lived in. She shivered involuntarily.

'This is eerie,' she said. 'It makes me feel . . .'

'Me too,' said Joe before she'd finished the sentence. He didn't know if she was going to say scared or creeped out or anything else, but he was feeling both of those things.

'Let us try a different house,' she said.

He followed her outside again. They went to the next house, which was identical both outside and inside, and then a third which was almost the same, except that there were more bowls and cups on the table. One of the bowls contained some mouldy fruit which was now frozen.

'I wonder who lived here,' said Kaia. 'And when.'

'Maybe the Carcassians found the abandoned houses and thought it would be a good place for the Loran,' said Joe.

'Maybe.' Kaia frowned, then looked around anxiously. 'Did you hear that?'

'What?'

The words were hardly out of Joe's mouth when there was a rustling noise from the fireplace of the house and then a large pulsating mass appeared in the grate. Before either of them had time to move it raised itself on to eight legs, scurried out and stopped directly in front of Kaia. It was a giant version of the spiders they'd encountered at the start of her run and its red eyes were fixed on her. Two antennae just above the eyes quivered as it swayed from side to side.

Kaia stood in front of it, not daring to move. Joe wasn't sure what to do either. He didn't want to anger the creature and make it go for Kaia, but obviously he had to distract it in some way. He looked at her questioningly and, very slowly, she began to slide her rucksack from her shoulders. But before she'd got it halfway down her arms the spider had moved closer to her.

'Stay still!' mouthed Joe. He began to remove his own rucksack. At the slight sound, the spider swivelled and turned towards him. A long silver thread snaked from the centre of the black body and wrapped itself around the rucksack. Joe felt it being pulled from his shoulders. He tried to hold on to it but the thread the spider was spinning was too strong. Joe couldn't prevent the bag from being yanked from his arms and gathered beneath the spider's body. It turned to Kaia and did the same with hers.

With the two rucksacks containing the Kerala and their only means of stunning the creature now concealed beneath it, Joe began to feel even more anxious. And then the creature's antennae lengthened and touched Kaia's hair, while another thread shot from the spider's stomach and wrapped itself around her waist.

'No!' cried Joe as she struggled against it. 'No!'

But the spider kept pulling her closer and closer. Joe looked around him frantically. There was nothing in the room to help. Nothing to stop her being pulled beneath the creature. And nothing to stop him being pulled in after her. Was this what had happened to the people who had lived here too? he asked himself. Had they all been killed by this revolting spider?

He looked out of the open door at the vast expanse of snow. And then he bolted out into the cold air, away from the spider and away from Kaia.

He heard her call his name as he tugged off the top of his tunic and wrapped it around his hands. Then he grasped one of the big icicles that hung from the rails. He pulled hard and it cracked, coming away in his hands so quickly that he almost fell over. He held it in front of him then ran into the room again and, without stopping, plunged the pointed end into the centre of the spider.

The creature immediately stopped pulling Kaia and began thrashing around. Joe pulled at the icicle again and it came out of the spider with a squelching sound. Then he slashed the thread that joined Kaia to it and grabbed her by the hand. The two of them ran out of the house together, the high-pitched shrieks of the wounded spider following them. They stood in the snow, as the shrieks grew quieter and quieter and finally stopped altogether.

'Oh, Sho.' Kaia was shivering, although Joe didn't know if it was from the cold or because she was as frightened as he was. 'That was horrible. Horrible.'

'I know.' He held her close to him. 'I know.'

'I thought you were running away from me.' Her look was shamefaced. 'I was thinking that you were leaving me to face it alone. And I was trying to come up with a plan but the creature was on top of me and it was hard to breathe and . . .'

'We're a team,' said Joe firmly. 'I won't leave you, no matter what.'

'Yes,' said Kaia. 'A team. And I will not leave you either, Sho Hun-ter.'

They made their way warily back to the house. The spider remained immobile on the floor as they cautiously retrieved their rucksacks from beneath it.

'And so you have killed a creature of Kanabia,' said Kaia. 'Even though you said when we encountered the spiders in the cave that you did not wish to kill anything at all.'

'I guess I've changed,' said Joe.

* * *

There was only one house left to explore in the settlement. It was slightly apart from the others and Joe and Kaia approached it warily. They were even more cautious when they realised that the front door was ajar. Kaia held her finger to her lips as she approached it as quietly as possible.

She gave it a gentle push and it scraped against the floor. She pushed it a little harder. It opened a little wider. But before she went any further, Joe stopped her. She nodded in understanding as he wrapped fabric around his hands again and broke two icicles hanging from the roof. He handed one to Kaia who held it in front of her as she stepped inside, Joe right behind her. She stopped immediately and let out a muffled cry. Joe gasped.

There was a long table in the centre of the room, with three spaces for Kerala crystals. But none of them was glowing, and there were broken shards from them on the ground. However, it wasn't the table or the shattered crystals that they were staring at in horror. It was the five frozen bodies in a seated position against the wooden wall.

With a sense of disbelief, Joe realised that the fifth body was Oani's. Her hair was coated in the same glittering frost as the others. Her face was an eerie shade of blue. Her eyes were open, staring at them.

'Maybe she's not dead,' he whispered to Kaia. 'I've heard about it, you know. People being frozen and coming back to life and . . .'

Beside him, a tear rolled down Kaia's cheek. She walked slowly and cautiously across the room, holding the icicle like a dagger in front of her. When she reached Oani she knelt down beside her and touched her. The other girl didn't move, but a piece of her frozen hair came away in Kaia's hand.

'Oh, Sho.' Kaia's voice trembled. 'She was so brave. She made it here even though she was injured. But . . . but . . .'

He knelt down beside her and took Oani's hand in his, rubbing it frantically to try to warm it up. Then he opened his rucksack and took out a bottle of Gira. He poured it all between Oani's slightly parted lips while Kaia watched. But Oani didn't swallow and the liquid dribbled slowly down her chin. A moment later it had frozen.

'I'm so sorry,' said Joe, his voice shaking. 'I liked Oani.'

'She was my friend.' Kaia was trying hard not to cry. 'She was my friend and she was a good Runner and this was not supposed to happen.'

'No,' agreed Joe. He whirled around suddenly, holding the icicle in front of him. But the noise that had startled him was only the door rattling in the wind.

'The others are Runners too?' he asked, even though he already knew the answer.

'Yes. Brin, Yva, Solder and Anama,' said Kaia. 'All good Runners. All strong. Why, Sho? This was not the final Loran for all of them. So why did they die? Why did the Runners in Zwemat die? What is the problem with the Kerala?'

'Maybe that spider had something to do with it here,' he said.

'The Kerala should have kept it away,' she said slowly. 'But - oh, Sho - this is like Zwemat again, although there were more bodies there. Is it possible, d'you think that this creature kills them and keeps them until it wants them?'

'I don't know.' Joe felt his heart beat faster. 'And I don't know if there are more of them . . .'

'We must leave.' Kaia stood up. 'It is not safe here. This Loran is useless. And that means that the only one which is maintaining the Shield must be at Lagat. Where Mihai is. If something has happened to him, if he did not make it, Carcassia is in the gravest of danger.'

'Should we do something with these bodies?' asked Joe. 'Just in case . . .'

'There is nothing we can do.' Kaia's voice was clipped and hard. 'They are dead. The ground here is frozen. We cannot bury them. We must go.'

She walked out of the house and Joe followed her. The wind was howling and the snow was flurrying around them.

'We can't get far in this,' said Joe. 'We need to shelter somewhere.'

'Not here,' said Kaia. 'I cannot stay here.'

'I don't want to either,' agreed Joe. 'But maybe—'

'We will go,' said Kaia. 'Come on.'

And without a backward glance she began to run.

She ran as though she were alone. Joe imagined this would have been how her entire Run would have been if he hadn't appeared. She set off at a steady pace and didn't stop, even when the wind howled around them and the snow whipped into their faces. She didn't stumble over snow-covered branches or icy patches. She was entirely focused on what she was doing and Joe was struggling to keep up with her.

But he didn't ask her to stop even though the hunger was gnawing at his stomach and he desperately needed to rest.

It was growing dark before she finally slowed down at a place where the forest petered out into a valley.

'This is where we will stop,' she said.

He looked around him. The snowy valley was bleak and desolate.

'We will use the Looban trees to make shelter,' Kaia said. 'They bend and we can tie them together.'

She dropped her rucksack on the frozen ground and grabbed the branch of the nearest tree. The snow fell off it and revealed tiny leaves on the thin branches. They were able to mould the branches any way they liked and in a very short time had made a basic shelter.

'Now can we talk about . . . about what happened at Domote,' said Joe as they sat inside it.

'There is nothing to say.' Kaia's voice was tight. 'It is clear that the Loran in Lagat is the one that is maintaining the Carcassian Shield. We must do everything we can to reach it and ensure that it is powered.'

'Maybe Mihai has already done that.'

'I hope he has,' she agreed. 'But my task is to make sure that there is another Kerala there. In that way I will be honouring the leaders of Carcassia and the memory of Oani and all the other Runners.'

'Kaia, we have to talk.'

'Why?'

'Oani should have kept running. Same for everyone at a Loran when it wasn't their last stop. They shouldn't have been there. They shouldn't have died.'

'Unless they were captured and released their Muqi,' said Kaia. 'Perhaps that is what the message in Zwemat meant. They had been betrayed. By the Haaken? And they took Muqi.'

'But we weren't captured. We escaped.'

'At Zwemat . . .'

'What?' asked Joe.

'When we got to the Resting Place I thought of sitting there with the other Runners,' said Kaia. 'You made me leave. But I felt . . . if you had not been there, I might have stayed.'

Joe stared at her.

'And in Domote I had the same feeling,' confessed Kaia. 'I wanted to sit down and stay. But because you were there I did not.'

'You think it's different because there are two of us?' asked Joe.

'It might be.'

'If that's how all the Runners feel it makes sense that they died,' said Joe slowly. 'But how is the Shield still in place if the Lorans aren't working?'

'Lagat must be different,' she said. 'The Runners who reach there succeed. I have always felt there is something special about Lagat.'

'I hope you're right.'

'I must be,' she said. 'Otherwise Carcassia is doomed. And so are you.'

27

There was a renewed sense of urgency about their Run through the snowy plains. Joe was trying to ignore the feeling of impending disaster that was gnawing at the edges of his mind. If the Loran at Lagat had failed like Domote and Zwemat, Carcassia and Kanabia would be at war and he and Kaia were in grave danger. Not that they weren't in danger already, he admitted to himself. Not that they hadn't encountered it on the way. And more importantly from his point of view, if the Loran had failed there was no possibility of him returning to Earth, with or without Kaia. He hadn't said anything more to her about coming to Earth with him. He knew she'd say no. But perhaps after she'd placed the Kerala she'd feel differently. He didn't know how she was feeling now. She kept her head down and ran without saying a word and ignored his attempts to make conversation on the only occasion that they stopped.

By the time the sun was setting and the light of the Qaan was becoming brighter in the sky, they'd covered a greater distance than they'd ever achieved before in a single day.

And quite suddenly, just as it had when they'd been running towards Domote, the weather changed. The snow stopped, the ground softened and the wind dropped from a howling gale to a gentle breeze.

The plain gave way to undulating hills. There were no forests, but there were copses of trees and tall grasses.

'And shelter?' asked Joe when Kaia took out the map to check on their progress.

'According to this there is a place up ahead,' she said. 'But I . . .' She sounded uncertain. 'I am not inclined to trust the map, Sho. You are right. It is a long time since it was drawn up. Things are not as they once were.'

'Let's have a look in that direction anyway,' he said.

They walked forward cautiously until they came to the shelter marked on the map. It was a rocky structure at the edge of a large pool. There seemed to be nothing inside the structure itself but both of them checked it out carefully, looking for spiders or any other kind of creature, before deciding it was safe.

'Warm and dry too,' said Joe. 'Which is a nice change.'

'Yes,' agreed Kaia. 'I am sorry, Sho Hun-ter. I have been preoccupied since the death of Oani Lupei. I have not been good company.'

'Don't worry about it,' he said.

'It is important that I complete the Run,' said Kaia. 'I am thinking only of that.'

'I understand.' He nodded. 'But I can't help wondering about Kanabia. It doesn't seem like a battle-ready country. Zwemat wasn't particularly nice, and we met some rough characters, but I didn't see any soldiers. Domote is practically deserted, though that's not a surprise if it's populated by those disgusting spiders.'

'Perhaps all of the Kanabi armaments are around Lagat,' said Kaia.

'Perhaps,' agreed Joe.

Kaia shivered suddenly. 'You are very right that we do not have enough information about life outside the Shield. You are also right that we should be able to report back through the Link. It is a major weakness.'

'Perhaps there was a way to return originally,' said Joe. 'Perhaps that's how I got through.'

'But we would know,' Kaia told him. 'The Leaders have all the records going back years. It is not possible they wouldn't know.'

Joe sighed. 'I wish there was an easy answer,' he said.

'Maybe we will understand more when we get to Lagat,' said Kaia.

'I hope so,' said Joe. 'Meantime . . . time for sleep again?'

'We are getting good at sleeping comfortably together,' said Kaia as she snuggled up beside him. 'At least this is one part of the Run that is working out all right.'

Joe put his arm around her. He wasn't going to disagree.

Joe felt a lot better the following morning. He bent down by the edge of the pool and sniffed at the water. Then he scooped some in his hand and tasted it carefully. It was cold and fresh and he drank some more.

'Stop!' Kaia, who'd been gathering the Kerala crystals

together, hurried over to him.

'I'm just having a drink,' said Joe. 'We're running low on Gira.'

'It may not be safe.' She took one of the empty vials out of her rucksack and filled it with water. Then she shook it and watched.

'What are you doing?' asked Joe. 'We've drunk water from pools and streams before.'

'Because the map said they were safe,' she replied. 'I know you do not trust it, but it has been right about the safety of the water. This a test,' she added. 'The glass will turn green if there is a problem.'

Joe wasn't worried. The water had tasted fine. And then the glass turned green. He felt beads of sweat appear on his forehead and he put his hand to his throat.

'What's the matter?' he said. 'What's going to happen to me?'

'Your lips will swell up and so will your eyes,' she said. 'And then your hands.'

'I think it's started to happen.' Joe was panicking. 'I can feel my tongue tingle. Kaia – can you do anything? D'you have some kind of antidote? The Vay powder?'

She shook her head.

Joe put his hand in his mouth and began to feel his tongue. 'I 'ink ish swollen,' he said with difficulty. 'Oh, Kaia . . .'

She started to laugh and he looked at her in astonishment. He was about to die and she thought it was funny!

'I am sorry, Sho,' she said. 'I know I should not have done it. But . . .'

''Ut 'at?' he mumbled.

'But I am playing a joke on you.'

'A joke?' Suddenly his voice was back to normal. 'You're playing a joke?'

'Yes.' She nodded.

'You think it's funny?'

She laughed hard as she nodded.

'I thought I was going to die.'

She laughed again.

'There have been enough times when I thought I was going to die and I really was without you making one up!' He gave her a dark look and then he grinned. 'I never thought I'd see the day that you'd play a joke on me.'

'Neither did I,' admitted Kaia. 'You said you had changed, Sho. I think perhaps I have too.'

They went back to the shelter to gather up their stuff.

'I am having to learn things on this Run every day,' Kaia said as she packed her rucksack. 'I did not expect to. I thought I knew everything I needed to know. I thought I had prepared well. But when I think of what has happened, I do not believe I was prepared at all. I believed that Vasila taught me well. But if she does not know what is happening here, how could she teach me properly?'

'Nobody has every answer,' said Joe. 'Mostly, I reckon we just muddle through.'

'I cannot muddle through, Sho,' said Kaia. 'I must complete the task.'

'I know,' he said. 'And I'm here to help you.'

She set off at her usual fast pace, Joe keeping up with her easily. Not only because of the extra speed and strength he had on Charra, he thought, but also because over the course of Kaia's Run he himself had become leaner and fitter.

After a long Run without any distractions, she stopped and held up her hand. The landscape in front of them hadn't changed, but there were more birds wheeling in the sky ahead, and a faint thudding sound in the distance.

'What's the matter?' he asked.

'I do not know,' she said. 'This place. It feels . . . different.'

Joe stood still and sniffed the air. He looked up at the birds in the sky and listened carefully. Then he grinned at her. 'I know what it is,' he said. 'At least I think I do.' He ran on ahead of her and then stopped and turned. His face broke into a smile. 'It's the sea. And a beach.'

'This is the end of the land?' Kaia stared at him. 'Where the great Vut meets it? I have not seen it before, Sho.'

'Come on.' He took her hand and ran with her to the top of the cliff. Below them, the sea was a broad expanse of blue, topped by choppy waves. It looked both familiar and different to Joe and he was gripped with a longing to be back on Earth, where everything was exactly the way he expected.

'It cannot be safe,' said Kaia. 'There must be a great creature beneath to make the water boil like that.'

Joe shook his head. 'There are lots of fish and other creatures in the sea but that's not what makes it move like that. The tides are caused by the moon.' He glanced upwards. The light from the Qaan was fainter at this time of the day, and the moons weren't visible at all. 'Well, here it would be the moons and the

Qaan, I suppose,' he said. 'It's to do with gravity. Everything pulling against everything else.'

Kaia looked at him in bemusement.

'It doesn't matter,' he said. 'I promise you it's not doing that because of a creature. We could paddle in it.'

'Paddle?'

'Walk at the edge of the water,' he said.

'I do not think it is safe.' Kaia took out her map and looked at it. 'Besides, it would take time to climb down and we cannot spare it. We are not supposed to go near the Vut. We should not be this close now.'

'Maybe there's been some erosion since the map was drawn.'

'Erosion?'

'The land falls into the sea,' said Joe.

'How do you know so much about this place?' Kaia's eyes narrowed.

'Not about this place,' he said. 'About geography and stuff. It's the same here as on Earth, more or less. And everyone loves going to the beach. You'd like to paddle, Kaia, honestly. You'd like the sand too.'

'There is no need for us to go there,' she said, turning away. 'And I think it is strange that you would want to risk your life climbing down to this beach place for no reason.'

'The reason is I like the sea,' said Joe.

'We have always been told that the Vut is dangerous,' Kaia said.

'It's only dangerous if you don't respect it,' Joe told her. 'And, Kaia, I'm thinking it might be safer to approach Lagat from the coast instead of inland. That way we wouldn't have to worry about being surrounded by Kanabians. We know they can't come at us from the direction of the water.'

She looked thoughtful. 'It depends on where the Loran is situated. We will be able to tell when we get closer. I think we should stick to the map today but make another decision tomorrow.'

'OK.' Joe didn't want to antagonise her any more.

Kaia turned and looked out over the water. 'It is . . . interesting,' she said as she watched the waves pound against the shore.

'At home, when people go to the beach for the day, they bring umbrellas and picnics and it's great fun,' said Joe. 'And of course if you go to somewhere hot you can lie out and sunbathe. You need sun protection for that, of course.'

'But the sun does not attack! You mean protection from enemies?'

'No, it's against the rays of the sun. It can damage your skin . . .' His voice trailed off. 'Our two planets are the same in lots of ways, but everything we do is different.'

Although maybe not everything. Joe thought of the news that seemed to carry stories every day about a war somewhere on Earth. And his mother watching the TV and shaking her head and asking what was so difficult about living in peace? And his father trying to explain whatever grievance the people were fighting about. He sighed.

'Are you all right, Sho?'

'Just thinking about home again,' he said.

'Soon we will place our Kerala,' said Kaia. 'And then, Sho, we will see if there is a way to get you back to your Earth where

239

you can go to the beach and paddle in the water.'

She smiled at him and leaned her head against his shoulder.

He put his arm around her waist. He wanted to believe that when he asked her again she'd agree to come with him. And that they could paddle together.

28

Their shelter that night was another rock formation. It was bigger than the previous one, and a good deal warmer. The weather had continued to improve over the day so that by the time they were ready to rest they were both hot and sweaty. Joe could hear the rhythmic sound of the waves on the shore in the distance, and he longed to get in for a swim.

'I have to go in there,' he told Kaia.

'It cannot be safe.'

'It is, I promise you.'

'I am the Leader here,' she said. 'And I am telling you not to go.'

'Kaia, you're not in charge of me. I'm not a Runner. I've done everything you wanted up to today, but now I want to get in for a swim.'

She said nothing and he ducked out of the shelter and strode towards the sound of the water. He'd just caught sight of it, gold and pink in the light of the setting sun, when he felt the Link bracelet tighten around his arm. He'd almost forgotten about the way it kept them together but now the pains were shooting through his arms and legs. He couldn't move. He couldn't even cry out. He crumpled to his knees.

'Sho.'

He felt her arms around him and then the shocks through his body lessening. He opened his eyes and saw her kneeling beside him, an anxious expression on her face.

'Why did you walk away from me?'

'I wanted to swim,' he said. 'That's all.'

'You should have known that the Link would stop you.'

'Seeing the water made me forget.'

'I will come with you to the edge of the water. Is that sufficient?'

'It's better than nothing. Thanks.'

He was still a little shaky but he pushed his way through the waist-high grass and then emerged a moment later at a long, sandy beach. The aquamarine water lapped against the shore, the waves much smaller and less vigorous than the previous day. Joe took off his shoes and walked barefoot on to the sand.

'It's lovely,' he said to Kaia. 'Come on.' He strode towards the water and only stopped when he was ankle deep.

'Do not swim, Sho.' She was still standing on the soft dry sand.

'This is paddling,' he told her. 'Not swimming. And it's great. Give it a try, Kaia. You'll like it.'

She looked at him hesitantly and then took off her shoes. She gasped as she felt the powdery sand between her toes.

'Come on,' said Joe. 'Get your feet wet.'

He peeled off his tunic so that he was in the light vest and shorts that he was wearing underneath, then he plunged into the water and swam until he was about ten metres offshore. 'It's beautiful, Kaia,' he called.

She watched him for another minute or two and then she tugged off her own tunic so that she was wearing nothing but her sturdy vest and shorts. She ran into the water and swam out to meet him.

Her strokes were unwieldy and it took her a while to end up beside him. But she smiled.

'You are right,' she admitted. 'It is lovely. And it is nice to feel water on my skin again. Although . . .' she ran her tongue over her lips, 'it tastes different.'

'The sea is salty,' said Joe. 'And we learned why in Geography too but I can't remember the reason.'

'As long as it is not because of the tears of a monster I do not mind,' said Kaia.

Joe laughed and splashed her. She splashed him in return and then swam away from him. But he caught her easily and dunked her under the water. When she surfaced, spluttering, he laughed at her.

'I will conquer this sea and be better at swimming than you,' she said. 'And then I will . . .' This time she was the one to dive and she caught him by the legs, pulling him underwater. He grabbed her by the arms and they broke the surface together, panting and laughing.

He'd never seen her laugh so much before, he thought, as he looked at her face, now clean from the dust and grime of the last few weeks, the streaks over blood over her eye washed away too. She looked like a normal teenager, as though she hadn't a care in the world – or at least, her cares weren't about saving her homeland and evading danger.

Even after the swim, dressed in their tunics, she looked more relaxed. He took out his phone and took a photo of her.

'You do not need another image of me,' she said.

'It's a nice photo,' he told her as he showed it to her.

She frowned.

'I look . . .'

'Happy,' he said as he put the phone away again.

'I am happy that we are getting closer to Lagat,' she agreed. 'But not that we have lost time. The Link does not have an allowance for swimming. So we must go now.'

'How long before the Shield fails?' asked Joe as they left the beach.

'Immediately the Kerala runs out of power,' Kaia replied. 'The thing is, we know now that only the Lagat Kerala is working. That means it might lose power sooner than it otherwise would. So if Mihai has failed, then we do not have much time.' She tightened the ribbon on her plait.

'Kaia . . .' he began.

'What?'

'If there's a portal for me . . . if I can get home . . . will you come?' Joe spoke urgently.

'I told you before. It is my destiny to die here.'

'It doesn't have to be,' he said. 'Vasila said that the Muqi is neutralised by going through the portal. If you come with me you won't die.'

She didn't say anything for a moment, then slowly shook her head.

'I cannot leave Carcassia,' she said.

'But you'll be dying in Kanabia not Carcassia,' Joe pointed out.

'If I fail we will be at war and I will have to fight.'

'You won't have time to fight!' cried Joe. 'You'll be dead. And that's such a waste, Kaia. You're a brave, intelligent person. You shouldn't end up like Oani or the other Runners. You have so much to live for.'

'It is our way,' she said.

'It's a stupid way.'

He turned away from her and started to run faster than he ever had before. He didn't look around to see where she was but he knew she was maintaining enough pace because the Link didn't tighten around his wrist again.

Eventually, as evening drew in, he slowed down and allowed her to catch up with him.

'Do not be angry, Sho Hun-ter,' she said. 'I have known all my life that it will be this way.'

'You've known all your life that there are three Loran keeping the Shield in place,' he said. 'And yet there aren't.'

'You said yourself that the theory and the reality are not always the same,' she reminded him. 'Things change over the years. The Leaders do not know that. So they cannot be blamed. It does not matter. We know the Loran at Lagat is functioning because the Shield is still protecting Carcassia. All that matters is that it continues to do so. What happens to me is irrelevant.'

'You are *not* irrelevant,' said Joe. 'And you matter to me.'

'You matter to me too,' she said. 'That is why we must get to Lagat, place the Kerala and get you home. You must get back to your own life. But I hope you will never forget me.'

There was no point in trying to pressurise her. But he hoped that at Lagat, and faced with the prospect of dying, she would change her mind. If only she wasn't so damn stubborn, he thought. But if she was any different, she wouldn't be such a good Runner.

29

They'd only run a short distance the following morning when they saw buildings shimmering in the sun.

'This is not Lagat,' said Kaia, pulling the map from her rucksack and looking at it.

'No, but it'd be surprising if there weren't other towns near the shore,' said Joe.

'We will have to be careful,' said Kaia. 'We must move away from the sea now.'

They changed their route so that they were walking further inland, but even so they began to see lots of small houses ahead. They were similar to the ones they'd seen in Zwemat – made of wood and shaped like the letter A, although the wood on this side of Kanabia was paler, and seemed to sparkle slightly under the strong sun.

'Perhaps it is time to get ourselves some new clothes,' said Kaia softly as the approached the nearest house, where a long line of washing fluttered in the breeze. 'We will need them when we arrive at Lagat, and if there are more settlements around the city it is better that we look like Kanabians.'

Joe knew she was right but he didn't like the idea of robbing clothes any more now than he had before. He and Kaia hid among the tall grass and observed the house which seemed to be deserted.

'Maybe they're all at the beach,' said Joe.

'Maybe.'

Kaia took a deep breath and ran to the garden. As quickly as she'd done before, she took a number of items from the washing line and then returned to their hiding spot.

'These are different clothes,' she said. 'They are not as substantial.'

'That's a sun-dress,' said Joe. 'And you've managed to get me shorts and a t-shirt. Which is a bit better than the trousers that didn't fit.'

They looked around for a place to change, and finally found some space behind a small clump of Roxana hedge.

'Kanabians,' said Joe, as they emerged again. 'More or less.'

'You look comfortable in Kanabian clothes,' said Kaia.

'Shorts and t-shirts are normal where I come from,' said Joe. 'I feel more like myself.'

'I feel like an idiot.'

The sun-dress was pink and yellow and shorter than anything Joe had seen Kaia wear. He'd never realised quite how long her legs were before.

'I wish I had some shades,' said Joe.

'Shades?'

'Sunglasses. You know, to protect your eyes from the glare. It's really bright now.'

She turned to him. 'It is not a problem for me.'

'That's because yours are different.' In the same way as they appeared green and helped her to see better in the dark, in the full light of the sun they were an almost indigo blue and Joe realised that they were effectively filtering the harsh light. 'The sun is making mine water.'

'How do these sunglasses work?' she asked.

'You put them in front of your eyes to protect them . . . like this.' He took out his phone and showed her a photo from the previous summer where everyone was wearing them.

'That is very strange,' she said. 'It is a design flaw in your eyes. The same as the design flaw in your ears.'

'I guess so,' he said.

'I might be able to fix it for you,' she said.

'My eyes or my ears?'

'Both.'

'Kaia! You never said that before.'

'You have not needed ear modification because of the Joq,' she pointed out. 'And for your eyes, there has not been a need either. We had glowsticks. And your phone device. However . . .' She took out one of the small crystals. 'I am not an expert, you understand,' she said. 'But these things were explained to us. The effect is not permanent. Come.'

They moved behind the Roxana hedge again. Kaia tapped the crystal on the ground, it glowed and then she placed it over Joe's right eye.

'Keep your eye open,' she instructed when she took it away and placed it on the other.

Joe was finding it hard to do, because a kaleidoscope of

colours was bursting in front of him. He was suddenly worried. Maybe this wasn't particularly safe. Then everything went black.

'I can't see. Kaia, I can't see!' He couldn't keep the panic out of his voice.

'That is good,' she said. 'You must wait.'

His heart was thumping in his chest. What if this didn't work? What if he'd been blinded for ever?

A sliver of light appeared at the edge of his vision. And then, like someone peeling back a strip of paper, he was able to see more and more. But now the landscape in front of him was sepia-tinted, exactly as though he was wearing sunglasses.

'It worked.' He breathed a sigh of relief. 'It really did.'

She smiled. 'I am glad. For most Carcassians, there is not usually a need for this modification. If the sun is very strong, it is the Shield that changes. But for Runners, it is done.'

'What about my ears?' he asked.

'There is no need to modify your ears because you are using the Joq,' she said.

'You could do it though?'

'If you wish.'

'Would it be permanent?'

She shook her head. 'These Kerala are not designed for permanent modifications,' she said. 'I can make your ears hear more strongly if you wish, but you will still need the Joq to help you understand and speak in Carcassian or Kanabian.'

'How long do the effects last?' asked Joe.

'I am unsure,' Kaia said.

'Do it anyway,' said Joe.

'If that is what you want.' She took a different crystal. 'I think there is some pain,' she said after she'd made it glow. 'But it should not last long.'

She took the Joq out of his ears. The sound from the Kerala was like nails scraping across a metal surface. His face contorted with the effort of not crying out and he grabbed Kaia's hand, holding it tightly, as the pain reached a crescendo.

'I am sorry, Sho,' she said as the tears flowed down his cheek. 'I am sorry. I did not realise . . .'

'Stop.' He sniffed and wiped away the tears. 'Stop. I can't understand what you're saying. But I can hear it perfectly.'

She waited until he'd put the Joq back in his ear.

'Are you sure you are all right? Perhaps I had this at too intense a level? I did not think it would be so painful, Sho.'

'It was worth it.' Joe touched his ears. 'I thought I was hearing great with the Joq. But this . . . this is a million times better.'

And then, because they were sitting close to each other and completely out of view, he kissed her.

30

After the kiss, Kaia didn't move. Joe was afraid that he'd offended her, but he hadn't been able to help himself. After all, she'd just adapted his eyes so that the constant glare of the sun wasn't bothering him, and more than that, she'd cured his partial deafness. He'd been delighted at how good the Joq had made it. But now, now he could hear sounds with a clarity he'd never expected. And it was all because of her. So she deserved a kiss.

He started to speak, to ask her if she was upset, but she put her finger to her lips in the universal sign for silence. Obviously her normal hearing was even better than his improved version, because a few moments later a group of about a dozen Kanabians came into view. They were dressed in a plain green uniform, with peaked hats, and they were marching in formation.

'You see,' whispered Kaia, after they'd gone past. 'They are warriors. Perhaps the Shield has already fallen and they are getting ready to fight against Carcassia.'

'Wouldn't your Link tell you if the Shield had fallen?' asked

Joe. 'Wouldn't it go completely white or release the Muqi or something?'

'I am not sure. But there would be no reason for us to live if the Shield fell, so you are probably right.'

'There's a good chance I am.'

'We must be cautious,' she told him. 'We will continue to walk through the fields. And Sho—' she looked sternly at him, 'if there are children caught in traps please do not try to rescue them. It might be a trick.'

Joe nodded again and followed Kaia as they circled away from the town and back towards the route that had been marked on the map. It wasn't possible to run in the stolen clothes, so they walked quickly, their heads down but their senses alert.

When Joe first heard the music he wasn't sure if it was real or not, because it was faint and distant and he'd never heard things in the distance before. But as they continued to walk it grew louder. Kaia looked worried. Then, as they reached the end of the field and arrived at a narrow track, they saw what the music was about.

Joe grinned, he couldn't help it. In another field – this time of short, dry grass – was a collection of coloured tents, with high pointed centres and fringed tassels around the edges. As well as the tents there were brightly painted wooden stalls dotted around the field. Kanabians in summer clothes were walking around, laughing and joking.

In the centre of the field was a long bench, divided into six sections. Above the bench were six painted targets. Beneath the bench was a trough of water. Some of the soldiers Kaia and

Joe had seen earlier were sitting on the bench.

'I do not know what this is,' she said. 'A training centre like Sanctuary? If so, it is not very secure.'

Even as she spoke, a line of Kanabians stood in front of the soldiers on the bench. They were holding small yellow balls. They started to throw the balls at the targets. Mostly their aim wasn't very good but when eventually one of the Kanabians hit the centre of a target, the seat beneath the soldier gave way and he was dunked into the water to much applause and laughter.

'What are they doing?' asked Kaia in bewilderment. 'Why do the soldiers sit there and allow this to happen? Why do they not take their revenge?'

'You don't need to worry about the Shield. It definitely hasn't fallen yet,' said Joe. 'They are playing a game. We do it on Earth too. It's fun.'

'These people are not very good at throwing,' said Kaia.

'Like I said, it's just for fun.'

Her eyes narrowed. Then suddenly she strode across the track and into the field. Joe rushed after her.

'What are you doing?' he demanded. 'I thought we were keeping a low profile.'

'I have the opportunity to defeat Kanabian Chan,' she hissed. 'I must take it.'

'Kaia! This is just a game.' Joe looked horrified.

'I wish to participate,' she said. 'How do I get these missiles?'

'You probably have to pay,' said Joe.

'No, no.' The well-built Kanabian woman who was handing out balls and who'd heard Kaia's remark smiled at her. 'Today is Hensie. It is a celebration day for our town. You can throw for free.'

'There are six soldiers,' said Kaia. 'I will need six missiles.'

The woman laughed. 'I like your attitude,' she said, as she handed her the balls which were soft and fuzzy, like tennis balls. 'Dunk all six and you get a prize.'

'And what are these prizes?' asked Kaia as she weighed a ball in her hand.

'Whatever Chai Donnat has on his stall,' said the woman. 'It is the one at the far end of the field. You are on holiday here, are you? From Lagat?'

'We're from Zwemat,' said Joe before Kaia could reply. 'It is our Time.'

'Zwemat!' The woman looked impressed. 'You have had a long journey. Not many people cross the territory these days. It is a difficult trip.'

'We are travelling to Lagat,' said Joe.

'For work?' the woman nodded. 'That is the place to be. But I thought people from Zwemat stayed in Zwemat.'

'My husband does a lot of travelling.' Kaia gave Joe a sudden mischievous smile and put her arm around his waist. 'He likes new experiences.'

'I am too old for that now,' said the woman. 'I leave the adventure to you youngsters. Well,' she said, turning to Kaia. 'Are you ready?'

'It is difficult when there are other people throwing missiles too,' said Kaia.

'Everyone likes to dunk a soldier.' The woman laughed. 'Fortunately they do not clap you in irons for it any more.'

Kaia snorted and then took up a position in front of the first target. She breathed in and out a couple of times, then threw the ball, which landed in the exact centre of the painted target and sent the soldier plunging into the water.

The crowd around the stand cheered and Kaia smiled.

'One down, five to go,' said the woman.

'Indeed,' said Kaia.

She stood in front of the second soldier, breathed in and out again, and then threw.

He also ended up in the water. There was more applause for her this time.

'Impressive,' said the woman.

'It is not so difficult,' said Kaia. 'It is a matter of co-ordination and strength.'

She moved to a place in front of the third solider. By now, the group of people watching had grown.

'Sock it to him, girl!' cried a voice.

Kaia steadied herself and threw.

There was a roar of approval as the third soldier found himself in the water.

'You are good,' said a tall, thin man at the edge of the group. 'Where did you learn to throw like that.'

'Zwemat,' said Joe before Kaia could even open her mouth. 'She learned in Zwemat.'

'She and her husband have travelled all the way,' said the woman.

'Really?' The man looked at them both curiously. 'Why?'

'Opportunity,' said Joe. He edged closer to Kaia. 'You should stop,' he told her quietly. 'You're attracting a crowd.'

'I am demonstrating my superior skills,' she told him.

'I'm not so sure that's a good idea,' said Joe.

'These soldiers deserve to get wet,' she said. 'And I am the one to do it.'

She took up her position again. The soldier beneath the fourth target was looking anxious. She threw the ball, it hit the target and he ended up in the water.

'Well, well!' said the thin man. 'You are a natural, Zwemat girl. No question.'

She shook her head and moved to the next position. Hardly bothering to steady herself this time, she flung the ball at the target. It hit dead centre and the solder was upended. The crowd cheered again.

'Hey, little warrior, if the High Command see you throwing like that they will conscript you!' cried a woman's voice. Everyone laughed. Joe caught Kaia by the arm.

'You're making people notice us,' he whispered. 'You're not supposed to do that.'

Kaia pulled her arm away from him and stood in front of the final target.

'Don't forget we have an early start in the morning, Wife,' said Joe loudly. 'Don't tire yourself out too much chasing after soldiers!'

There was more laughter from the crowd. Kaia looked at Joe. Her fingers curled around the ball. She lifted her arm and threw it. But it hit the edge of the target and rolled aimlessly away. The soldier gave a thumbs-up to the crowd, who groaned loudly before starting to disperse.

'Hard luck,' said the woman. 'But nobody has ever

got five before.'

Kaia turned to Joe who was hustling her away. 'You pushed me,' she said. 'I would not have made an error like that.'

'This isn't the time or the place,' said Joe. 'You're not supposed to be noticed. But everyone was watching you. And if you'd actually won a prize . . .'

'I would have deserved it for drowning the Kanabian—'

'Kaia!' He interrupted her. 'What's wrong with you? We're nearly at the end of your Run and you're going to ruin it all and risk being captured just for the joy of knocking Kanabian soldiers into a trough of water?'

'Hard luck!' The tall, thin man had pushed his way through the remainder of the crowd and now stood in front of them. 'You throw very well.'

'It was a fluke,' said Joe. 'When we play catching games at home she never throws well.'

'Really?' said the man. 'I thought she looked almost professional.'

'There is no profession in throwing balls at people,' said Kaia.

'No, but there is Klijan,' said the man.

'Klijan?' Joe looked puzzled.

'Even Kanabians from Zwemat play Klijan,' said the man. 'In fact, if your wife can throw like that, I am surprised she is not on the national team.'

'I will not allow her to play sports,' said Joe. 'It is . . . unbecoming.'

The man laughed. 'I thought you were an enlightened couple,' he said. 'Travelling across the country together. But it seems I was wrong. However . . .' He put his hand in his pocket and produced a card. 'If you change your mind, you can come and visit me. Perhaps have a trial for the Flox team.'

'Flox?' asked Joe.

'This town,' said the man. 'We are second in the national league at the moment. Zwemat is bottom. But that is not a surprise, they do not have the talent. Maybe that's because all the good players come to Lagat.'

'That's true,' said Joe. 'There are not many players where we come from.'

'Come to me,' said the man to Kaia. 'If you change your mind. If he lets you!'

He was laughing as he melted into the crowd again.

Neither Kaia nor Joe spoke for a moment. Then Kaia released a long, slow breath.

'I am sorry, Sho Hun-ter,' she said. 'You were right and I was wrong. I let my pride and my desire to punish Kanabians take control. I should not have taken part in that game. I should not have made us known to these people. We should go as quickly as possible.'

'I think the better thing to do is just walk around for a while as though we're enjoying ourselves,' he said. 'Someone might notice if we just disappear. Maybe we could try another game and do badly at it. Act like a newly married couple. Like we did in Thalia.'

'Yes,' agreed Kaia. 'That is what we should do.'

They walked across the bumpy ground and stopped in front of a stall. It was brightly painted in blue and white and said 'Chai Donnat. Collect your prize here.' Lined up on shelves behind a heavy, red-faced man, were wooden toys, brightly coloured cushions, and books in the Kanabian script which Joe didn't understand.

'Here to collect a prize?' he asked.

'No, unfortunately,' said Joe. 'My wife nearly managed to drown all our good soldiers, but in the end she failed.'

'Haha!' The man beamed at them. 'You cannot mess with the military, young lady. Who would protect us from marauding Carcassians if you did that?'

Joe felt Kaia stiffen beside him and he grabbed her hand.

'Our brave soldiers live to fight another day,' he said. 'And we must bring our day to a close. It has been very busy.'

'There's dancing on the beach later,' said the man. 'That's a better bet than throwing balls at soldiers.'

'Sounds good to me,' said Joe, and led Kaia away.

'I do not wish to dance on the beach,' said Kaia. 'I allowed myself to get caught up in this carnival and I regret every second of it. But I will not dance with Kanabians.'

'No,' agreed Joe. 'All the same we should go there anyway. We might hear information that'll be useful.'

'I do not need information, Sho,' said Kaia. 'I know what I must do.'

'What I'm thinking,' said Joe, 'is that if we figure out a way to send messages back to Carcassia, any information we learn would be useful.

'That is a good point.' Kaia nodded. 'But we have not come up with a way to send messages.'

'I know,' said Joe. 'Because we've been afraid to mess with the Link. But when we get to Lagat I think we should try again.

In the meantime, though, can we have just a little bit of time at the beach.'

'A short time,' said Kaia. 'Then we must go.'

The beach reminded him of Earth. There were wicker sun loungers beneath umbrellas made from the long grass. The Kanabian men were wearing shorts. The women were in one-piece costumes with very short skirts.

'Chairs and umbrellas,' said a Kanabian to them. 'You wish to hire?'

'No thanks,' said Joe. 'We won't be here long.'

But it was so lovely there that even Kaia didn't want to go, and the sun was beginning to set before she said they had to leave. The Qaan was bright in the sky and one of the moons was visible near the horizon.

Then, from the far end of the beach, they heard music and Chai Donnat, who'd been behind the prize stall, got up on a small stage on the sand. He was talking into a large cone which amplified his voice, and every so often the crowd that had gathered around him cheered wildly.

'What's he saying?' asked Joe.

'I cannot hear. We are too far away,' replied Kaia.

They walked closer until his words were clearer.

'The other good news is that the Kerala cultivations have improved significantly over the last cycle,' he continued. 'We are hopeful that one day we will produce a strain to rival that of Carcassia!'

This statement got the biggest cheer yet.

'And when we do we will rid them of their Shield and

we will take back the things that are rightfully ours!' cried Chai Donnat.

'Kanabia for ever!' yelled a voice in the crowd.

'Kanabia for ever!' cried Chai Donnat.

The music started again and everyone in the crowd began to sing. Joe realised that it was probably the Kanabian anthem. He could feel Kaia trembling beside him but he didn't know if it was from fear or from rage. Either way, he reckoned he had to get her out of here before she said or did something she'd regret.

The anthem seemed endless, and it was accompanied by a set of arm movements that everyone seemed to know.

'Hey,' said a young male Kanabian who was standing close to them. He was wearing faded shorts and a blue v-necked shirt with wide gaps for the arms. 'Show your loyalty to Kanabia. Make the moves.'

Joe immediately started to copy them, but Kaia did nothing.

'She has a sore shoulder,' said Joe, hoping that this feeble explanation would excuse her.

'Not much,' said the Kanabian. 'I saw her earlier. She is the one who dunked five soldiers.'

'And not the sixth,' said Joe. 'Because she hurt her arm.'

The Kanabian looked doubtfully at them. Joe did the arm movement with even more intensity while Kaia stood and watched.

'Let's get out of here,' said Joe when the music stopped and everyone started cheering again.

He and Kaia slipped through the crowd and made for the dunes. Even though his night vision was significantly better since Kaia's treatment, Joe occasionally stumbled over a buried rock. But Kaia didn't falter. She kept going, strong and confident.

And then, in the middle of the sand dunes, they saw three Kanabians standing in front of them. One was the male who had told them to join in the anthem. The others, one male and one female, were about the same age. The female was wearing a soldier's uniform.

'Here they are,' said the Kanabian in blue. 'The disloyal citizens of Zwemat.'

'We are not disloyal citizens,' said Kaia.

'Yet you did not sing the anthem,' he said. 'And you did not participate in the moves. So, I ask myself, what kind of Kanabian are they breeding in Zwemat?'

'Peasants, Thano Melk,' said the girl.

'Peasants who do not know how to be a good Kanabian, Thana Gryl,' he replied.

'Or spies from Zwemat?' suggested the guy standing beside her.

'Which would be a bad thing, Thano Bouk,' said Melk.

'I think the Councillors would be very interested in Zwemat spies,' said Gryl.

'Oh for God's sake, you know we're not spies,' said Joe. 'There are no spies in Zwemat. You're just trying to pick a fight.'

'A fight.' Bouk grinned. 'Now that is a good idea. The peasants of Zwemat against three of Flox's finest.'

'You are their finest?' There was derision in Kaia's voice. 'Then I pity this town.'

'How dare you!' Melk moved forward and swung a fist at her, but Kaia sidestepped, grabbed his arm and tossed him on to the ground.

'You think that is funny?' Bouk went for Kaia but, in almost the same way, she caught his arm and upended him.

'Where did you learn moves like that?' asked Gryl.

Moves. Joe realised it now. The actions that they'd been doing when they were singing the anthem were meant to be fighting moves.

'I am a peasant,' Kaia said. 'I taught myself.'

'In that case,' said Gryl, 'you are no threat to me.'

She jerked her arm sideways and a knife gleamed in her hand. Joe gasped.

'So come along, little peasant girl,' taunted Gryl. 'Let us see what you're made of. Oh,' she added as Kaia moved towards her and she evaded her, 'did I tell you that I am the best cadet in the Lagat Security Force? I did not learn moves myself. I was taught them. By the Masters.'

Kaia straightened up and looked at her. Then she glanced at Bouk and Melk who had pulled themselves to their knees. She rocked slightly from side to side, then ran at the two males, kicking them both in the face with her bare feet. Before they'd landed on the ground again, she spun in the air and kicked Gryl's knife from her hand.

'What exactly do they teach you in the Lagat Security Force?' she asked. 'To be an easy target?'

Gryl cried out in anger and rushed at Kaia, who bent low and flicked the other girl over her head. Gryl landed with a sickening thud on the ground and was immediately still.

'Oh God, Kaia,' said Joe. 'I think you've killed her.'

'Impossible,' said Kaia. 'I used very little force.'

'But she's hit her head on the ground.' Joe's expression was worried as he kneeled down beside Gryl.

'She should not have fought me,' said Kaia. 'I was defending myself.'

Joe felt the girl's pulse and looked at the side of her head.

'She's not dead,' he said in relief. 'But she's out cold.'

Melk and Boku were beginning to sit up. Kaia ignored Joe, went over to the two of them and banged their heads together so that they both collapsed again.

'What are you doing!' cried Joe. 'D'you want to kill them all?'

'Actually, yes, I do,' said Kaia. 'They are Kanabian soldiers and not even good soldiers at that.'

'You can't just murder them.' Joe was angry. 'I can't believe you'd even think like that, Kaia.'

'I could,' she said. 'However, I will do no more with these Kanabians now.'

'We have to help them.'

'Help a soldier? Are you crazy?'

'No, but—'

'What do you want me to do? Carry her back to the beach?'

'She needs medical treatment. They all do. They're probably concussed.'

'A Carcassian would not have been rendered unconscious by such actions,' she said. 'These Kanabi are weak. But I will revive them. They can make their own way to the beach.'

She took out the last slim bottle of Gira and dabbed it on to

265

Gryl's lips. The girl moaned slightly. Then she did the same to Melk and Boku.

'They will revive within minutes,' she said. 'I promise you, Sho. But we should not be here when they do.'

Joe watched as the Kanabians began regaining consciousness. Then he picked up his rucksack and followed Kaia into the night.

31

'It was a mistake to go to that carnival,' said Kaia as they walked through the field. 'I let myself be distracted from my mission and I have endangered both of us. I am not fit to be a Runner. Maybe that is why the Leaders did not send me to Lagat first.'

'It's my fault,' said Joe. 'I persuaded you. And I did it because I wanted to do something that wasn't running for a while.'

'I should not have listened to you,' said Kaia. 'However, we did learn something useful.'

'That they're not as good at fighting as you?'

'That they are cultivating Kerala. That they are trying to improve their crop. And that they will attack Carcassia when the time is right. So, Sho Hun-ter, this is information that would be good to send to Carcassia if we can work out a way to do that. Our Leaders need to know that the threat from the Kanabian Chan may increase.'

'I didn't get the impression that would happen any time soon,' said Joe. 'I thought Chai Donnat was trying to fire everyone up.'

'Fire up?'

'Get them excited,' said Joe.

'Perhaps. But the last thing Carcassia needs is excited Kanabians. And, more worryingly, we have engaged with them by my attack on Thana Gryl.'

'You should have walked away.'

'I know. But I did not. Now she and her companions will be able to describe us. And I think the security forces will not be happy that one of their agents was defeated by a peasant from Zwemat. Perhaps fleeing from a murder scene would have been better after all.'

'You can't mean that.'

'I do not know what I mean,' said Kaia. 'However, I do think we are going to have to be even more cautious, Sho. We will leave the track. We will not follow the route on the map. We will approach the city from a wider angle. This may take us more time but it will be safer.'

Joe nodded.

'We must change from these Kanabian clothes, Sho,' said Kaia. 'We must run. And we must run as quickly as we can.'

They ran through the night, alert to the possibility of Kanabians searching for them. But they saw nobody and eventually stopped as the sun rose and bathed the country in a soft golden light.

The sunlight meant that they could now see buildings in the distance. Joe could make out some of the A-shaped houses, but there were also taller buildings and some long, tapered spires that reached for the sky.

'Lagat.' Kaia stared at the city. 'The centre of Kanabian power.'

'Journey's end,' said Joe. He shivered with excitement and fear.

Kaia took out the map and looked at it. The location of the Loran wasn't highlighted yet so they continued running until they were on the outskirts of the city. There were proper roads now, and lots of houses. There were also people, more formally dressed than those they'd seen at the carnival or even Zwemat. The men were wearing loose tunics, mainly in pale shades like blue and soft pink and topped by gold- or bronze-coloured waistcoats. The women also wore tunics, though instead of waistcoats they wore multicoloured scarves around their necks.

They looked happy and prosperous, thought Joe. It was hard to think of them as warmongers.

'We need to find fresh clothing again,' said Kaia as she looked at them. 'We cannot go into the city in these garments. Or our tunics.'

There were no fields now, just roads, tracks and more and more houses. But this time they were surrounded by walls and fences. Kaia and Joe slipped through laneways that separated the houses, watching out for Kanabians, as they continued towards the centre of the city. They couldn't keep in a straight line as they had to weave in and out of the streets to avoid bumping into people, which was making Joe feel more and more anxious. Sooner or later they were going to be seen. And he knew that they didn't look in the least bit like the population of Lagat.

'Here.' Kaia kept her voice low. 'Here is a place for clothing.'

They were at the corner of a road of houses. On the opposite side was a shop. Displayed in the window were tunics, scarves and waistcoats.

'We don't have money to buy them,' said Joe.

'We do not need money,' said Kaia. 'I will retrieve this clothing for us.'

'How?'

She opened the rucksack and took out a small transparent stone.

'That's not a Kerala crystal,' said Joe.

'No,' said Kaia. 'But it will help us. Wait here.'

Joe stood in the shadow of the wall as Kaia crossed the road. As she reached the entrance to the shop she threw the stone inside. Nothing happened for a moment, then pink smoke started to pour from the building and three people rushed outside. As they did, Kaia slipped in. The smoke grew denser and billowed in the wind, engulfing the shop completely and beginning to drift along the street. People ran out of their houses to see what was happening, while the two men and a woman who'd fled the shop stood in middle of the the road, rubbing their eyes. A moment later Kaia emerged again with a bundle of clothes in her arms. She glanced at the Kanabians who were shouting at each other, and then hurried to where Joe was waiting for her.

'That's a new trick,' he said.

'These smoke bombs were developed by the Kanabians themselves,' said Kaia a little breathlessly. 'They used them in the war. Cadres of Kanabians would rush into our cities and throw these bombs into homes. When people ran out, they killed them.'

'Horrible,' said Joe.

'I am hoping that the people in the shop will think that Kanabian thieves are responsible. And I am sure that there will be more people around here very soon so we should go.'

They hurried through the warren of laneways until they found a quiet spot where they dressed in the Kanabian clothes. Once again, Joe's trousers were a little too big for him around the waist and a little too short in the legs, but the waistcoat itself, in soft gold with threads of scarlet, fitted perfectly. And, as always, Kaia's clothes looked wonderful on her. The pretty pastels in the scarf brought out the blue of her eyes and the darkness of her hair.

'We must walk with confidence through the streets,' said Kaia. 'We do not want to look nervous in any way. I am a little worried about these.' She indicated the rucksacks. 'I have not seen a Kanabian carrying anything like them. But we will try to keep them out of sight.'

'Which way?' asked Joe.

'The map is not clear. But it has always been said that the Lagat Kerala is in the centre.'

Joe grimaced. 'Why on earth did the Carcassians think the centre of the enemy city was a good place to put your Loran?' he asked. 'It seems crazy to me.'

'To be honest, I think it is crazy too,' admitted Kaia. 'But they must have had a reason.'

'And like every Carcassian reason, not one I have the

faintest idea about,' muttered Joe as they began to walk towards the city centre.

There were fewer houses now, and most of the buildings seemed to be warehouses or offices or shops. They were all built in a cream stone and many had brightly coloured awnings over the doors and windows. Trees (Umqo trees, Kaia said) lined the roads and there was a floral scent in the air.

Most of the Kanabians seemed to get around the city either by walking or on oddly designed bicycles, but occasionally one of the pedal-operated Zaals trundled along one of the streets. Nobody took any notice of either Joe or Kaia as they walked among the crowds, and finally they arrived at a large plaza in front of a long three-storey building. A wide flight of steps led up to the first floor of the building, which had an outside balcony surrounding it. A banner hung around the balcony.

'This is the centre.' Kaia took a brief glance at the map before quickly putting it away again. 'The Loran should be here. And that building . . .' She looked at it again. 'According to the banner that is the Headquarters of the City and Security Council of Lagat.'

'That's not what I wanted to hear,' said Joe. 'Is the map showing you the Loran?'

'Once again I am sad to inform you, Sho Hun-ter, that the light from the map is not shining.' Kaia turned to look at him, her eyes filled with anxiety. 'And given our experiences in Zwemat and Domote, this makes me fear for the Shield and fear for Carcassia.'

'If the Shield had failed we would definitely know, even

without something happening to your Link,' said Joe. 'They wouldn't have been talking about "one day" at the beach party. They would've been talking about now. And that security forces girl would have known too.'

'I would like you to be right,' said Kaia. 'But the reason there were no lights on the map before was because there were no Kerala sending a signal to it. The fact that this Loran is not sending a signal worries me deeply.'

'There must be something wrong with the map,' said Joe. 'Look at this place! Nobody here is geared up for waging a war.'

Kaia looked around her. The plaza was filled with people sitting at tented cafés. They were drinking juice and chatting among themselves. It looked very peaceful. Then, as they watched, the sound of a whistle broke through the air. Immediately all of the conversation stopped and the plaza was eerily quiet. Joe and Kaia heard the sound of marching feet and a column of at least fifty soldiers marched through the square and up the steps of the three-storey building. The people in the plaza saluted the soldiers respectfully. The doors opened as they reached them and the soldiers marched inside. The doors closed again and the noise and chatter of the people in the plaza resumed.

'You see,' murmured Kaia. 'There is an outward show of peace here but the truth is that it is a military nation.'

'I wanted to believe that the Carcassians might be wrong about Kanabia, but that was a scary sight,' said Joe. 'We need to find the Loran as quickly as possible.'

'I do not think it can be inside,' said Kaia. 'Surely they would have noticed it before now?'

'I hope you're right. Wherever it is it's going to be difficult to find in all these buildings,' Joe said. 'Unless your map starts to light up I don't know how we're going to locate it.'

'That will be a problem,' agreed Kaia. 'We will wait for darkness and then begin our search.'

'In the meantime we'd better find somewhere to rest and to eat,' said Joe.

Kaia nodded and they walked away from the plaza. After about ten minutes they came to a small square surrounded by single storey buildings all of which seemed to be closed up. There was a stone bench on one side of the square and so they sat there, took the last of their Gira and Cheebas from their bags and settled down to wait.

It seemed to take for ever until darkness fell. By then both Kaia and Joe were stiff from sitting around and they welcomed the opportunity to walk back to the centre of Lagat. The streets were faintly illuminated by the same kind of lights as they'd seen in Zwemat, but they were much better lit by the Qaan and the two moons which were high in the sky.

There were very few people around and the plaza was deserted. The buildings were closed, their awnings pulled back. Joe and Kaia stood at the corner of the plaza and looked at the map. There was still no signal to show the location of the Loran.

'What do you think?' asked Joe.

'I have been considering this a lot,' said Kaia. 'The Loran must have been constructed before the buildings. That means it cannot be in one of them now. Or, if it is, it is in a basement or somewhere difficult to access. I wonder how Mihai found it. If he did.'

'If he didn't, if it wasn't because the Loran was destroyed like the others, what would he have done?' asked Joe.

'He would have gone to the next Loran.'

'But how long would he have looked here?'

'I do not know,' said Kaia. 'We never discussed not being able to find the Loran. We talked about not being able to access it, because of Kanabians or Haaken. But nobody ever believed that would happen to them. The Shield has been secure for generations. We all had to assume that the Runners did their job.'

'And yet we now know that there were problems in Zwemat and Domote,' said Joe. 'So this is the only one that's working. But we don't know where it is.'

Kaia rubbed her forehead. 'The other Runners must have found it,' she said. 'It is the only way. Therefore it cannot be hidden too much.'

'Let's check out all the streets around the plaza,' said Joe. 'Maybe we'll see something.'

They walked along the streets, looking at every building, trying to find any possible place that might be, or might lead to, the Loran.

'This is futile,' said Joe after they'd been looking for over two hours. 'We need some kind of clue.'

'Maybe in the daylight . . .'

'We didn't see anything earlier,' said Joe.

'There must be something,' said Kaia. 'We were not looking for it, that is all. We will check tomorrow.'

'OK.' Joe sighed. 'And tonight? Where are we going to go tonight?'

'We will have to find an empty building.'

'There are plenty of those,' said Joe. 'But none unlocked.'

'It is not cold,' said Kaia. 'Perhaps we can find shelter in a doorway.'

'My mother always told me that if I didn't apply myself in school I'd end up sleeping on the street,' said Joe, when they found a suitable place in a narrow road. 'I never believed her. But she's ended up being right.'

32

They took it in turns to rest because even with a motion sensor Kaia didn't want both of them asleep at the same time.

'As soon as it is light we will search again,' she said. 'You sleep first, Sho.'

He nodded and closed his eyes but it was impossible to truly fall asleep in a doorway. Whenever he felt himself drifting off he would jerk awake again, convinced that someone was nearby. He was glad when it was his turn to keep watch and Kaia closed her eyes.

He sat propped against the wall and tried to figure out the mystery of the Carcassian Shield and where the Kerala might have been placed. It had to be hidden enough that no Kanabian could find it and yet accessible to the Runners who were looking for it. But he couldn't for the life of him imagine where that might be. More and more he thought that the whole concept of the Shield and the Runners was ridiculous and that the Carcassian leaders needed to change how they did things. Communication with the Runners would be a start. Allowing them back home would be even better. He didn't care what Kaia said about not being able to return, there must be a way.

He watched the sky begin to lighten and then he took the map from Kaia's rucksack. Slowly, so as not to wake her, he lifted her finger and touched the arrow icon. The map zoomed in on the centre of Lagat and he saw their position marked by a pulsating red dot. Totally like Google Maps, he thought, as he traced his finger over the route they'd taken through the city. He supposed it had been a much smaller place when the war had taken place and, with everything he knew about Earth's wars, the city had probably been destroyed by the Carcassians. Life would have been chaotic. But the Carcassians had to have been in control when they placed the Kerala. They would have needed time to set up the Loran.

So where would they have been? Where would they have thought of as the centre? Would there have been some kind of fortified building they were holed up in? With a basement perhaps?

An old building, he was thinking just as Kaia woke up. That's what we have to find.

'You must be right, Sho,' she said when he shared his thoughts with her. 'Also, the place must be inaccessible to ordinary Kanabians and not built over. And it must be in some way meaningful for Carcassians.'

'This map doesn't tell you what's meaningful and what's not,' said Joe. 'All it does is show buildings and streets.'

'We will find it, Sho Hun-ter,' said Kaia.

'I suppose if that idiot Mihai worked it out, we can too,' agreed Joe.

'Perhaps he did not.' Kaia's voice was serious. 'Perhaps he is already dead, having failed.'

'How long do we have left?' he asked.

'I do not know exactly.' Kaia glanced at her Link. The jewel was now a very pale pink. 'But I hope we have long enough. I do not want to die before serving Carcassia.'

And I don't want either of us to die at all, said Joe. But he didn't speak the words out loud.

They walked towards the square again. In the early morning it had fewer of the tented stalls in its centre. The Headquarters of the City and Security Council of Lagat looked grim and forbidding without the gaiety of the stalls in front of it.

'It'd be just our luck that it's inside there,' said Joe.

'I do not think it can be,' said Kaia. 'If it were, it would have shown on the map by now.' But she gazed at the grey building, a worried frown on her face.

'Maybe there are shields so that we can't pick up its signal,' said Joe. Then he laughed. 'I think I've watched too many sci-fi movies.'

'I do not know this sci-fi. But I also do not think that the Kanabians have enough Kerala for these shields.'

'Probably not,' agreed Joe.

'However, it would be good to check out this building,' Kaia said.

Joe groaned. 'Tell me you're joking.'

'I do not joke.'

'You did back at the pond,' he reminded her.

'That was different. I do not joke about my mission.'

'We can't walk in there,' he said. 'We'll be captured and then what'll happen to the mission?'

'*We* will not walk in there,' she said. 'I will.'

'I'm not letting you go alone.'

'I understand what you are saying,' said Kaia. 'But I think I will do a better job of not talking to Kanabians than you. Besides,' she added, 'I will not bring the Kerala in there without finding the Loran first. You will need to stay outside and guard it.'

'But Kaia—'

'Let us sit in the shelter of this tree and wait,' said Kaia. 'The Kanabians are setting up their stalls. The building will open soon, I am sure.'

'I wish we had something left to eat and drink.' Joe rummaged in his rucksack as they sat down. 'I'm hungry. And thirsty.'

'Here.' Kaia took out a bottle and gave it to him.

'You have Gira left?'

'No, this is the water I gathered before,' she said. 'I kept some of it. The Gira is rationed to last until a Runner's arrival at the final Loran. It should allow some extra time here but of course we lost time on our way. And at the beach.'

'I'm sorry for pressurising you about the beach,' said Joe.

'It was fun.' She smiled at him and her whole face lit up. 'Not afterwards with those Kanabians, but at first. I swam in the sea and I liked it, Sho. I wish . . .'

'What?'

'I wish all days could be such fun. I wish we had a place like it in Carcassia. I wish . . .'

'What else do you wish?' Joe was listening to her but he was also watching the people setting up their stalls and opening their cafés.

'I wish that it was different,' she said finally. 'I wish that there was peace between our countries.'

'Wow.' Joe turned to her in amazement. 'What about wanting to kill Kanabian Chan?'

She sighed. 'I do not know how I feel about this. There are bad people here. But perhaps not everybody is bad.'

'So would it be such a disaster if you didn't place the Kerala and the Shield failed?'

'Of course!' She looked horrified. 'Some Kanabian people might be all right but you can see that the country is ruled by the military and the one thing I know about military people is that they train for war. They say that they want to keep the peace but the truth is, Sho, that if you train for war then you want the opportunity to use that training. And so if we lowered the Shield Carcassia would be attacked because that is what military people do.'

'I guess you're right. Look, Kaia, they're opening the doors to the Security building now.'

Two uniformed guards had unlocked the big double doors to the front of the building. They stood either side of them as people started to walk up the steps and enter. Most of them seemed to be ordinary Kanabians but some were dressed in the uniform of the soldiers while others were in different uniforms.

'They do not seem to be searching people,' said Kaia after a while. 'But nor do they allow them to bring in bags.'

'I was thinking about your plan,' said Joe. 'And I feel we should change it.'

'How?'

'I'll go in,' he said. 'We can't afford for you to be captured.'

'I will not be captured.'

'You might be.'

'I will not,' she said. 'And if I am I will fight my way to freedom.'

'Kaia—'

'That is all,' she said. 'We will wait for the busiest time and then I will enter the building.'

Joe said nothing.

They sat in silence and kept watching.

Finally the square was full of people, a great many of whom seemed to have an appointment at the City and Security Council Offices.

'There is just one thing,' said Kaia suddenly.

'What?' asked Joe.

'If I go too far inside the building without you the Link will fade and . . .'

'Why do I keep forgetting about this damn Link?' Joe looked at the bracelet around his wrist. 'That settles it. We're going in together.'

'No,' said Kaia. 'We cannot.'

She looked at him for a moment and then bowed her head.

'We must press the circles on each other's Link at the same time,' she said. 'That will sever the connection.'

'Are you sure?'

She nodded.

'You just thought of this now?'

'I thought of it when we were at the carnival,' she confessed. 'I realised that the circles symbolised togetherness. To press them both will break them apart. But I was afraid . . .'

'. . . afraid of what?'

'That you would not come here with me. That you would try to find another way.'

'Why would you think that? We're a team.'

'I know you say this but I am a stranger to you,' she said. 'Charra is not your planet and Carcassia is not your concern.'

'We're a team,' he repeated. 'Whether we're linked or not I'm not going anywhere. We're in this together. So let's do it.'

They both pressed the circles on the Link. The green jewels flickered and went out. Then they glowed a very pale yellow.

'That just means that there are two Links close to each other,' said Kaia. 'We are no longer joined, Sho Hun-ter.'

'There's a part of me that's sorry.' He smiled at her. 'I felt safe when I was linked to you, Kaia Kukura. But now that we're separated you have to let me go inside. You know it's the sensible thing to do.'

'I agree,' she said reluctantly. 'But please, please, be careful, Sho. Just look around and come back.'

'No worries,' he said. 'And, Kaia?'

'What?'

'If I don't come out before sunset, then you're on your own.'

'I do not wish to be on my own, Sho Hun-ter,' she said. 'I wish to be with you. I will wish you good luck.'

'Thanks,' said Joe.

He left his rucksack with her and walked up the steps to the building.

33

Joe could feel his heart thumping in his chest. He could feel it pounding in his head. He'd never been more terrified in his life. Not even when he'd been accosted by Niall and Greg, or Mihai, or the whale or the spider. Because he hadn't been able to avoid them. But he didn't have to do this. He could walk away. And yet he couldn't.

He reached the top of the steps. He was in a small group of people and he stayed close to them as they approached a security check. Joe suddenly thought of ID. What if they asked for it? What would he say? What would he do?

But they didn't ask. Instead they took his fingerprints. Joe worried that Kanabians might have very different fingerprints to humans but it seemed that they were similar enough not to cause any trouble. Joe was waved through to another guard who frisked him. Then he moved to another guard who had a clipboard in his hand.

'Name?' he asked.

Joe was just about to reply Sho Hun-ter when he remembered

that the Kanabians used either Chai or Chaia in front of their name. The younger Kanabians and the girl who was in the security forces had used something else but Joe guessed they were military titles. So he said he was Chai Sho. The guard frowned.

'You do not have an appointment,' he said.

Joe felt his heart thump even more.

'Are you sure?' he asked. 'I spoke with officials last week.'

The guard shook his head. 'Is it about enrolment?' he asked.

'Yes,' said Joe, hoping he wasn't making a terrible mistake.

The guard wrote something on his clipboard and then nodded at Joe. 'Down the corridor on the right,' he said. 'Chai Lexo is today's official. Good luck.'

'Thank you,' said Joe.

He felt dizzy with stress as he walked along the corridor. It was lined with noticeboards all covered with information that Joe couldn't read, and crowded with young people queuing outside Chai Lexo's office. The crowd was a mixture of male and female, all talking eagerly about the enrolment process and how they would one day serve Kanabia.

Joe noticed that there was an emblem on the wall in front of the door. It was a castle on top of a mountain and beneath were more words that he couldn't read. And now that he noticed that, he realised that the castle emblem was also on the notices which were pinned on the walls.

'I am looking forward to going to Kama for training,' he heard one of the young men say. 'I reckon I can beat anybody.'

There was a burst of laughter from the girls beside him.

'You're so vain, Chai Mex,' said one. 'I am sure that after training I will beat you.'

There was a lot of laughter at this which suddenly stopped as an oversized man trundled past them and into an office. Joe couldn't read Kanabian writing but he guessed this was Chai Lexo. A young and pretty Kanabian girl came to the doorway. She was also holding a clipboard.

'Chai Lexo will see appointment number one. Chai Mex,' she said.

'Number one, that's me,' he said as he followed her into the office. 'When I return you will call me Thano Mex.'

Joe sidled away from the group, walking slowly along the corridor until he came to another one which intersected it. He turned up this deserted corridor. There were offices on both sides. All of the doors were closed.

Joe stopped outside one of them and listened carefully. He could hear no sound from within so he turned the handle as softly as he could. The door opened and he stepped inside. He realised that he was sweating as he closed it behind him.

In the office was a desk, a chair and some filing cabinets. On the wall was a map. Joe went over to it and looked at it. He immediately identified the city of Lagat. And on the outskirts, the symbol of the castle on top of the mountain. He looked at it thoughtfully. Then he slid one of the drawers of the filing cabinet open. It was full of folders, each stamped with the castle symbol and all full of unreadable pieces of paper.

He walked to the door again and listened carefully before opening it. He made his way down the corridor, pausing at every door, opening them all and seeing every office empty.

They were all laid out the same way, and all had the map on the wall. At the end of the corridor were two doors leading to a staircase. They were both locked. Joe rattled them a couple of times but there was no way he could open them. And there was no other way out of the corridor other than going back the way he'd come.

Just as he turned into the area outside Chai Lexo's office (which was still busy with people wanting to enrol), two uniformed officials headed down the corridor. Joe sighed with relief. He looked around him a little more, realising that there were very few places people could get to without being stopped either by guards or locked doors. Obviously the only reason he'd made it into the corridor was that it was empty.

But he didn't think it mattered any more. He was pretty sure he knew where the Kerala was. And it wasn't in the City and Security Offices. It was in the castle. Where the Security Forces were trained.

Joe decided that there was no point in staying in the security offices and that he would go back outside and tell Kaia what he'd seen. He edged his way past the crowd and back to the main exit.

'Where are you going?' asked the security guard.

Joe felt his heart sink.

'You must sign out,' said the guard. 'Your prints.' He pushed the large sheet of paper with everyone's prints on it in front of him.

Joe dipped his fingers in the ink and pressed them on the paper again.

The guard looked at them and then nodded at him.

'You can go.'

Joe didn't wait but headed down the steps as quickly as he could. The plaza wasn't as crowded as before but he couldn't see Kaia. He looked around anxiously. For the first time he noticed that the pennants fluttering above most of the stalls also carried the picture of the castle. He knew he was right about it. But where the hell was Kaia so that he could tell her?

He walked slowly around the plaza, past stalls selling fruit and vegetables, bread and cool drinks. Others sold clothes like the ones he and Kaia had stolen the previous day. He spent some time in front of one of the clothes stalls, pretending to be looking at a waistcoat but still searching for Kaia.

And then he heard her voice in his ear and he turned around.

'I was worried about you,' he said.

'You? Worried about me?' she smiled at him. 'I was not the one risking my life. And probably for nothing.'

'What d'you mean?'

'I think I know where the Loran is,' she said.

'So do I.'

'The castle,' they told each other at exactly the same time.

34

'What made you think of it?' asked Joe as they left the plaza.

'The image,' she said. 'On everything. And we learned at Sanctuary that there was a castle in Lagat where there was fierce fighting but that the Carcassians captured it. It would not have been the centre of the city physically but it would have been the centre of everything to do with the city. And then I heard people talking about training for security officers at Kama. Kama is another word for Loran.'

'That settles it,' said Joe. 'We're off to the castle. Where there will be hordes of security officers. Great.'

'We will defeat them,' said Kaia.

There's confidence and there's craziness, thought Joe. And if Kaia thinks that two of us can defeat heaven knows how many trained Kanabian guards she's utterly crazy. But I can't stop her. And I won't let her go alone.

'It's not as bad as I thought,' said Joe when they got their first view of the castle. 'It's on a hill, not a mountain.'

'Still high enough to see over everything,' said Kaia.

'And surrounded by a wall,' added Joe. 'But, hey, at least we're heading in the right direction.'

'I hope,' said Kaia.

'I'm sure of it,' said Joe. 'How many guards do you think there'll be?'

'Lots,' said Kaia. 'It is where they train, after all.'

'I was afraid of that,' said Joe. 'It's just like Sanctuary.'

'It is not!' exclaimed Kaia. 'In Sanctuary we learn to defend ourselves, not to attack our enemies.'

'Maybe that's what the Kanabians learn too.'

'And I know you are joking, Sho Hun-ter,' said Kaia. 'Because you said that there were people enrolling to be soldiers in the security offices. We do not have soldiers in Carcassia. Only the Shield. So we are not warmongering people.'

'I thought you said some of the Kanabians were nice,' said Joe.

'I was probably wrong,' said Kaia, and walked on ahead of him.

It was growing dark by the time they reached the bottom of the hill and, much to their dismay, they saw that torches were being lit at regular intervals along the castle walls.

'Not going to be easy,' said Joe.

'No,' agreed Kaia. 'But I am ready. And we will do this tonight.'

The nearer they got to the castle the more they realised how big it actually was and Joe wondered how easy the Loran would be to find. Then, as they came within a hundred metres of the outer walls, Kaia gave an exclamation.

'We were right, Sho!' she cried as she unfurled the map. 'It is here.'

A golden dot was pulsating at the centre of the castle.

'It is the symbol of the Kerala. It is there. It is working.' She beamed at him. 'Oh, Sho, this time everything will be all right.'

'Is it working because Mihai got there first?' asked Joe.

'It does not matter. I will place my Kerala. There is a space for it, you know that,' she said.

'What about the spare ones?' he asked. 'The ones you should have placed in Zwemat and Domote?'

'There will be a place for a second one anyway.' The excitement left her voice. 'Where Oani should have placed hers.'

Joe nodded.

'And perhaps we will use the third to send you home.' She smiled again. Then she flung her arms around his neck and kissed him on the cheek. He looked at her in surprise. 'I like your way to express happiness and affection,' she said. 'And Sho . . .' she looked at him solemnly. 'I *will* find a way home for you from here. I promise.'

'Thank you.' He kissed her back. 'Now let's see how we're going to get into this place.'

They waited until it was completely dark and then they made their way slowly and carefully up the hill towards the castle. There were plenty of boulders on the hill that they could hide behind, but it seemed to both Joe and Kaia that although the castle was protected there weren't armed guards patrolling the walls. In fact everything was very quiet and very still. It was only the flickering light from the torches that indicated the castle was occupied at all.

It took them over an hour to reach the walls and another hour to walk around them. Then, when they were almost back at the place they'd started – the huge gated entrance to the castle – Kaia put her finger to her lips and stopped. Joe looked at her questioningly.

'There,' she whispered. 'A doorway in the wall.'

'Where?' Joe couldn't see anything.

'I thought I fixed your eyes,' said Kaia. 'Look carefully.'

Joe stared at the place she'd pointed to and then, very gradually, he saw what she'd seen. It was a slight discolouration in the wall, the size of a small door. And he realised that she was right and it really was a door, because around the edges it glowed with a faint green light.

'OK, it's a door,' he agreed. 'But does it open? And where does it lead to?'

Kaia walked over to it. She stood in front of it and then ran her fingers gently over each individual stone. At the sixth stone she stopped. She placed both her palms in the centre of it and pressed firmly. The door slid open.

Joe was expecting Kanabian guards to pour out, but there was nothing but total silence.

'Come,' whispered Kaia as she stepped inside.

Joe followed her.

They were in a narrow passageway. Except for the green glow of the walls, it was totally dark. Joe waited for his eyes to adjust but even after they did, there was very little to see. He realised that the green light was from moss growing on the walls. The same moss covered the roughly hewn floor.

Joe could barely make out Kaia who was standing just ahead of him. He took his smartphone from his rucksack and pressed the torch app. Immediately the light from the moss began to sparkle. He reached out and touched it. He'd expected it to be springy but it was like dried seaweed. Kaia was looking at it with awe. And then she straightened up and said that they must move forward.

She led the way through the passage which ran in a straight line for quite a distance before turning abruptly to the left, then to the right, and ending in another blank wall.

Kaia took the map from her rucksack and opened it. The golden light indicating the Loran was fixed and steady.

'We are there.' She could hardly keep the excitement from her voice. 'We have found it. And I will complete my Run.'

She reached out to touch the wall in front of them, even as Joe put his smartphone back in his pocket and said, 'Kaia, wait. There's a—'

But he was too late. As Kaia's fingers came in contact with the green wall there was a flash of dazzling white light and a loud bang which flung both of them across the passageway.

Joe felt his head thump into it and he cried out in pain. He was blinded by the light and couldn't see anything. He felt around him for Kaia's hand but instead his fingers curled around his phone. He put it into his pocket. Then he closed his eyes to try to block out the green and white starbursts. He wished Kaia had seen the sensor light in the wall.

The same sensor light that had set up the Shield in Zwemat.

'Welcome, Carcassian spies.'

He heard the words and he opened his eyes again. The starbursts had faded but his head was pounding. He rubbed the back of his neck and then looked at the people who were standing in front of him. They were four Kanabian guards and two of them were already holding Kaia upright between them.

'Kaia,' said Joe. 'Are you all right?'

'I think so,' she said, although her voice was weak.

'Quiet, Carcassians,' said another guard as he hauled Joe to his feet.

Joe blinked a few times. The passage was now filled with light coming from a room behind the wall that Kaia had touched. The room was made of smooth white stone. There was a small plinth in the centre, with a carved hollow in its centre. In the hollow was a single Kerala crystal which glowed faintly.

Joe turned to Kaia who was staring at the Kerala, an agonised expression on her face. It was clear that the power from it was fading and it needed to be replaced. Which meant that Mihai hadn't been here. Which meant that Kaia's Kerala was the one needed to keep the Carcassian Shield in place. But that wasn't going to happen now, was it? Not since they'd been captured by Kanabians.

And then the realisation hit Joe. The Kanabian military knew about the Kerala. They knew about the Run. They'd been waiting for them.

Kaia had been betrayed.

* * *

The guards pushed Joe and Kaia to a corner of the room. Then one of them waved his hand over the wall. The exit to the passageway closed and another door on the adjoining wall appeared. The guards walked out of the door, leaving Joe and Kaia alone.

'Are you all right?' asked Joe again.

'My head hurts,' said Kaia. 'And . . .' Her eyes filled with tears. 'I have failed, Sho. I have walked into a Kanabian trap. I was supposed to be the best of them and I allowed myself to be captured and now Carcassia will fall. Because of me.'

'Not because of you,' said Joe. 'You can't blame yourself.'

'There is no one else to blame,' said Kaia. 'I have let my people down.'

'No,' Joe said. 'Kaia – don't you see? They already know about the Kerala. They left it there. That means they must be OK with having the Shield in place. Why? Why haven't they removed the Kerala and let the Shield fail? Why haven't they attacked Carcassia already?'

Kaia stared at him. 'I had not thought of that. How could I not think of that? I am so stupid.'

'You had a bang on your head,' said Joe. 'And worse than me by the looks of things.'

He pushed back a lock of Kaia's hair. There was a large bump on her head and he could see that it was bleeding.

'You need medical help,' he said.

'I will be fine.'

But Joe could see that blood was now running down Kaia's cheek.

'Sit down,' he said.

She sank to her knees beside the wall. Her face was very pale. Joe was worried. He wished the guards had left them with the rucksacks so that he could use the paste on Kaia's head to stop the bleeding. But he had nothing.

She took the pretty scarf that she'd taken from the shop along with the other Kanabian clothes and handed it to him.

'Wind this around my injury,' she said. 'It will help.'

'What d'you think is going to happen now?' asked Joe when he'd tied it as tightly as he could.

'We escape,' said Kaia.

'How?'

Joe walked to the wall and began to wave his hand in front of it as the guards had done. But it remained firmly closed.

'The Kerala should control the doors,' said Kaia. She stood up and walked over to it, studying it from all angles. Then she turned to Joe.

'Do you see what is wrong here?' she asked.

'No.'

'Think of the other Loran,' she told him.

'None of them worked,' said Joe. 'All the Kerala were broken.'

'Yes,' said Kaia. 'All of them. And there was space for all of them. But this Loran only has one space for one Kerala.'

'And?'

'And because of the bump to my head I did not think of this before, but it is not what was designed by the Carcassians.'

'Huh?' Joe stared at her.

'You saw it yourself. The plan is always that there will be

space for three Kerala in each Loran. Even though one will maintain the Shield, the more there are, the safer it is for us. There should be space here for three Kerala but there is not.'

'Design flaw?' suggested Joe.

Kaia gave him a withering look just as the wall swung open again.

A tall man in a military uniform, and flanked by two guards, stepped inside.

'Hello, Carcassians,' he said.

Joe and Kaia stayed silent.

'It is a long time since we have seen a Carcassian in Lagat,' he said. 'Your disguises are poor. Those markings are of old Kanabians. People your age do not have so many circles these days. We have evolved, it seems.'

'Who are you?' asked Kaia.

'I am Thaxo Mabai,' he said. 'I am the Authority of Kanabian security.'

'Does that make you a Leader?' asked Kaia. 'I wish to speak to a Leader.'

'Such impoliteness in a visitor.' Thaxo Mabai smiled at her, but it was a cold smile. 'There is a way to address me. It is Excellent Authority.'

'You are not my Excellent Authority,' said Kaia. 'You are a murdering Kanabian.'

'My, my,' said Thaxo Mabai. 'A firebrand.'

'What are you going to do with us?' asked Joe.

Thaxo Mabai looked at him thoughtfully.

'You do not sound Carcassian,' he said. 'Your speech, the patterns, they are not as we know.'

'He is not,' said Kaia. 'He has nothing to do with us. You should release him.'

'If not Carcassia, then where?' asked Thaxo Mabai.

'He is from further away,' she said. 'He is no threat to you.'

'Oh but I think he is,' said Thaxo Mabai. 'And I think you are too, my pretty little firebrand. So I will have to deal with both of you. Come.' He clicked his fingers and the guards grabbed both of them. Kaia struggled but the guard was too strong for her. Joe twisted a little but gave up when he decided that there was no point in trying to free himself underground.

'Let's wait,' he said softly to Kaia. 'We may get a better opportunity.'

Thaxo Mabai laughed. 'You will not,' he said. 'You will not get any opportunity at all.'

They were ushered back along the passageway by the guards, up the steps and into another part of the Castle. There they were brought to another almost empty room. In the centre was a table and two chairs. The guards pushed Joe and Kaia on to the chairs and secured them with a thin rope. A man that neither of them had seen before walked in and placed Joe and Kaia's rucksacks on the table.

'So,' said Thaxo Mabai. 'It is an honour to meet a Carcassian Runner. We must thank you for bringing Kerala to our country.'

'So you have the Kerala,' said Joe. 'Now what?'

'I will place it in our grid,' said Thaxo Mabai. 'And I will wait for you to die. That is what happens with Carcassians in Kanabia. They die.' He pointed to the Link on their wrists. 'This is the killing device of Carcassia. I will let your country kill its own. As barbarians do.'

There was a knock at the door and a woman in uniform walked in.

'Ah, Thana Gryl,' said Thaxo Mabai. 'I believe you are already acquainted with our visitors.'

Joe looked at her. Her blue eyes were hard and cold and her expression fierce. She was wearing a plaster over the side of her face.

'These terrorists tried to kill me and my friends,' she said.

'And they will shortly die themselves,' said Thaxo Mabai.

'But I would like the opportunity to deal with them first,' said Gryl. 'To show them that you cannot attack a soldier of Kanabia.'

'It is a Kanabian's right to exact revenge for injury,' said Thaxo Mabai. 'You may do so, Thana Gryl. However, you may not kill them.'

He nodded to the guards, who tied both Kaia and Joe's arms behind their backs.

'When you are finished, Thana Gryl, please come to me in my rooms,' he added as he took the two rucksacks. 'We have a lot to talk about.'

'Of course, Excellent Authority,' said Gryl.

She smiled as he left the room, followed by the guards. Then she turned to Kaia and Joe.

'So which of you first?' she asked.

35

'We are two and you are only one,' said Kaia from her chair. 'That hardly seems fair.'

Gryl laughed. 'I think you will find that I have sufficient skills to deal with two Carcassians trussed like Jakas,' she said. 'And I must have my revenge.'

'Why?' asked Joe.

'You attacked me and you must pay,' said Gryl. 'There are Kanabians who like to talk. Thaxo Mabai believes that talking can be useful. I do not. I believe in action.'

She strode across the room and stood in front of Kaia.

'You injured me, Carcassian,' she said. 'Now I will injure you.'

'No,' said Joe. 'You won't.'

Using all of the extra power he had on the planet, he pushed himself forwards and upwards. The chair came with him as he launched himself directly at Gryl and slammed into her back. She toppled forward on to Kaia who immediately head-butted her. Gryl rolled to the floor, dazed.

'Here,' said Joe. 'Undo my wrists.'

He manoeuvred himself and the chair so that Kaia could reach the rope that tied him. It took her a few seconds to release him and in that time Gryl had got to her feet again.

'That was some feat, Carcassian,' she said. 'Of course the rumours are that you are not of Carcassia. Or that they are breeding a new type of fighter. Is that true?'

'Might be,' said Joe, as he stood opposite her.

'Well, let us see,' said Gryl.

She rushed at him and he got out of the way enough so that her elbow only grazed the side of his head and didn't get him directly in the face as she'd clearly intended. Then she went for his legs but he managed to jump high enough to avoid her. She looked at him in astonishment. Joe grinned. He realised that, even though he was terrified and even though he knew he was in a terrible position, he was enjoying himself. He'd never come close to winning a fight before. This time he rushed at her. It was a mistake. She caught him by the arm and slowly began to twist it.

The pain shot through him and he nearly screamed. If she kept on with this she was going to break it. Suddenly he wasn't enjoying himself any more.

Then it was Kaia who, having managed to remove her own bindings, attacked Gryl. She came at her from the side, slamming her foot into the other girl's shoulder. Gryl cried out and released Joe's arm. He staggered backwards into the upturned chair. He felt his knee twist as he fell. The pain was excruciating. He blinked the tears from his eyes and tried to get up again but he couldn't.

Meanwhile Kaia and Gryl faced each other. Their eyes were locked.

'Come, Kanabian,' said Kaia. 'Try me.'

'I will defeat you,' said Gryl.

'I will take pleasure in killing you,' Kaia said in return.

And then, while Joe watched, the two of them attacked each other with a flurry of fast and furious kicks. It was hard to know who was getting the better of the exchanges but Joe fancied Kaia's chances. At least until a well-aimed blow from Gryl caught her where she'd bumped her head. The makeshift bandage was dislodged and Kaia stumbled as blood began to pour down her face.

'And now, Carcassian . . .' Gryl smiled at her.

Joe tried to stand again but his knee was too painful. He felt utterly helpless and he watched Kaia, the side of her face almost completely covered in blood, try to steady herself.

'I will have my revenge,' said Gryl.

'No you won't!' Kaia stood up straight and jumped into the air. Her kick landed exactly in the centre of Gryl's face and the Kanabian went down on the spot.

Kaia turned to Joe and smiled.

'I told you Kanabians were weak,' she said and fainted.

Joe made a choice to tie Gryl before attending to Kaia. He'd seen lots of movies where the hero is busy looking after an injured comrade and is then attacked again by someone who was supposed to be unconscious. He wasn't going to let that happen. So he used the Kanabian rope to secure Gryl's arms to her body before turning to Kaia.

He wiped the blood from her face with the sleeve of his tunic. Then he felt in the pocket of her trousers, hoping to find the Vay ampoule, which she'd put there after her Gosekka bite. There wasn't much in it but he prised her mouth open and sprinkled the last few grains on her tongue. For a moment nothing happened and then Kaia opened her eyes.

'Sho,' she said. 'What of the Kanabian?'

'Out for the count,' he said.

'Weak, weak, weak.' Kaia was already trying to sit up.

'We need to do something about that cut,' said Joe.

'It is nothing.' Kaia was dismissive. 'A flesh wound.'

'It's bleeding a lot,' said Joe.

'It will stop. I have had these injuries before. However . . .' She looked at the belt that was around Thana Gryl's waist. There were small pouches hanging from it. She opened them one by one and put the contents, which were mainly types of bandages, into her tunic pockets. When she found a rectangular plaster she pushed her hair out of the way and told Joe to stick it over her wound.

'And now,' she said when he'd done that and the blood had stopped pouring down her face, 'our objective is to retrieve the Kerala.'

'And do what with it?' asked Joe. 'It seems pointless to replace it.'

'We cannot leave the Kerala in the hands of Kanabians. We must retrieve the crystals and find a way to return to Carcassia, Sho.'

'And how will we do that?'

'We will run,' said Kaia. 'We will try to make the Link work to communicate with them from outside to warn them of the danger. But if we cannot, we will stop the new Runners as soon as they come through the Shield so that they do not bring fresh Kerala to Lagat. Perhaps we can form a group to work on the problem. Maybe we can be resistance fighters. For you, I do not know how we can do this, but perhaps putting the Kerala near the Shield will generate a portal for you to go home.'

'It's a plan, I guess,' said Joe. 'But I'm not sure how we're going to manage it. We're still in the castle and there are lots of guards. Plus you're hurt and I've crocked my knee. And you've forgotten about the Muqi. When will that be released, Kaia?'

'I have not forgotten,' she said as she looked at the Link. 'But there is still time. If we leave now and run very fast, not using the route back to the departure point but going directly to the nearest part of Carcassia, perhaps we can get there before the Muqi is released.'

Joe looked at her doubtfully. 'All through the Run you've talked about being behind schedule, and the Link has been getting paler and paler. Surely we don't have enough time?'

'Maybe not,' she admitted. 'But we have to try.'

He realised that it was futile. That they'd never succeed.

'I have a better plan,' he said. 'We find the portal that will get us back to Earth.'

'That will not save Carcassia,' she said.

'We know Carcassia isn't in danger right now,' Joe reminded her. 'The Kanabians only have the old Kerala and the ones you brought. That's not enough for them to power anything. If we get back to Earth maybe I can find the portal that got me here in the first place and we can reach Carcassia that way.'

She stared at him.

'That is a possibility,' she acknowledged. 'Let us decide when we find the Kerala.'

'OK,' said Joe. He grimaced as he tried to move.

Kaia took a bandage from Gryl's tunic pocket. She wrapped the strip around his knee.

'I wish you had not given me the last of the Vay,' said Kaia. 'It would have helped you. But we will manage, Sho Hun-ter. We have done well so far. There is just one more thing.' She took out a roll of bandage and used it to gag Gryl.

'She can breathe, can't she?' Joe sounded anxious. 'I don't want her to suffocate.'

'She was going to kill me,' said Kaia.

'I know,' said Joe. 'But . . .'

Kaia shook her head. 'I do not understand you, Sho,' she said. 'However, I have not deprived the Kanabian of air. She will not die. Nevertheless . . .' she smiled, 'she will have a very bad headache when she wakes up.'

With that she opened the door to the room and peered outside. The passageway was deserted.

'The Kerala must be with Thaxo Mabai,' said Kaia. 'We will find him and take it from him.'

'You're making that sound easy,' said Joe.

'He is a Kanabian,' said Kaia. 'Of course it will be easy.' She winked at him although he could see that there was worry in her eyes.

Joe limped as he followed Kaia out of the room and into the deserted passageway of the castle. The light was faint and the ceiling high. They made their way as silently as possible along the faded red carpet that lined the stone floor. It was Joe who first heard a low murmur ahead, and put his hand on Kaia's shoulder. They stepped into an alcove just in time to avoid two uniformed Kanabians.

'The Kerala has done a good job on your ears,' whispered Kaia. 'I hope those two do not find Thana Gryl.'

'We're in big trouble if they do,' said Joe.

Kaia peeped into the passageway again, and seeing it deserted she beckoned Joe to follow her. They walked past a number of big rooms, none of which had doors, before turning into a narrow passage, this time lined with closed and studded wooden doors.

'Crap,' said Joe. 'I'm sure they'll make a noise to wake the dead if we open them.'

'We will go past slowly,' said Kaia. 'If we hear anything behind one of the doors we will go in and subdue whoever is inside.'

'Subdue?' He looked at her doubtfully. 'I can hardly walk and you've got a bruise the size of a Kerala on your forehead. I'm not sure we'll be subduing anyone.'

'No problem,' said Kaia as she started to walk along the passage.

They heard no sounds of people, but behind the third door a gentle hum was audible.

'Let us check it out,' said Kaia.

Joe felt his entire body tense as she turned the circular handle to open the door. He was ready for it to squeak loudly but in fact it opened quietly. There was a soft light inside, again generated by the small Kerala stones that the Kanabians used for power. Kaia and Joe could see a wooden desk, a few armchairs and a large bookcase full of scrolls. There was also a fireplace with glowing embers in the grate. Over the mantelpiece hung a huge portrait which Joe recognised as Thaxo Mabai. The noise they'd heard came from something that looked like an old-fashioned gramophone player. It sounded like falling rain.

'Tranquillity music,' said Kaia. 'We also use this in Carcassia to help children to sleep. And if this is Thaxo Mabai's quarters I am not surprised he needs it.'

She looked around. Two more doors led off the room. She tried the handle to one and again it opened quietly and easily.

'Sho,' she said softly. 'I think this is what we want.'

He limped over to her. Behind the door was a corridor, this time in the same white stone as they'd seen before.

'Come,' she said.

Joe took a deep breath and once again followed Kaia. The corridor led to a set of spiral steps leading downwards. Kaia continued ahead of him. Joe was tense as he stayed closely behind her.

She stopped abruptly and he nearly walked into her. He peered over her shoulder and his eyes widened. In front of them was a room. The floor and ceiling were white but the walls were covered entirely by the green moss substance they'd encountered earlier. In the centre of the room was a long workbench and on the centre of the workbench were the three Kerala crystals and their rucksacks.

'We have found it.' Kaia smiled at Joe. 'I told you we would.'

She stepped into the room and walked over to the workbench.

'I can't believe this place isn't guarded,' said Joe as he followed her. 'Kaia – don't you think . . .'

But he didn't get to finish the sentence. Because at that moment one of the walls slid back and Thaxo Mabai, flanked by two security guards, entered. They saw Kaia and Joe at once and reached for their belts, withdrawing what appeared to be truncheons.

Behind them a dozen young soldiers trooped into the room. They took up positions around the walls.

'This doesn't look good,' said Joe.

'You are right, Carcassian spy,' said one of the soldiers. Joe recognised him from the group that had been signing up the previous day. 'The time of your end is near.'

'We have failed.' Kaia turned to Joe, a haunted expression in her eyes. 'I cannot save my country and I cannot save you. I am sorry, Joe. The only thing that matters now is getting the Kerala.'

'And doing what with it?' asked Joe as the two guards advanced towards them.

'Destroying it!' she said. 'Perhaps this is what happened at Zwemat and Domote. My fellow Runners were trapped like we are. And like them, I must prevent Kanabia from having the power of the Kerala for when war begins.'

She launched herself across the room and towards the workbench. The guards tried to stop her but she managed to evade them. Then Thaxo Mabai made a grab for her, but Joe, forgetting about how much his knee hurt, leaped across the room and banged into the Kanabi leader so that both of them crashed into the opposite wall. Thaxo Mabai hit his head and fell to the ground with a low grunt. Joe slammed into the wall and felt the green moss react to him as it suddenly sprouted long tentacles which wrapped themselves around his arms and legs.

'Kaia!' he cried.

But she didn't hear him. She was too busy trying to avoid the guards. Meanwhile the other soldiers took a step forward in unison.

Joe felt as though electricity was running through his entire body. Sweat began to pour down his face. He watched as Kaia suddenly feinted to the left, got past the guards and reached the first Kerala crystal. She picked it up in both hands and lifted it above her head.

'I am sorry, Sho!' she cried. 'I really am.'

Then she threw it as hard as she could above the heads of the approaching Kanabians towards the wall behind them.

Time slowed down. Joe watched as the Kerala came spinning towards him, over his head. He felt it impact the wall and then the tingling of the electricity running through him became stronger and stronger. His entire body was twitching and jerking and all he could see was the bright light of the crystal exploding above him. And then, suddenly, nothing but darkness.

36

'Sho. Sho. Can you hear me?'

The voice came from far away. Joe wanted to respond but he couldn't. His body felt as though it had been run over by a truck. Every part of him hurt. His head was pounding. All he wanted to do was sleep.

'Sho. Joe.'

His eyes flickered but he couldn't open them.

'You're doing well, Joe. Come on now, buddy.'

He tried again and this time his eyes opened.

'Oh, Joe! You're awake at least.'

This time it was a female voice but it wasn't Kaia. He recognised it though. It was his mother. And she was laughing and crying as she stood over him, relief etched all over her face.

'Oh, Joe, we were so worried.'

'How'you doing?' His father stood beside his mother.

Joe was too shocked to speak. He couldn't be here. Not now. Kaia needed him. He had to save her. He struggled to get out of the bed but a white-coated doctor who'd been standing behind his parents put his hand on Joe's shoulder.

'Whoa,' he said. 'You've got to stay there for a bit.'

'I can't.' Joe was frantic. 'I have to get back. I have to save Kaia.'

His parents exchanged worried glances.

'Do you remember what happened?' asked the doctor.

'Kaia.' Joe's voice was a croak. 'The Kerala. An explosion.'

'And before that?'

'The Crystal Run,' said Joe.

'Mrs McGoldrick saw you.' His mother spoke. 'You were running and two boys were running after you. Did they do this to you? Did they?'

Joe looked at them impatiently. 'It was the security guard,' he said.

'OK, pal.' The doctor smiled at him. 'I'm just going to talk to your mum and dad for a minute, then we're going to bring you for a scan.'

The adults stepped outside the curtain surrounding his bed. Joe sat up slowly. Every bone in his body ached. There was a drip attached to his arm too. He was wearing a hospital gown and a pair of grey shorts. On the locker beside his bed was a bottle of water, his phone and a green wristband. He reached out gingerly for the wrist band. It was covered in tiny symbols. It looked different now because there were no jewels on it, but Joe knew it was the Link. He reached out for it and slid it on to the arm without the drip. None of the lights on it was flashing. In fact, he couldn't see where any light would be. He picked up his phone as well and was just about to scroll through it when the doctor returned. He slid the phone into the pocket of his shorts.

'We'll bring you for that scan,' he said. 'It's nothing to worry about.'

How was he going to get back to Charra when he could hardly move? Joe asked himself. When his body hurt so much and when he felt like a weight was pressing down on him? How could he save Kaia? He tried not to think that it might already be too late.

His mum and dad stayed with him until a hospital porter arrived with a wheelchair. A nurse removed Joe's drip and then helped him into the wheelchair.

'How are you feeling?' asked his mum.

'I'm fine,' he said. 'I just need to get back.'

'You'll be home soon,' she promised him. 'And we'll have a big party. With cake.'

Joe said nothing. His mum walked alongside as the porter wheeled him through the corridors of the hospital and then into a lift which took them down to the basement.

'You'll have to wait here, Mrs Hunter,' said the doctor who greeted them outside the Radiology department. 'But don't worry, we'll take good care of Joe.'

The nurse wheeled him through a set of double doors.

'We're going to do a CAT scan,' said the nurse. 'It won't take too long.'

Joe wanted to get up but his body felt too heavy. He couldn't move.

The nurse made him lie on a narrow table. At the end was a big circular ring.

'The table will move you through the ring so that we can take pictures of your head,' said the nurse. 'I have to go outside. I'll talk to you through a microphone. It'll be all over in a couple of minutes.'

Joe nodded. At that moment, it was all he could do.

He heard some whirring noises and then the nurse's voice over the mike telling him to keep his arms by his side and to stay perfectly still. He did as he was told. He couldn't do anything else. He felt the table start to move.

And then he felt the Link on his arm begin to pulsate. He could feel the pressure coming and going. He lifted up his arm. A transparent jewel had pushed its way through the plastic. It grew brighter and brighter until it was shining a bright yellow. A yellow jewel meant that someone else with a Link was nearby.

'Sho!' He could hear her voice. 'Sho!'

'Joe!' This time it was the nurse. 'Joe, you have to lie still.'

The big circle of the CAT machine was directly over his head. It was lighting up just as the Link had done. Joe felt a huge pressure on his arm, then a blast of cold air hit him in the face.

And once again he was in darkness.

He was freezing when he woke up but that was because he was wearing only the hospital gown and his shorts. He was still lying on the table, but this time in a room with white walls and a white ceiling. And then, as his eyes adjusted, he saw that the white light was coming from a row of small Kerala crystals at the bottom of the wall. He could see that the room was divided in two by a white screen. He got up from the table. The enormous weight seemed to have lifted from his body. It still ached, but not as badly. And his knee wasn't hurting at all.

He looked at the Link on his arm. The jewel was still glowing.

Joe walked around the dividing screen. There was another table behind it. Lying on it, eyes closed and arms crossed over her chest, was Kaia. There was a long cut across her forehead and he could see a large bruise under her eye. Joe rushed over to her. The jewel on her Link, black to signify that the poison had been released, was beginning to flicker. The ruby stone was completely white.

He felt a lump in his throat. The Muqi had been released. She was dead. He had failed her.

'Kaia!' He whispered her name. 'Kaia . . . I'm so sorry.'

She didn't move. She didn't open her eyes.

He took his phone from the pocket of his shorts. He tapped it and opened the photo album. He looked at the photo he'd taken of Kaia on the beach, smiling and happy. Confident that she would complete her Run. Confident that she would save Carcassia.

But it hadn't worked out that way. By now the Shield must have fallen. And Carcassia and Kanabia were at war again.

He didn't want to be here. Not if they were at war and not if Kaia had died. He needed to get home. He looked around him. He saw his tunic, neatly folded on a shelf, and he put it on. At least he felt warmer now. He put the phone in the pocket.

'Sho.'

He whirled around.

But Kaia was still lying there, not moving. She couldn't have been the one to say anything.

'Sho Hun-ter. Save me, Sho. Save me.'

Her voice was coming from the Link. But she wasn't speaking. She was still totally immobile.

'Kaia,' he whispered. 'It's me, Kaia. It's Joe.'

'I am here.' Her voice was soft. 'But it is difficult.'

Suddenly, her eyes snapped open. They were so dark they were almost black.

'Kaia,' he said. 'I'm so glad you're all right.'

'What are you doing here, Carcassian?' Her voice was hard and cold.

'It's me, Kaia,' he said. 'It's Joe.'

'You are an enemy of Kanabia. You will die.'

'Kaia.' Joe was frightened now. 'What are you saying? What have they done to you?'

'I am enlightened.' Kaia sat up. 'I am . . .' She stopped speaking and stared straight ahead of her. 'I am Kanabi. I will fight to the death for my country.'

'Kaia, you can't mean that!' Joe was horrified. 'You're a Carcassian Runner! They've brainwashed you.'

The door to the white room opened and a tall, thin man walked in, carrying a silver case.

He looked shocked to see Kaia sitting up. And even more shocked to see Joe standing beside her.

'How did you get here?' he asked. He stepped towards a panel in the wall.

'No you don't!' cried Joe. Without even thinking, he launched himself at the thin man, taking him completely by surprise. He fell to the floor instantly, and lay there knocked out.

'Let's go, Kaia,' said Joe. 'I don't know what's happened to you but I'm going to fix it. Somehow.' He took the silver case, gathered up the Kerala crystals and put them inside. Then he grabbed Kaia by the hand. She didn't say anything.

'Come with me,' said Joe. 'I'm going to get you out of here. And now that I know it's possible for me to get home, even if I don't know how it happened, I'm going to try to get you home too. Back to Carcassia.'

'I am home,' she said. 'I am Kanabi.'

'Oh, Kaia.' He looked at her in frustration. 'You're not. I don't know what they've already done to you or what they plan for you in the future. But it's not going to be good. You've got to come with me.'

'I must remain,' she said. 'I must complete . . .' her voice broke off and she frowned. 'I must complete . . .'

'Don't talk now,' said Joe. 'You've been through a lot.'

'Why am I here?' She looked around. 'Am I being punished? Am I no longer a warrior?'

'You've been sick,' said Joe. 'But you'll get better. You always get better.'

'I am a Runner.' Her voice was stronger.

'Yes you are,' said Joe.

'We ran together,' said Kaia.

'Yes, we did.'

'I must run again?' She looked at him, a dazed expression in her eyes.

'Yes,' said Joe. 'But this time your Run is different, Kaia. This time I'm going to save you. Because this you're running for yourself.'

Keep reading for a
sneak preview of the sequel!

THE CRYSTAL RUN

SHIELD
OF LIES

Joe Hunter was beginning to sweat.

A few minutes earlier, he'd felt very cold, so either the dimly lit room had started to heat up, or his temperature was rising because he was worried. And Joe had a good reason to be worried. He was on another world and he'd just attacked a man who was now lying unconscious on the stone floor. But it wasn't really the thin man with the severe face that concerned him. It was the girl sitting on the doctor's table in the centre of the room. The girl the man had come to see. Her name was Kaia Kukura and Joe needed her to trust him. He needed to rescue her before anyone knew he was here.

'Come on, Kaia,' he urged. 'We've got to get out of this place before that guy regains consciousness.'

She said nothing. Her wide eyes were almost black. That frightened him. Kaia's eyes adapted to the light. In the sun, they were usually a vivid blue. In a dim room like this they turned green. He'd never seen them so dark and expressionless before.

'Trust me,' he said. 'We need to find a way to get you back to Carcassia. We have to save you and your country. Trying to save Carcassia is what got you here in the first place, remember?'

She frowned.

'You must remember, Kaia,' he said. 'You were training for the Crystal Run when I suddenly turned up. You all thought I was a spy or a terrorist but I was sent through the Shield with you.'

She kept staring straight ahead as Joe continued talking, desperately trying to get through to her.

'You were supposed to put Kerala crystals in sites called Loran to keep the Shield powered up,' he said. 'But the Loran were destroyed and we discovered the bodies of the other Runners there. It was horrible. Then we were captured and—'

'You lie,' said Kaia in a voice that still didn't sound like her own. 'No one can pass through the Carcassian Shield. You are trying to trick me.'

'I would never trick you,' he told her. 'I care about you.'

Her eyes seemed to lighten for a moment and then she gritted her teeth. 'I do not need anyone to care about me,' she said. 'I am a warrior.'

'Even warriors need other people,' said Joe. 'We were strong together before, Kaia. We can be again.'

She said nothing.

'We need to get out of here,' he said. 'We should head for the Carcassian border. From there we can try to communicate with your Leaders. That is if I can modify our Links to use as transmitters. We have to tell them that everything they've taught you about the Run is wrong. They have to try powering down the Shield long enough for you to return.'

'The Loran,' she said slowly. 'We are betrayed.'

She was echoing the words that had been carved into the walls of the ruined sites deep in the enemy territory of Kanabia. When they'd seen them, they'd both known that the Crystal Run wasn't working out the way it was meant to.

'We are betrayed,' she repeated. 'And the Runners must die.'

Joe looked at her and shivered. Once again, her eyes were pools of black in her pale face. Her Kanabian markings, the ones she'd painted on herself as a disguise, stood out more clearly too. He noticed his own wrist for the first time. His markings had been almost invisible back on Earth but now they were stronger and brighter in the faint light of the small crystals set into the floor of the room.

'You're a Runner and I don't want you to die,' he said.

'The Carcassian Runner died when the Muqi poison entered her bloodstream. I am reborn. I am Kanabi.'

'Oh, Kaia . . .' He was close to tears. 'You seemed to remember earlier. You called to me to save you. You want to help Carcassia. I know you do. You're not a Kanabian. You never will be.'

'Get away from me, traitor!' She suddenly leapt from the table and stood in front of him, a fierce expression on her face. Then she took a few steps back before running at him and kicking him in the stomach. Joe stumbled backwards and fell over the thin man who was still unconscious on the ground.

'Kaia!' he gasped. 'Stop!'

She was close to him now and put her hands around his

neck. For the first time since they'd met, Joe was truly afraid of her. He grabbed her wrists and tried to break her hold on him, but she was stronger than she looked. He kicked out as they rolled across the floor. Once or twice he connected with her body, but she didn't seem to notice.

She was going to kill him. After everything they'd gone through together he was going to die in a Kanabian prison because of Kaia Kukura.

'Please.' His voice was a croak.

And then, just as he'd expected her to tighten her grip still further, she let him go and doubled over in pain.

Joe looked at her warily as she staggered across the room and knelt down beside the unconscious jailer. With trembling fingers, she opened a concealed section of the silver case. It was lined with red velvet. Small glass vials shaped like teardrops were set into individual spaces. Kaia took out a vial of orange liquid, broke the top and then swallowed the contents. Almost at once she started to groan.

Then she crawled to a corner of the room, where she sat, doubled over, occasionally crying out in pain. Joe wanted to comfort her, but every time he approached her, she moved away from him. So he waited. After what seemed like forever, she pulled herself to her knees and began to retch violently. Steaming black liquid poured from her mouth and nose and pooled around her. Joe watched her anxiously but did nothing.

Finally, the retching stopped. She edged backwards until she was leaning against the wall. Her face was paler than ever and covered in sweat. This time Joe went to her.

'Kaia?'